GOOD ROCKIN' TONIGHT

A Novel By

STEVE YOUNT

RALEIGH, NORTH CAROLINA

Good Rockin' Tonight

COVER DESIGN BY DAVE YOUNT

ISBN-13:
978-0615749433 (Wry Whiskey Press)

ISBN-10:
0615749437

Printed in the U.S.A.

Wry Whiskey Press
Raleigh, North Carolina

www.WryWhiskeyPress.com

This book is dedicated to my mother and father, sisters and brothers, and my son.

Acknowledgements

I owe thanks to Margaret Dardess, Ramona DuBose, and Peggy and Phil Carter for editing assistance, and Dave Yount for contributions extending well beyond his graphic creativity and technical proficiency.

All of humanity's problems stem from man's inability to sit quietly in a room alone.

Blaise Pacal 1622-1663
Penses

CHAPTER ONE

Jeff Stuart navigated his mother's 1949 Plymouth station wagon through the gravel parking lot of The Hitching Post, searching for a spot large enough to berth the beast. Young, cocksure greasers and weathered old rednecks leaned against their machines and snarled as the Plymouth kicked up dust that settled on freshly washed hoods and windshields. The station wagon was a drab elephant in a jungle full of sinewy tigers.

"There's one over there," Chuck Brady, riding shotgun, pointed to a parking place close to the building. Jeff ignored the front row spot and passed up several more before pulling in between a shiny '54 Chevy and a '52 Ford pickup in the back row.

"Don't you think we oughta park in the same county as the club?" Chuck asked. "We got a three hour hike, up hill, against the wind, in enemy territory."

Marty Ryder, son of a Baptist preacher, summed up the legal and moral perspective from the back seat. "We're under-age, our wheel-man's been drinking, and we're publicly consuming intoxicating beverages. I can see why Jeff isn't eager to display our sins to God, the management, and every Neanderthal in the county." Marty took a last pull off a warm Pabst Blue Ribbon and slipped the empty can into the paper bag at his feet. "We got time for another beer before we storm this place?"

"Hell, no." Chuck said, always ready to charge Hell with a wet hand towel. "Let's bust in there with steely eyes and brass balls and straighten the joint out."

Jeff shook his head. "*If* we get through the front door, I'm gonna become invisible. I just want to listen to the music and drink a beer. And if anybody gets in trouble," Jeff looked squarely at Chuck, "I don't know you."

When the boys climbed from the Plymouth, they were greeted by a June breeze carrying hints of beer, perfume, and auto exhaust. Chuck and Jeff peeled off their football letter sweaters and tossed them in the back seat. Marty, using the driver's side mirror, tilted his glasses to what he considered "maximum virility" and ran a comb through his lank, black hair. He pushed the sleeves of his red nylon jacket back halfway between wrist and elbow and turned the collar up. Lighting a Winston, he let it dangle wickedly from the side of his mouth. Satisfied, he presented himself. "How do I look?"

Chuck was unimpressed. "Real good, Marty. You *might* pass for fifteen." Marty whipped out his comb and tried to coax maturity from features that adolescence refused to surrender.

As Chuck rolled his Marlboro pack up into his shirtsleeve, Jeff leaned against the Plymouth and scanned the grounds. The few poles that housed working lamps scattered enough light to display a small carnival of depravity in the parking lot. Good ol' boys of all ages passed whiskey bottles across car hoods, some laughing in glee, others shouting in anger, while several back seats hosted vigorous wrestling matches between brazen lovers. A small crowd gathered around a fistfight about twenty yards off to the right of the roadhouse. A riot of car radios, each seemingly tuned to a different station, competed for the last word.

None of the boys seemed eager to leave the sanctuary of the car and commit to the uncertainty of the no-man's-land that might well lead to confrontation at the roadhouse door. Jeff took a deep breath and struck off toward The Hitching Post and destiny. Short, stocky Chuck fell into step, and the gangly Marty bounced along in the rear. They marched single file, each armed with a cigarette behind his ear, projecting an attitude of hostile indifference.

That posture served them well until they drew close enough to read the sign posted above the dance hall entrance:

HITCHING POST
POSITIVELY NO ONE UNDER TWENTY-ONE ADMITTED!
THIS MEANS YOU!

The boys pulled up short to consider the message. Marty scratched his head, "It looks to me like they intend to discourage—".

WHAM! The door of the roadhouse burst open and a huge, bald man wearing a torn blue work shirt charged out. He was carrying an unfortunate patron by the collar of his bowling shirt and the seat of his pants, looking for a place to deposit him. Spotting an opening, the bouncer took half a dozen running steps into the parking lot before nimbly pirouetting in a tight circle and launching the ex-bowler in a soaring arc that terminated in a sprawling nose-first landing and a short slide. The bouncer drew a line in the dirt with the toe of his shoe, and walked off the length of his toss, counting each pace aloud. Five paces, fifteen feet. Satisfied, he smiled as he clapped the dust from his hands and hustled back inside the bar.

The boys stood in stunned silence, smoking and occasionally stealing a glance at the moaning body.

Marty threw his cigarette butt to the ground and stepped on it. "Apparently the club is full," he said, as he rubbed the back of his neck. "Why not get another six-pack, stop by the Snack-Bar, pick up some fries and a foot-long—

"I got your foot-long . . . hangin'." Chuck snapped. "We're here, I say we try to get in."

"I'm not sure I'm ready to risk my ass just to hear some hillbilly sing 'Old Shep.'" Marty countered. "This ain't Elvis Presley we're trying to see."

Chuck looked to Jeff. "You're driving. What do you say? Stay or go?"

Pressed up against his manhood like that, Jeff had little choice. "What the hell," he said slowly, "what can they do besides ask us to leave?"

The battered carcass behind them moaned loudly.

"They sure as hell ain't gonna let the three of us walk in arm-in-arm," Chuck said. "Let's match for it."

Three quarters tumbled through the air, were caught and slapped upon left wrists: Chuck and Marty showed heads—Jeff had tails. "Give me another cigarette," Jeff said. Chuck produced a Marlboro and offered fire. Jeff nodded grimly and walked toward the entrance. "If I'm not back in two days," he called over his shoulder, "feed my dog and tell Mama I loved her."

The band played "The Wild Side of Life" as Jeff walked through the door of the Hitching Post; everyone standing, smoking, and talking in the cramped lobby looked as though they'd been dragged through those lyrics for years. Jeff joined a staggered line that led to a wooden table with a sign taped to the front: ADMISSION $1. One buck to get your hand stamped and pass through the tattered black curtain into an oppressively loud, blindingly smoky cavern where you traded your money and respectability for the possibility of injury and arrest and the certainty of a torturous headache, a poisoned stomach, and hours of misery the following day. All in all, everyone in line agreed, a fair swap.

Behind the table, taking money and stamping hands, sat the bouncer, "Burt," identified by the patch on his torn blue work shirt. Jeff fought off the urge to flee and fell into the slow moving line. Burt maintained a running stream of chatter with everyone standing, coming or going. "Hey, Leon! You wanna lay some seerus money on that race Sunday. I'm willin' to betcha twenty that Ol' Fireball Roberts gonna blow the doors offen that Junior Johnson Ford." Everybody in the lobby, save Jeff, offered up a defiant opinion on the subject. When the band struck up "My Son Calls Another Man 'Daddy'," folks slowly filed back into the club.

Jeff, the last in line, sidled along and extended his bill to the bouncer. He frowned slightly, in an attempt to create some wrinkles in his forehead, and spoke in a deep voice, "I'm bettin' on Speedy Thompson. Nobody's gonna outrun that Chevy on Sunday."

As Burt slowly raised his gaze from the till, Jeff felt precious years melt off his face and collect in a shallow pool on the desktop. "Son," Burt asked, "just how old *are* you?"

Numbers bounced wildly around Jeff's brain. Seventeen? Twenty-five? Twenty-one—

"THAT'S MY GAL, YOU SONUVABITCH!"

The hysterical shrieks, shouted threats and splintering glass inside the club emptied the lobby with a speed usually reserved for gunshots and police sirens. Burt slammed the metal cash box inside the table and locked the drawer with a small key tied to a string around his wrist. Within seconds, he was at the far side of the stage surrounded by overturned tables and chairs and a rising tide of bodies. When Jeff peeked around the black curtain, he saw Burt the bouncer raising knuckle-bumps on every head within reach.

Jeff hastily stamped his left hand and slipped into the club. Moving quietly along the wall, he found a deserted table in a darkened corner. Half a dozen tables separated him from the dance floor, but he could still see the band from the waist up on the raised stage. He pushed aside the empty beer bottles and found a single cigarette inside a crumpled Camel pack. He lit up and stifled a cough just as a beefy, brunette waitress appeared at his table.

"Bottle of Miller High Life, please," Jeff said quickly.

The waitress appraised her new customer. "Whip it out, Honey," the waitress said.

"Uh, beg pardon?"

The waitress leaned on the table and shook the back of her hand in Jeff's face. "The stamp, Sweetcakes."

Jeff displayed his mark.

"What the hell," she said, as she shunted empty bottles from the table to the tray she balanced in her left hand. "But you damn sure better be a good tipper, Sonny."

Jeff nodded eagerly. "Not much of a fight," he said, implying he'd seen hundreds.

The waitress shrugged. "It's early."

Up on the bandstand, "Restless Bill Terwilliger & His Footloose Ramblers" ground out yet another of Bill's favorite World War II vintage ditties: "Filipino Baby." But to anyone who cared to look closely, it was obvious the young lead guitarist did not share his boss's enthusiasm for the Asian girl whose "teeth are bright and pearly, and hair as black as jet."

"Christ on a crutch," Cody Hunter muttered to himself, "if I have to play one more whiny, drag-ass, three-chord, shit-kickin' song, I'm gonna walk over and piss in Restless Bill's hat." Cody had auditioned the day before, and got the job because he was the only player who showed up with an electric guitar and amplifier. Bo, the new bass player, shared Cody's opinion of the music. When the two exchanged a glance, Bo wrapped his skinny, blue-veined arms around his doghouse bass, shut his eyes and feigned sleep.

When Restless Bill segued into "The Tennessee Waltz," Cody breathed a sigh of relief. Break time. Soon he could sneak out to his car and drink as much bourbon as he could pour and keep down in fifteen minutes. With the aid and comfort of a pint of Old Crow, he might just make it through the gig.

"Thank ya, thank ya, thank ya," Bill responded to the smattering of applause. "I'd like for you kind folks to put your hands together now for the band. On the fiddle, we got my old partner, been playin' with me since back before Pearl Harbor, Mack McLaurin. Let's hear it for Mack." Polite applause greeted the grim Mack as he sawed off a verse of the waltz.

"On the bass," Bill continued, "playin' with us for the first time tonight, we got Bob....well, we just call him Bob." Bo shook his head, and beat out a few measures on his stand-up bass before Restless Bill cut him short. "Thank you, Bob. You're a doin' a fine job back there." Bo snarled and finished his run before fading the bass.

Restless Bill turned to the husky guitar player with the long black hair and sideburns. "Now I know all you gals out there are wondering who this good-lookin' blue-eyed feller is. Ain't that the truth? Let's give a big hand to Cody Hunter."

Most of the audience was heading for the john or outside to sneak a drink, so the anemic applause fell far short of what the guitarist felt he deserved. Indignant, Cody stepped forward and picked up the beat. After only a couple of hot licks, Mack, the fiddle player, pulled his instrument from his shoulder and stared at Cody then at Bill.

"Mighty fine, son, mighty fine." Bill said quickly, stepping all over Cody's break. "Now, we gonna be right back—and I promise to play that song I wrote about ol' Hank Williams adyin' first thing—but we been workin' hard for you, and we need to take us a breather. Thank you." Restless Bill raised his right arm out shoulder height and then dropped it to his side abruptly.

But Cody didn't back off his guitar run, and when Bo sensed where the beat was headed, he jumped on for the ride. Hands froze on door knobs while folks listened up as the "Tennessee Waltz" galloped across the stage of the Hitching Post.

Jeff had finished his beer and was admiring a buxom young cowgirl who appeared to be having trouble sitting upright when he was pulled from his reverie by the throbbing guitar. He had ignored Restless Bill's mumbled introductions but now stood up to get a better look at the musicians. Bill and the fiddler glared at the long-haired guitar player who was hunched over his instrument, oblivious to anything but his six string universe.

The three couples that had been waltzing abandoned the dance floor in disgust. Jeff smiled and nodded when the bass player grabbed hold of the beat and filled in the bottom, leaving the guitarist free to strike off into new territory. Soon they were playing a raucous song the radio could not get enough of lately. When Restless Bill made a motion toward the sound equipment, the guitarist stepped defiantly in front of the amplifier. The frail old man muttered something about an old war wound that prohibited combat, then stomped off the stage.

Everybody in the audience had an opinion, but for every "Go man, go," Jeff heard a volley of "Cat-ass" and "Greaser." The guitarist smiled broadly, then moved to the front of the stage and took The Word to the people: a full-throated, note-for-note rendition of *Blue Suede Shoes,* as good, to Jeff's ear, as Carl Perkins's or Elvis's.

Jeff did not consciously decide to walk from his table down to the stage front, but merely responded to an impulse akin to a cave man's desire to stand next to the fire. Cody danced wildly across the stage kicking his feet as high as his head, displaying those trademark shoes. The crowd divided along generational lines, as the men who had come to the roadhouse, not exactly looking for a fight but certainly unwilling to walk away from one, searched and found each other.

When the first beer bottle shattered on the wall behind him, Cody's head snapped back like it was on a hinge. The guitar man scanned the audience and found that everyone who didn't have a longneck beer bottle raised to throw appeared to be looking for one. As fistfights raged across the floor, Cody and Bo beat an ungainly retreat, the sound of shattering glass dogging their steps out the back door of the club.

When the glass barrage eased, Jeff followed the musicians through the back exit. A cherry-red 1950 Ford raced across the gravel parking lot and slid broadside in front of the two musicians. The bass and the guitar were tossed in the back seat, and Cody and Bo piled into the passenger side of the car. The driver, a dark-haired, full-breasted babe, dropped the clutch and left a spray of dust and gravel on Jeff's shoe tops. The Ford leapt onto the two-lane blacktop, and in little more than a heartbeat disappeared into the moonless night.

CHAPTER TWO

Rose Stuart cooked her Sunday dinner and set the table with the efficiency and dispatch one might expect from a woman who ran a tight office, a spotless home and hadn't gained a pound in twenty years. Rose placed the fried chicken next to the lima beans and mustard greens at the center of the table. Her meals were uniformly delicious though lacking in variety or romance. She cooked the food she was raised on—a menu that leaned heavily on fried meat and pork seasoned vegetables—and her father-in-law and son rewarded her by taking second helpings and returning clean plates. Jeff, since childhood, would eat anything set in front of him, but Granjack would reject outright any dish that was not standard, rural fare dating from the War of Northern Aggression. Rarely did a tablecloth go into the wash without a gravy stain.

Whenever Rose was tempted to stray into new culinary territory, her memory would flash to the dinner scene of the Sunday before Christmas, 1954. Harried to distraction by a Sunday school Nativity play she was directing at the First Baptist Church, she attempted to replace the traditional Sunday chicken dinner with a frozen TV dinner that had been recommended highly by the ladies in her missionary society. She shuddered each time she recalled the sight of her father-in-law scooping up the metal tray and flinging it against the wall. The sound of the hard, lime-green peas striking the windowpane reminded her of hail stones ricocheting off a tin roof. Afterwards, she had scrubbed her hands raw trying to remove the stain left by the off-colored carrots. Even now, a year and a half later, when the late afternoon light filtered through the dining room window just so, Rose would swear she could see the green-yellow tinge—a color unknown to nature—on the dining room wall.

"Jeff," Rose called into the living room, "tell Granjack dinner's ready." The old man lived alone in the rock house about a hundred yards down the dirt road that ended at his doorstep. Jeff, still a trifle hungover, roused himself from a prone position on the couch and walked out the back door

Rose set the hot biscuits on the table just as Jeff and his grandfather walked through the door. Jack Stuart was a half-foot shorter than his grandson and stocky as an oak stump. His face, tanned and gnarled from a lifetime of working outside, was set up carelessly around a large, bent nose the old man claimed had broken more knuckles than he sported on both hands. Four furrows ran parallel across his forehead, the lines cut so deep four carpenter ants could march abreast in them and never catch sight of one another. Charging into his late sixties, Jack still had a head of mostly-black hair he slicked back with Vitalis hair oil and covered year-round with a cap. His eyes loomed large and dark behind glasses as thick as transparency would permit. The old man was dressed, eternally, in a long-sleeved white shirt and baggy Pointer overalls.

When everyone was seated, Rose recited the prayer. Although only a salutation and two brief lines, Granjack's hand was fondling a chicken breast before the "Amen." There was rarely much conversation at the table. Granjack attacked his food with an urgency learned when sharing meals with lumberjacks at a forty-foot table. Rose ignored the old man's grunts and slurps, having long since accepted that his table manners were as irredeemable as his all-mighty soul. He ate everything with a spoon, except meat which he speared with a fork. Lately, Jeff had grown almost as taciturn as his grandfather. Rose longed for a dinner table like that on "Father Knows Best," where even Bud, the teen-age boy, gushed with ideas and opinions.

When the silence grew oppressive, Rose ventured a question. "Did you go to the movies last night?"

Jeff, eager to finish and head over to Marty's house, was packing away food at a trencherman's pace. "Uh, yeah," he replied. Was that where he said he was going?

"What did you see?"

"'The Ten Commandments. At the drive-in.'"

"Oh, I'd love to see that. It was good, wasn't it?"

"Not bad. But I heard the book is supposed to be better." Jeff was willing to be sociable, if that was what it took to keep Rose from discovering he was lying through his teeth.

Rose laughed. "Did you take Vicky?"

"She's still at cheerleader camp."

As quickly as the name passed Rose's lips, she regretted it. The girl had been a source of pain and contention for over two years. Rose knew as surely as God made home-grown tomatoes that Vicky Parrish was not nearly good enough for her son. Bad family, bratty kid. Of course, she would have been hard put to locate a female who was worthy—Rockton being a small town in only the medium-sized state of North Carolina. Slim pickings.

Not another word was spoken until Granjack removed his napkin from under his chin and placed it on a plate scraped so clean it scarcely needed washing. "Law took that Carswell boy off. Said he robbed a gas station in Richardson. Leaves Ab two men short a crew on the Adair land."

"Wrong time of year to look for help," Rose said. "Every man in the county willing to work is working."

"I reckon it's time for Jeff to cut," Granjack said. He reached over and snatched a half-eaten biscuit from Jeff's plate. He salted the biscuit as he did every scrap of food he ate.

Rose placed her knife and fork on her plate. "He can work with the crew after he graduates. He's got plenty to do around the lumberyard."

"Don't need a lumberyard if we got no lumber," Jack countered.

"I don't mind working with the crew," Jeff said. "It'll get me in shape for football."

His words were ignored.

"Needs to learn the business from the ground up if he's gonna run it," the old man said. He scavenged a piece of chicken skin off the serving plate.

"But those men..." Rose shuddered at the thought of introducing her only son into the rogue's gallery of slack-jaws, felons and miscreants she paid off in cash every Saturday. "More of them have been to prison than to fifth grade."

"Oh, they'll drink and fight till hell wouldn't have it, but Jeff don't have to follow them around on a Saturday night. Ever one of 'em got somethin' to teach him," Granjack said, pushing away from the table.

"Like where to find a bail bondsman at two o'clock in the morning," Jeff offered.

Granjack frowned and Rose's head dropped to within inches of her plate.

"I'm going over to Marty's," Jeff said, as he carried his plate to the kitchen sink. "I'll start with the crew in the morning."

Rose sat alone in the dining room with half a plate of food, no appetite, and the realization that when the sun rose in the morning, her baby boy would be sailing off with the pirates.

CHAPTER THREE

Jack Stuart sat on the running board of his old Ford pickup, dawn's light at his back, and stared off toward the Blue Ridge Mountains. Although more than forty miles distant, and obscure to even the eagle that circled overhead, the old man believed he could see the very pinnacle that towered over the cove where he had been born. He recalled the smell of the cabin he shared with his mother, father and two sisters. The feel of wet grass under bare feet, the sound of the creek, the taste of blackberries.

Jack's great-great-grandfather, Robert Stuart, was descended from one of the contingent of Scotsmen dispatched by the British government in the 17th century to establish a beachhead of Protestantism and civil order among the ungovernable Catholics of northeast Ireland. Jack's bedtime stories had been populated with skirmishes between valiant Scots defying English treachery and Irish ignorance and prejudice. The tale of Robert's flight, with wife and son, from famine and bigotry in 1772 to the promise of American prosperity never failed to stir the young boy's blood.

After docking in Philadelphia, Robert and a company of kinsmen set off on the Old Wagon Road for the northwest Carolina frontier—a feral mountainous land that harked back to the Scot Highlands that all revered but none had ever seen. They settled and hunted the dense forests, fished the swift waters, and planted their first crops around the roots of felled trees. Legendary were the tales of battle with Cherokee Indians, bear, wolf and wildcat. No less sinister to the Scots-Irish was the specter of Government that would inevitably intrude, impose ideas, extract taxes.

Jack's father, James, would dutifully recount stories of the following three generations of Stuarts, but the boy's memory and imagination never strayed far from the pioneer Robert. To strike out across sea and over mountain to an unknown fate in uncharted territory would be young Jack's life. He would not be shackled by land and family. "The will to do, the soul to dare," in the words of Sir Walter Scott.

The tragic death of James Stuart in 1899, could be considered traditional for the Scots-Irish in that it involved whiskey, guns, and an assumed breach of honor. James' death left wife Mary with three children—Jack being the youngest—to raise. After a mourning period that many in her church considered unnaturally brief, Mary sold the Stuart land to the Pennsylvania Timber Company for little more than enough to pay the family's debt at the general store. Anxious to leave behind a clannish and spiteful settlement, she prepared for a new life. She had seen a poster promising housing and a generous weekly paycheck to men, women and children willing to move to a "Model Community" centered around a church, a school, and friendly neighbors. Down the mountain, the Rockton Textile Company was hiring all comers.

Jack was nine years-old when he walked the eleven miles to the railhead. As the man of the family, he resisted crying and attempted to comfort his two sisters. He remembered how the earth shook as the train rounded—

"Ready to go, Granjack?" Jeff called.

The old man jumped at the sound of the voice. "Hell, yes," he said, as he pulled himself up on the truck mirror. "You already farted away the best part of the morning. If it wadn't your first day, I'd have Ab fire you."

Jeff climbed into the driver's seat and waited while Granjack hauled his five and a half feet of stiff joints into the cab. The key was in the ignition; the old man had lost it so many times he'd quit taking it out.

Jeff rolled past his mother's house at a snail's pace to avoid kicking up dust, and Rose's ire, and accelerated only slightly as he drove down the three hundred yards of winding, wooded driveway that ended at the paved road. A quarter mile to the left lay Stuart Lumber—a wood frame office building out front, a cabinet shop and four sheds of machinery and stacked lumber behind an eight-foot chain link fence. The old man pointed to the right.

After rolling over miles of twisting pavement, Jeff followed Granjack's hand gestures up a series of dirt roads, all leading deeper into the hills. Driving the old truck was always a trial for Jeff since the Ford's clutch was at best tricky and at worst devilishly cunning. The steering wheel had anywhere from a quarter to a half revolution's play—it varied according to temperature, humidity, and moon phase—so he never knew when an attempted turn would actually take place.

After a long, silent twenty minutes, the old man jabbed a crooked index finger to the right. Jeff turned the truck up a steep red clay logging trail that had been cut through a heavily wooded forest. The trail was narrow, rutted, and still wet from a light rain the night before. He downshifted into low gear, knowing it would take every bit of engine left in the old pick-up to climb the hill.

The Ford pulled resolutely up the slope with the driver scanning for the path of least resistance while monitoring the engine's whine. Jeff heard the oncoming roar only seconds before the loaded two-and-a-half-ton lumber truck flashed into view. The deuce-and-a-half was barreling down the hill, and nothing short of a brick wall could stop it. On instinct, the boy hit his brakes and steered hard to the right. The pickup slid into the side ditch just as the lumber truck flashed by.

"Damn it, boy, he missed you by better'n two feet. You coulda eased her over to the side, kept her rollin'." Granjack exhaled a long, tired breath, sounding more disappointed than angry. "See if she'll back out, then take her to the bottom."

Jeff gripped the wheel tightly to keep Granjack from seeing his hands were sweating and shaking. The fact that both could hear the whine and groan of chain saws just up the road rubbed salt into the boy's wound. He nearly flooded the engine when he tried to restart it, and he had to rock the truck from low to reverse repeatedly to get it out of the ditch and rolling down the hill.

The long ride backward gave the old man plenty of time to think about the trouble with kids who had grown up after the Depression. Having pulled a man's load since he was twelve years old, Jack knew if you waited until a boy was sixteen or seventeen before you worked him daylight to dark, you had no better than a Chinaman's chance of ever making anything worth a shit out of him.

Starting anew from the bottom of the hill, Jeff drove up the logging trail in silence and parked in the clearing alongside a flatbed truck. He grabbed Granjack's ancient chainsaw from the truck bed and followed the old man toward an ear-ripping riot of saws, trucks, and tractors. Above the cacophony, Jeff could make out the shouts of the foreman.

"Goddamn it, Leon, are you goin' to fiddle-fuck with that hickory tree all day? Cut the somebitch up and be done with it!" yelled Ab, the boss. "Lester, Goddamn it, if you ain't gonna do no work, at least stay out of everbudddy's way. You damn near cut Moe's arm off, and then I'd be forced to give him the rest of the day off."

When Ab saw Granjack and Jeff approaching, he turned his roar on them.

"Hell's bells, Jack, can't you get me any better help than this triflin' bunch? I know you come out here to raise hell at *me* when all I got to work with is this bunch of waterheads. If this is the best you can scare up, I'm goin' back to usin' mules."

Ab was over fifty years old and carried the baggage common to men who spent their lives in the timber business. He walked with a brutal limp from a leg mangled by a felled tree, lacked several fingers on each hand, and he'd rather chew off and swallow his tongue than utter two consecutive sentences unleavened by profanity. Every machine that deals seriously with wood degrades the ear, and Ab compensated for his deafness by shouting like a revival preacher.

Ab and Jeff knew each other on sight, since Ab regularly passed through the lumberyard, but they had never done more than nod. Ab's speech impediment kept him out of the office, the domain of Rose, Jeff, and a part-time girl who typed and filed. Ab blushed every time Rose said, "Good morning."

"I brung you some help," Granjack said, nodding toward Jeff.

"Hell, Jack," Ab snorted, shifting his weight from good leg to bad in an agitated sort of buck and wing. "I need three hairy-ass convicts and you give me a file clerk. I'll have to put two men on him to see he don't cut his own damn leg off. Sure as he does, Miss Rose will take a saw to my ass."

The old man stared Ab directly in the eye till the foreman managed to keep both feet on the ground simultaneously. "He'll be alright," Granjack said flatly.

As Jeff poured gas and oil into his chainsaw, Granjack directed Ab's attention to a lumber truck taking on logs. "Why the hell you got trucks runnin' *down* that road? We cut you a road takes you across the ridge and drops you right on Highway Ninety." The old man pointed to a steep trail running straight up the hill. "You could cut better'n half hour off the trip."

"I noticed your damn road right off, Jack," Ab said, and spat tobacco in that direction. "I ain't blind. But which one of these lame-dicks do you think is gonna drive it when it's slick as owl shit? They all got wives and whores to go home to. I'm three men short a crew now, and none of 'em I'd trust to drive so much as a goddamn kiddy car at the county fair."

Granjack sized up the crew. He pointed to a stocky man wearing an Army fatigue shirt and ball cap. "He can drive,"

Ab shook his head and scratched his crotch. "He just started last week. Didn't say shit about drivin' truck."

Granjack nodded. Ab put two fingers in his mouth and whistled over the din of chain saws and trucks. Everyone within forty yards looked up. Ab pointed and shouted, "Hunter! Haul ass!"

Cody Hunter cut off his saw and set it on an oak stump. Wiping the sweat and dirt from his forehead with his sleeve, he ambled toward the truck. He appeared to Jeff to be about five-foot-ten, broad shouldered and possessed the bluest eyes he'd ever seen on a man. When Hunter took off his soaked cap and ran his fingers through his long black hair, Jeff was instantly thrust back into the Hitching Post watching that guitar-playing cat rock that redneck crowd into a riot.

"You ever drive truck?" Ab bellowed, although Hunter stood no more than three feet away.

Hunter nodded.

"Can you drive *that* truck over *that* hill?" Ab asked, aggressively jabbing half an index finger at the truck, then at the hill.

Hunter repeated Ab's gesture. "Is *that* truck worth a shit?"

Ab nodded emphatically. "Good goddamn truck." Ab limped over to the truck and shouted at the man inside. "Piney, take your lunch."

Piney grabbed a brown paper bag from under the seat and climbed out of the cab. Cody crawled in. After two men secured the logs with heavy chains, Cody cranked up, gunned the motor a couple times, and pulled slowly away. Nobody laid down his saw, but every man on the crew kept an eye on the truck as it approached the steep, slick hill. Several times the truck appeared to stop, the rear end slipping visibly before grimly inching forward.

Piney, standing next to Jeff, unwrapped a boloney sandwich and chewed loudly as he watched the agonizing ascent. When the truck cleared the crest of the hill, the displaced driver couldn't help but express his admiration. "That damn Cody," Piney grunted, "fight, fuck, or run a foot race, it don't make no nevermind to him."

Jeff had been led to believe that slavery had been abolished in the United States—he recalled hearing about a war being fought over the issue. But if that were true, then why were all these men sweating bucketfuls in the summer heat, working dawn to dusk for a wage scarcely sufficient to keep a wiry body fed and a tin roof overhead. The crucial difference, Jeff decided, was that a logger *could* quit if he managed to scrape together enough money to chase another job that required no education, no skill, and no qualification other than the willingness to perform dangerous, gut-busting labor for eleven hours a day.

Jeff had played varsity football for the past three years, freshman through junior, and had endured August practice in full pads; he'd assumed that was as close to Hell as he was likely to get without dying. Logging was a damn sight worse. The only break you got on a logging crew was thirty minutes for lunch and the few minutes it took to fill your chain saw with gas and oil a couple of times a day. In order to avoid the wrath of Ab, you had to work at the speed of the crew; unfortunately, the loggers had internalized the pace of the chain saw—a ruthlessly efficient tool as contemptuous of silence and idleness as the profane foreman. And the innate, off-hand vulgarity that flowed with every audible breath from the loggers made locker room obscenity sound as civil as Baptist Sunday School chatter.

On that first day, Jeff made just about every mistake a new man could make, short of maiming himself or another. A badly notched walnut tree had split on the stump, ruining many board feet of valuable wood; his chain knot had slipped off a log causing the tractor—called a "skidder"—at the other end of the chain to lurch forward and nearly topple down a hill; finally, misjudging the lean of a white pine, he dropped it so close to Ab that the foreman had to scramble away as fast as his leg-and-a-half could manage. "Goddamn it, boy," Ab sputtered, grabbing his hat from under the limb that had snatched it off his head, "be patient. You ain't worked here long enough to wanta kill me!"

Jeff knew every eye was grading his performance. He worked as fast as he could with Granjack's old saw, but he lagged well behind the rest of the crew. Light was fading when Ab called the crew in with three blasts of the truck's horn. The loggers trudged back to the clearing and silently gathered around the tall metal water cooler on the back of the truck. The workmen filled up any container they could find and gulped down the warm liquid. Some placed their mouth on the spout and sucked water until they were pushed away. Jeff sat on the ground and leaned against the truck tire waiting for his shot at the cooler.

The next-to-last man in line tilted the cooler above his head and savored the trickle that dripped into his mouth. "Dead soldier," he pronounced, and bounced the water can across the truck bed. Jeff bowed his head, hoping no one could see how desperate he was.

"Holy shit, boys, you gone water-soft on me." Ab said, tossing the dented cooler into the passenger seat of the truck. "Back when I was cuttin', that much water would last us two days. You lame-dicks cut half the wood and double up on water."

Everybody cussed Ab and the old days as they clambered onto the back of the flat bed. Ab was cranked and in gear when Jeff attempted to pull himself aboard the chest-high truck bed. The truck rolled downhill, but Jeff's arms refused to respond to the demand. He stumbled along but felt his grip slipping. He avoided disgrace and injury when a strong hand grabbed the seat of his pants and hauled him aboard.

"Don't wanna lose you," Cody Hunter said, smiling down grimly. "You make the rest of us look good."

CHAPTER FOUR

Jeff, Marty and Chuck stared down at the green felt pool table in grudging admiration as Rabbit banked the seven ball cleanly into the corner pocket. The cue ball kissed the rail and spun off at an oblique angle, giving Rabbit the shape he wanted. The eight ball was an easy tap into the side pocket as the cue ball nudged the nine off the rail toward the corner pocket. Rabbit's shot on the money ball was a gimmee.

"I got lucky on that seven ball," Rabbit said, as he tapped the corner pocket with his stick before sinking the nine ball. "I was just framming away hoping it'd find a hole to hide in."

"Right," said Chuck, as he flipped his half dollar on the table. "The closer you get to the nine ball, the luckier you get."

Jeff rubbed the two quarters in his hand together and considered the sweat and energy expended behind a chain saw to earn the money Rabbit had effortlessly extracted. "Well," Jeff sighed, tossing the quarters on the table, "easy come, easy go."

"Let's get outta here," Chuck said. "Find some action."

Jeff and Marty nodded. They had only intended to pass enough time in the cramped, smoky poolroom to allow the air to turn black outside. Each boy, since leaving his home around seven o'clock, had harbored that Saturday Night Feeling, the gut belief that something exciting, something *big* was going to happen—you just didn't know what, where or when. But all knew it wouldn't happen in the poolroom.

The boys hung up their cues and descended the long dark steps that led to the sidewalk of Main Street. "You know," Marty said, still puzzled, "that guy didn't shoot that good when we were watching him."

"Yeah," Chuck sneered, "but once the money hit the table, he didn't miss. You notice how when *we* made a ball, our next shot was harder. When *he* made a ball, his shots got easier."

The view confronting the boys when they spilled through the propped door at the foot of the stairs did little to encourage their fantasies. Rockton's business district, a single row of two-story red brick buildings that ran for three uneven blocks along Main Street, could not have appeared more desolate had there been tumbleweeds blowing down the sidewalk. To the north stretched a series of locked store fronts, relieved only by a single lighted building—the City Cafe was open but nearly empty. A block to the south, the Main Theater had already admitted an audience to view a Dean Martin—Jerry Lewis film. Having just left the pool room and disdainful of the movie, the boys had exhausted every public entertainment in Rockton.

The sporadic traffic on Main Street rolled through the gauzy, humid twilight with weary indifference. The only purposeful action in sight was centered across the street and beyond the railroad tracks where Rockton Textiles' workers sweated out their shift before slouching home to the Mill Hill at midnight. Three men and two short, wiry women, all covered with a dusting of cotton lint, stood on the mill's loading dock. They alternately smoked and coughed, taking a break from the stifling heat and ungodly clatter inside.

"Ain't nothin' shakin' but the leaves on the trees," Marty said, as he lit up a Winston. Since his father was the pastor of the First Baptist Church, Marty felt honor-bound to offend the ancientry at every public opportunity.

Rockton had grown up around the cotton mills and furniture factories that arrived with the railroad shortly before the turn of the century. The first dirt road, and the railroad tracks that paralleled it on a north-south route through town, were designed to promote swift passage of goods from Rockton factories to the two larger towns—Oak City and Richardson—which lay about seven miles from Rockton's city limits at opposite ends of Main Street. Stores sprouted on the east side of Main Street, but the placement of the railroad tracks dictated that at no point could public shops face each other over picturesque tree-shaded streets in the classic small town tradition. Industry had prospered, jobs were available, but there was little in Rockton to tempt a visitor to settle and raise a family, or even to tarry and shop.

Jeff reached through the open window of his mother's station wagon and turned on the radio. Marty paced the sidewalk smoking as fast as he could raise and lower his arm. Chuck shadowboxed with his reflection in the Western Auto's plate glass window. The boys had time to kill. Being under-age, they had to wait until pitch dark before pulling around to the back lot of the Village Diner in Oak City. There, an embittered middle-aged curb-hop would charge them an extra dollar per six-pack for the privilege of buying Pabst Blue Ribbon Beer. Only Pabst Blue Ribbon. Keep them in their place. Stuck in summer's interminable twilight, the boys could do nothing but wait conspicuously in the middle of town in hope that someone would cruise up with a better offer—guys with tale of a party, girls with a suggestion of romance. It could happen; it just never did.

Rockton's Saturday nights had once teemed with commerce and sociability. The town had grown steadily throughout the first three decades of the century, and endured stubbornly through the Great Depression, but had peaked in population and vitality shortly after World War II. Throughout the half century, Rockton had been self-sufficient, with clothing, hardware, furniture and dime stores thriving quietly in the center of town. Three cafes, a poolroom, and a couple of store basements sold beer to farmers and factory workers while their wives shopped. Behind the old courthouse, an area called the Hog Wallow had attracted men eager to swap horses, guns, whisky, lies or what-have-you. Soapbox preachers railed, while neighbors exchanged opinions and, occasionally, blows.

This Garden of Redneck Delights came to an abrupt halt in 1950. A newly-elected mayor, haunted by the ghost of his derelict father and offended by the drunkenness and affray that commonly resulted when alcohol metabolized through the Scots-Irish temperament, joined with the town's preachers and chased alcohol and its public consumers out of town.

Unfortunately, that prohibition coincided with the dramatic increase of automobiles that rolled into the area with post-war prosperity. The trip to the large, diverse, dynamic and decidedly "wet" Oak City became fast and fashionable, taking business revenue and city taxes with them. Slowly, inevitably, businesses leaked from the town's center. By 1956, nearly a quarter of the red brick storefronts on Main Street were vacant and the sidewalk frequently empty.

Finally, the tidal wave of television receivers that flooded Rockton in the early 1950's dramatically reduced the number of folks who traditionally turned out on warm summer nights to socialize. Although nobody in town complained, and few seemed to notice, you could fairly accuse Marshall Matt Dillon of "Gunsmoke" of shooting a hole directly through the heart of Rockton's Saturday night.

While Fats Domino crooned, "Blue Monday," Jeff walked to the front of the station wagon and eased up on the hood. "Damn," he said, "I'd love to hear some rock 'n' roll tonight. Somebody's got to be playing somewhere, and we just don't know about it." Jeff mimicked playing the guitar and singing "Blue Suede Shoes."

"What's so damn hot about that Hunter guy?" Marty asked, irritated. The whole Hitching Post experience remained a sore point for both Marty and Chuck. They had been chased from the parking lot and forced to sit beerless in the station wagon while Jeff reportedly had a blast inside. "You've heard Carl Perkins and Elvis sing that song. You're not telling me that guy can sing better than Elvis."

"I've heard Carl Perkins and Elvis sing *on a record*," Jeff said slowly. "I heard Cody Hunter sing it *in person*. No more'n ten feet away. It's the difference between..." Jeff struggled for comparison, "seeing a picture of a naked woman, and seeing a naked woman."

The analogy struck Marty right between the eyes. If there was a subject the preacher's boy knew thoroughly—backwards and forwards, you might say—it was pictures of naked women. Inside Marty Ryder's bedroom closet, secreted in a cache so obscure and discrete only a burglar could truly appreciate its subtlety, rested the finest collection of pornography in the town of Rockton. Marty's archive had grown so large and diverse he'd been forced to store the overflow in the bomb shelter behind the parsonage.

"Let's go get the beer," Jeff said, sliding off the hood. "Drive around. See what happens."

The three piled into the Plymouth, and Jeff eased back into the street. The loud wail of sirens approaching at high speed forced Jeff to pull forward quickly. Each boy had his head out of a window in time to see a cherry-red 1950 Ford flash down Main Street trailing two police cars in desperate pursuit. All heads jerked back inside the car and exchanged expressions of wonder.

"Good God, Gertie." Chuck said, shaking his head. "There's at least one man in this town who ain't bored."

Cody Hunter roared down Main Street at eighty miles per hour, a song in his heart, a pint of Old Crow in his lap, and a prayer on his lips. "O Lord, if you get me through this light, You won't have to worry about me no more, cause I'll lose these lame bastards."

Cody sailed through the green light, "Praise Jesus!" at the Main Theater and slid the Ford sideways as he made the slight right turn that took him off Main

Street. He forced a farmer in a pickup off the road before straightening out and aiming his machine down the winding asphalt two-lane that led to a web of dirt roads west of town. Once on dirt, Cody knew there wasn't a cop in the state who could stay within pistol range. Even Parrish—and Cody knew damn well one of the cop cars tailing him was piloted by Police Chief Ray Parrish—was getting too old to lean into the curves like he had five or six years back when they had first swapped paint and dents on those roads.

Cody felt cocky, coasting at eighty-five and catching only an occasional glimpse of the black and white cruiser in his mirror. He was lining up the particulars of a night of debauchery—music, liquor, women—when his right front tire busted, as he later described, like a cheap rubber. The Ford lurched, slid, and nearly rolled. In the expanded time that crisis creates, Cody sized up factors of machine weight, road surface and terrain as he fought for control. He presumed throughout the ordeal that he would wrestle the car to a gentle stop then tear ass into a patch of woods and disappear.

Anger and betrayal flared in Cody when the Ford's passenger side slid heavily into the side ditch. His body slammed against the steering wheel, and his head cracked the driver's side window. He was barely conscious when the lights and sirens engulfed him, but he recognized his nemesis. The Chief jerked the door open and hauled the driver out by his shirtfront and flung him to the ground. Then Parrish beat Cody with his nightstick until two deputies pulled him off.

As he lay in a bloody heap, Cody moaned, "Harder, Parrish, harder."

CHAPTER FIVE

Cody Hunter never had a chance. Any hope his mother and his pastor entertained concerning a life of Christian probity for the boy was destroyed by a pair of occurrences even a Rationalist, if one could be found in Rockton, might term diabolic. Both incidents befell Cody in early adolescence, and in each case the boy was selected into a situation that would have tempted a saint.

Cody won prizes at the Free Will Baptist Church for attendance and scholarship, and most assumed he would become the church's pianist as soon as arthritis finally forced Mrs. Emmylou Kent to relinquish her stony grip on the keyboard. Alienated from a stern father who fumed at the prospect of his only son turning into a mollycoddle, Cody found acceptance and security in the bosom of the church.

Cody might have walked the steps of righteousness throughout his life had his path not crossed the back yard of Lula Shoal's mill house. One warm spring morning on his way to school, eighth-grader Cody was lured into the home of ninth-grader Lula. Cody cheerfully agreed to help Lula free a puppy she claimed was trapped behind her heavy couch. Once inside, the boy was confronted with a vision that he knew not, understood not, but compelled him mightily. Red-haired, freckled, lush and loose, Lula wore a nightgown fashioned from a Martin Brothers' feed sack that did little to confine the creamy flesh that strained the wide, black-threaded stitches. Emblazoned in a semicircle arced across her high breasts to slightly below her waist was the mill's motto: "Get Your Grinding Done Here."

When Lula slowly pulled the sack over her head, her ample body shimmied in the rosy sunlight that streamed through the open window. Cody watched the flesh roll till he feared his own body might burst into flame. Although fascinated by the entire vision, Cody couldn't tear his eyes away from a perfect triangle of fiery hair where he had never imagined such a growth. As Lula turned and beckoned, Cody fought the urge to flee. Instead, he faced temptation head-on. Several times. Although he was unsure of exactly how the game was played—what was expected of him, how all the parts fit together—Lula was operating seasoned equipment and didn't mind helping Cody break his in.

After a torturous night of guilt and recrimination, Cody returned to Lula's door and pallet the next morning. Thereafter he did not miss a weekday morning session, often arriving so early he had to wait for Lula's father to leave for work before stealing inside. By the third week, Cody's guilt had mutated into an active resentment against those holy folks who would have denied him this bliss. He began to suspect they might have lied to him about other things—perhaps, *everything*.

Although sorely tempted, he told none of his friends of his conquest, and few noted a whit of difference in his behavior. His mother, however, was pleased by how easy it had become to get her boy out of bed and off to school, while Cody's math teacher noted the boy had developed a problem keeping his mind on fractions first thing in the morning.

In less than a month, Cody's love nest was broken up when Lula's father returned for the lunch he had mistakenly left in the icebox. Cody managed to avoid a certain mauling by diving half-naked through an open window, but Lula's father beat her as he would a mad dog with mange, then shipped her off to relatives in Alabama for moral rehabilitation.

Cody never again looked at the world in the same way. The Lula experience had imparted an awareness rarely visited upon one so young. That awareness clung to Cody like a second skin, an aura apparent to some men, but virtually all women.

Cody's slide into dissipation was greased shortly after he started high school. Ira Hunter's single concession to his wife, Carrie, was an annual reunion for her family, the Hagens, at the Hunter home. Following the late afternoon picnic, Ira retired sullenly to his room, and the Hagens gathered in the parlor with a piano, several guitars and a standup bass.

Cody had long been accepted by the Hagen clan as a prodigy and the heir-apparent to their musical legacy, but out of deference to Carrie they had restricted the boy's participation to the early evening hours of their music-making sessions—hymn time. Once night fell and the men began the short trips to their cars to commune with the bottles that lived in brown paper bags—no liquor in the house—the music would descend to the secular, and the room would be cleared of children and sensitive women.

After the last chorus of "Onward Christian Soldier," Uncle Dolman rose from the piano to make the first of many visits to his car trunk. Cody seized the instrument and launched into a spirited version of a song he'd heard on KWKH's "Louisiana Hayride." As the women chased the kids outside, Cody performed "Lovesick Blues" just like that Hayride regular, Hank Williams sang it. Nobody challenged Cody's right to stay for the party after he flashed that hole card. When the piano was occupied, several uncles were eager to teach the boy guitar runs.

Shortly thereafter Uncle Dolman began stopping by the Hunter house on Friday or Saturday nights to take young Cody to the high school football games, or bowling, or cat fishing. Carrie was glad to have her brother spend some time with her son. Father Ira and Cody had grown openly hostile, and she understood the boy needed a man to teach him, well, man-things.

And teach the boy, he did. Good ol' Uncle Dolman took Cody straight to "Rambler's Inn," a local honky-tonk. Although still a minor, Cody had that way about him, that awareness, that convinced everyone he was older than he looked. He knew when to keep his mouth shut and how to make himself scarce when trouble, or the law, was afoot. Soon he was sitting in with the band.

Dolman attempted to keep Cody away from the vilest temptations at Rambler's Inn. But being only human, and prone to take a drink he occasionally lost track of the boy. Then, Cody would be left to defend himself against alcohol, tobacco, and the sort of woman who had nothing better to do than sap the precious bodily fluids of a handsome, young boy. Perhaps Cody tried to defend himself against that onslaught of vice; if he did, the effort passed unnoticed. Left to explore a wonderland that could have been lifted from the collective unconscious of the male adolescent, Cody acquitted himself with all the honor and virtue one might expect from a fifteen year-old. That being none, or right next to it.

By the time Cody's parents rescued their son from the honky-tonk life, the boy had gained such insight into the human condition there was very little reason to believe he would ever be satisfied with singing "Hail to Rockton High" at the homecoming football game, holding a steady job, tithing, or saving redeemable coupons to purchase patio/lawn furniture. In short, the odds were surpassing long young Hunter would ever develop into a respectable citizen. The die was cast in lead, the mold discarded, for even the Angels despair of redeeming souls cursed to live out their teen-age fantasies.

CHAPTER SIX

Jeff climbed the steps to the front porch and raised his right hand, ready to play his own peculiar version of "Lady or the Tiger." As the setting July sun burned a hole in his back, he rapped three times. Taking a step back onto the WIPE YOUR FEET mat, he braced for the worst.

Ray Parrish, all six-feet three-inches and two hundred fifty-five pounds, glared through the screen door. Resplendent in sleeveless ribbed T-shirt, plaid Bermuda shorts, and black socks, Rockton's Chief of Police was off-duty but on-alert. The face that red meat, blended whiskey and high blood pressure had stained pink was frozen in an expression of hostile inquisition demanding: Why in hell, is this punk standing on my doorstep with a handful of flowers?

"Is Vicky ready, Sir?" Jeff's voice was level, his gaze direct.

The Chief snorted and stomped back into his den. Jeff waited for the trail to cool before following. The Chief sat in an armchair facing the television, a folding meal tray with a plateful of food in front of him. A floor fan, turned full-blast and aimed point-blank, did little to slow the canals of sweat that rolled from the Chief's blonde crew-cut into his T-shirt. Jeff assumed a chair to the right and behind his host, closest to the door.

Jeff stared absently at *You Asked for It*—an animal trainer was wrestling a huge anaconda in a shallow pool—until he heard quick steps descending the staircase. Vicky Parrish was a teenage vision in a sleeveless white blouse and navy blue skirt cut two inches higher than any other respectable girl in town dared. What a package: Blond hair, blue eyes, skin as smooth as glare ice, and a figure that provoked tortured adolescent dreams throughout Rockton. Thirty years later middle-aged men would still recall that body with awe.

"You look great," Jeff said. He ached to touch her, but kept his hands pinned to his sides.

"So do you," she said, accepting the flowers. "You're so tan."

"Did your mother say you could wear that?" the Chief asked, craning his head around.

"Yeeees, Daddy." Vicky said. The pair rushed out the door.

"Eleven o'clock or there's hell to pay," the Chief shouted.

"I'm sorry I wasn't at the door," Vicky said. They held hands as they crossed the lawn. "I didn't hear your car."

"That's alright. At least he wasn't cleaning his gun tonight."

"Yeah, Mama talked to him about that."

When they reached the stop sign at the end of the block, recognized as the limit of the Chief's eyesight and jurisdiction, they exchanged several kisses. At Woody's Drive-In, Jeff wolfed down a sliced barbecue and a cheeseburger as Vicky nibbled and spoke breathlessly about cheerleader camp.

"It was the best two weeks of my *whole, entire* life. I didn't know there was so much to learn. The people in this town just *think* they've seen cheerleading. Just wait till September. I even found out some things I can do with those two clumsy little sophomores. I'll stick them out on the ends, they called it the 'wings' at camp—"

If anything in life could be termed predestined, then surely it was Vicky Parrish's rise to the top of the cheerleading pyramid. Perhaps God could have stopped it, but he would have had to drop everything else for awhile. In the Parrish family album there was a snapshot of five-year-old Vicky in a home-sewn outfit, feet wide-spread, tiny fists resting on hips, chest out, chin up, eyes confidently transfixing the camera—Born to Lead Cheers!

There were prettier faces in the high school than Vicky's. However, owing to a glorious quirk of Nature, her face projected the indefinable spark that can propel a dancer from the chorus to the lead or thrust a country preacher from a twelve-pew church into a massive revival tent. She had a smile capable of making every male in a crowd feel as though it were targeted at him. Although too short at five-feet three-inches to be taken seriously as a model or a dancer, her body was sublimely round and supple when viewed from any angle; when wedded with an allure Vicky accessed only when performing, the elements so mixed in her that Nature might stand up and shout: "This is a Cheerleader!"

"Do they still have you working out in the woods all day?" Vicky asked abruptly.

The question jerked Jeff back to the present. During Vicky's monologue, Jeff's thoughts had wandered off to his own plans for the night. Their last date before Vicky's pilgrimage to camp had left Jeff with the hope, the belief their relationship, after years of slowly creeping foreplay, fiveplay, six-, eight-, ten-play, would finally be consummated. Jeff had found it tough to think of anything else for the last fortnight. He had crammed his billfold full of Trojan condoms in anticipation.

"Uh, yeah," Jeff said, "it's not so bad. I'll be in good shape for football."

Vicky slid her hand under Jeff's short sleeve and squeezed the biceps that Jeff reflexively tightened into a baseball-tight muscle.

"I was thinking we might go to Chuck's place on Sugar Beach for awhile," Jeff said. "They'll have the ski boat out and there'll be a bunch of kids there. Sounds like fun." Of course, by sunset Chuck's folks would be tanked-up and disinclined to chaperone anything but a tumbler of bourbon. Friends, free food and beer, an unsupervised boat. And eventually there would be time to slip off to the woods—

"Oh, Jeff," Vicky said, as she lifted his arm and slid under it. "How about if we just go to the drive-in. There's a movie, all the girls at camp talked about it, *Love Is a Many Splendored Things.* It's on at the Starlite."

Jeff stiffened. Vicky pressed on quickly. "After the movie there'll be time to go somewhere, lay the back seat down," she purred into his ear, "and see what happens."

Jeff shifted uneasily. "They won't start the show till dark, it'll be too late—"

"It's not a long movie, and we can leave early if it's no good. It's just that," Vicky rubbed his chest lightly, "I don't want to share you with anyone else tonight."

Jeff acceded, staying focused on his larger plan for the night. But he did not know Vicky remembered their last date just as vividly. She had decided Jeff must be denied this particular night. He was just taking too much for granted.

They went to the drive-in and watched the sappy, bullshit movie that Vicky attended to as though it were Holy Writ. After enduring previews of coming attractions, two cartoons, and a movie split by an intermission, Jeff had to speed to deliver Vicky home at 10:58. He refused the offered goodnight kiss and swore to himself he would find something to do with the guys the following weekend.

CHAPTER SEVEN

"Sweet Jesus, it's hot," Ab moaned aloud, as he pulled out his pocket watch. Even though the watch was the heaviest thing he'd lifted all day, Ab was drenched in sweat. At twelve o'clock sharp, he sounded the truck horn and the woods fell silent. The loggers slouched toward the truck carrying their chain saws like crosses. They formed a sullen line to the big water cooler on the back of the truck, each man trying to slake his thirst before resorting to his own jug. When the men climbed on the back of the flatbed truck at sundown, there would not be a drop of consumable water on the site.

Jeff got his mouthful of water, grabbed his lunch, and looked for a place to collapse. Often, a raucous blackjack game would break out on back of the flatbed, but on this particular July day, no one appeared capable of lifting fifty-two playing cards. Jeff was looking for shade and a stump to lean against when he spotted a shadow sitting under a beech tree some forty yards in the distance.

Cody Hunter always sat alone. Each day he wolfed down his lunch, then stretched out on the ground with his ball cap over his face until Ab blew the horn to start work again. He got along with everyone on the crew, joined in the general bullshit, and accepted and doled out his fair share of abuse. When Cody showed up one Monday morning with a battered face that looked like it belonged on a "Mr. Potato Head" doll, and confessed he had been cornered, captured, and pummeled by the law-dogs, the crew ragged his ass for allowing himself to be taken alive. Fighting the law was the recreation of choice for the loggers. Jeff assumed he was the only person on the crew who was not on a first name basis with every bail bondsman in the county.

"Mind if I sit down," Jeff asked.

Cody glanced up briefly and shrugged as he unwrapped a Moon Pie and popped the top on a hot Royal Crown Cola.

Jeff sat off to the side so they could talk without having to watch each other eat. "I heard you play at the Hitching Post a while back," Jeff said, biting into his ham and cheese sandwich. "Sounded real good."

"As I recall," Cody said, gazing straight ahead, "not everyone agreed."

There was a long silence as both men ate a little and drank a lot. The woods were quiet as a cemetery, the workmen eating or sleeping, the birds driven away by five solid hours of angry chain saw.

"You playin' anywhere now?" Jeff asked.

"Workin' somethin' up with some guys." Cody said, around bites of an apple. "You pick?"

"No," Jeff said. "But let me know the next time you play. I'd like to be there."

Cody turned his head slowly and took a long hard look at Jeff. "You got a drivin' license?"

Jeff was more than a mite bewildered as he attempted to follow the carelessly drawn map Cody had scribbled on the back of a greasy lunch bag. After wandering over miles of featureless red clay back roads, he was ready to turn the Plymouth around and point it toward home when he caught sight of two wild cherry trees flanking a wide path that might charitably be called a road. He followed tire tracks up the overgrown trail for about fifty yards before emerging into a clearing that held an old wood shingle house and two cars.

Jeff was relieved to see Cody's cherry-red '50 Ford parked next to the house. He knew anybody so devoted to privacy would not look fondly upon a stranger wandering up his driveway. He had been raised to respect the solitude of the folks who had separated themselves for personal or commercial reasons. On several occasions when hunting grouse or quail in these hills, Jeff had stumbled on the rusted remains of deserted moonshine stills. Once he and Granjack had crested a ridge and found themselves within sight of a working still; Granjack grabbed his arm and wordlessly ushered him into a hasty retreat. Granjack didn't even whistle for their dog until they were beyond the range of a high-powered rifle.

Jeff parked between Cody's Ford and a 1946 Studebaker rattletrap whose engine hung suspended from an oak limb above the hood. Engine parts, hub caps, and various wood and metal tools shared the overgrown yard with a rusty wringer washing machine. He spotted some ripe tomatoes growing in a small garden patch renegade weeds had overrun.

A large hound of mixed parentage appeared from under the raised porch. The dog rolled his head and cleared his throat as Jeff walked slowly, carefully toward the stacked concrete block steps. The hound sensed the man did not covet his shady resting spot and considered nothing else worth defending. He bayed once then dropped in a boneless heap into instant, noisy sleep.

Just as Jeff stepped onto the porch, a female voice rang out from inside. "Cody! Ya drivah's heah."

Jeff was surprised by both the pitch and the accent. Cody had never mentioned a girl friend and took much abuse from the other loggers who spoke in lurid detail of their appetites and conquests. The voice was decidedly Yankee, the sort of accent Jeff heard only on television or radio. It was a voice you might hear on "The Goldbergs," or, it flashed into Jeff's mind, a female version of a boxing announcer at Madison Square Garden.

The screen door swung open, and a short, buxom, black-haired woman motioned for Jeff to enter. She wore a halter-top designed for someone with less dramatic cleavage, and a pair of cut-off jeans altered so severely no trace of pant leg remained. Her skin was dark and her hair so shiny and black it appeared wet. Jeff found her face attractive without being "pretty"—the kind of girl who wouldn't be elected homecoming queen, but would never lack for a date on Saturday night.

"C'mon in," she said, "he's still primpin'. He's worsena beauty contestant. Sometimes I gotta separate him from the mirra with a crowba."

She turned quickly and Jeff followed the swaying hips down a short hallway and into a room so cluttered it made Jeff dizzy to stare into it. There were several distinct smells borne on a gentle breeze that flowed under a raised window, but none was unpleasant. Jeff heard a radio playing more static than music, but he couldn't locate the source.

"I'm Naomi," she said, and then pointed to the sofa. "Park it ova theah. You wanta beah?"

"Ma'am?"

Naomi held up an open bottle of Schlitz and shook it. "Do..you..want.. a..beah?" she said, speaking to a foreigner.

Jeff nodded quickly. "Yes, please."

As Naomi walked into the kitchen, Jeff cleared a space on the couch, moving items as various as a baseball bat, issues of Confidential magazine and "Voodoo" comic books, and automobile carburetor parts. Naomi reappeared holding two bottles of Schlitz in her left hand and a church key in her right. She popped the cap and handed the overflowing beer to Jeff. "Don't worry," Naomi said, as he tried to stanch the flow with his thumb, "it'll keep the dust down."

Naomi sat down in a kitchen chair facing him. The boy took a long swallow of beer and consciously averted his eyes from the various cleavages that appealed for admiration. Resistance was futile; all his sight lines seemed to intersect at one lush crease or another.

"So," Naomi said, after knocking down half a beer in one tilt, "how old *are* you?"

Jeff coughed but was spared answering by Cody's appearance in the doorway. "How's it hanging, man?" He wore dungarees but was shirtless, shoeless and still wet from the shower. Cody had the upper body of a middleweight boxer. Not the bulky, showy build of the gym mule, but distinct, striated, cord-like muscles with no fat to hide the blue veins snaking down his arms. He took a drink of Naomi's beer as he toweled off his hair. "You and Naomi gettin' acquainted?"

Jeff nodded. Crossing the room quickly on the balls of his feet, Cody planted himself in front of a mirror, and whipped out a large metal comb from his hip pocket. He took a deep breath and put the finishing touches on his ducktail, Cody noticed the flawed music. "Can you tune that in, baby?"

"Do it yerself." Naomi said, lighting a cigarette and shifting position in the chair. "I'm entertainin' ya friend."

Jeff choked on his beer as he jerked his head away from the peep show. He focused on an unfinished painting that leaned against the far wall.

"You sure you don't want to come along?" Cody asked. He tuned a table model radio attached to an eccentric sculpture of wire, metal coat hangers, and aluminum foil snaking up the wall to the ceiling.

"Naah," she said, managing to sound both hostile and indifferent. "I don't get no kicks stayin' up all night listenin' to you guys play one song ovah and ovah."

"Suit yourself." Cody said, "When we get our shit together, you may have to pay your way to see us."

"By the time ya get your shit together, I'll be too old to care," Naomi said, releasing a thunder cloud of cigarette smoke.

Cody flopped down on the floor to put on his shoes and socks. "OK, Jeff, if you'll grab that amplifier over there—pick it up by the bottom, the top's missin' a screw—and carry it out to the car, we'll get this show on the road."

Jeff had the amp halfway out the door before his heritage asserted itself. He turned to face his hostess and bent slightly at the waist. "It was nice to meet you, Naomi," he said. "I hope to see you again."

The sulleness drained from Naomi's face. "Yeah, right. You, too." Southerners, she thought. You never knew whether they meant it or not.

Jeff opened the Plymouth's trunk as Cody walked out of the house carrying an electric guitar and four beers. "Whoa, Hoss," Cody called from the porch, "let's take the Ford. That old stationary wagon wouldn't pull a greasy string out of a cat's ass."

As Jeff situated the amplifier in the Ford's trunk, Cody laid his guitar on the back seat. "You took a pretty good lick," Jeff said, patting a brutal dent on the passenger side.

"Yeah, that was back when I got my ass lawed. Blew a tire and ditched it." Cody smiled as he opened a beer and handed it to Jeff. "Then the cops beat me till it just wasn't no fun for either of us anymore."

Jeff climbed in under the wheel and gazed through the cracked windshield. He turned the key, and the roar and crackle from the glass-pack muffler thrilled and scared him. He pumped gas to the twin carburetors and felt the power rumble through the frame. The Ford quivered like a high-strung race horse at the gate, eager to show its stuff.

"You oughta feel honored." Cody said. "Fastest wheels around. Every cop in the county's layin' for it. Another beer?"

All trace of smile fled Jeff's face. Driving an outlaw car with a beer in his hand and Public Enemy #1 riding shotgun. Ooooh Mama. He shifted the floor stick into first and cautiously fed the engine gas. The Ford leaped forward like a lion on an antelope.

"Easy now, Hot Shot," Cody laughed, as Jeff wrestled the Ford under control. "Just feel her out for a few miles. Up ahead we got some road where you can *really* kick her in the ass."

The number ten washtub, full of beer when the guys started playing, reluctantly surrendered an icy brew to Jeff's unsteady hand. The dirt-floor garage was cramped and hot, and the beer and still air had generated streams of sweat from the boy's face and body. His ears rang from the point-blank assault of amplified sound. His aching body cried for sleep. And *still* the band played on.

Jeff lowered himself gingerly onto the ground and reluctantly looked at his watch. Three thirty-five! He'd listened to Cody, Bo the bass man, and Sam the drummer, rehearse half-a-dozen songs for over six hours. Jeff waved his arms in surrender.

Cody unstrapped his guitar and leaned it against the amplifier as Bo and Sam continued to work on the rhythm. "What do you think, Hoss?" he asked, as he ran his hand around the washtub and extracted the last bottle of beer. "We worth a shit?" He opened the beer bottle with a church key he carried on a chain around his neck.

"Sounds great, man, but we got work. I shoulda been home..." Jeff's voice trailed off in despair.

Cody rolled the cold bottle across his forehead and turned Jeff's wrist so he could see his watch. "Whoooooa," Cody groaned loudly, as he emptied the beer bottle in three swallows, "it's time to take it home and put it to bed." Jeff nodded and bent over to unhook the amplifier.

"Slow down, son," Cody said, as he strapped on his guitar. "It won't take more'n fifteen minutes to clean up the bridge, then we're outa here."

Jeff sat down heavily, trying desperately to believe he would soon be headed toward a bed and a couple hours of sleep. He fought to chase away the thought of sunrise and chainsaws. Even worse was the obstacle that lay slumbering in his front room. Waiting, worrying.

CHAPTER EIGHT

Rose Stuart dozed fitfully in her armchair until the sound she'd waited hours for finally woke her. *The Search For Bridey Murphy* slid from her stomach to the floor when she stirred at the sound of a distant automobile drawing nearer. By the time the car pulled to a stop, Rose had collected her thoughts and tendered a silent prayer of thanks. The relief she felt quickly gave way to rising anger when she noticed dawn had leaked around the curtains of her window.

After several attempts, Jeff managed to unlock and fumble the front door open. The form that shuffled inside appeared so pitiful and bedraggled Rose's anger mutated reluctantly to concern. "Jeff, are you alright?" she asked, rising from her chair. "Where have you been?"

Half-formed thoughts and random sensations leaped wearily from Jeff's brain like sparks off wet firewood. Throughout the drive home his sluggish mind had reeled when asked to justify the unreasonable. Finally, he'd decided he would simply face the questions when they came and make up answers on the spot. Granted, a piss-poor plan, but the best he could do.

"I don't feel so good, Mama." Jeff said. He closed the door then leaned back against it. "Coulda been something I ate...I was listening to some guys play music in a garage, and they just wouldn't quit playin', and I couldn't leave because I was drivin' one of their cars, and I couldn't call because it was a garage..."

"Have you been drinking?" Rose asked. She pulled her robe tight.

"I had a couple beers."

"Jeffrey, you're under-age. They could put you in jail for that." There was a short silence while Rose untangled the explanation. "Why were you driving someone else's car?"

Jeff was framing his response when the back door opened. Mother and son waited as the footsteps approached the living room.

"Runnin' kinda late, ain't you, boy?" Granjack asked. He stood in the door with a cup of coffee.

"Kinda." Jeff said, relieved to have another party in a conversation that desperately needed variety.

"Well, you better get into work clothes and get there pretty damn quick." Granjack said grimly. "Ab won't abide you showin' up late."

Jeff looked to his mother, hoping for a reprieve he knew he didn't deserve.

"Get ready for work." Rose said. As Jeff walked across the room, she concluded, "You won't be using the car for a week."

"When you cut tall timber at night," Granjack said, as he observed a family tradition extending to a new generation, "there's always stumps to pull in the morning."

Jeff rubbed cold water on his face at the kitchen sink.

"It's a man's own business what he does with his time," Granjack said, as he scooped coffee into the percolator, "so long as he always shows up for work."

While Jeff changed clothes, Rose tried to impose order on a day ruined before sun-up. She took bacon and eggs from the Kelvinator and lit the gas stove to heat the water for grits.

"He won't have time for a sit-down meal," the old man said, opening the morning newspaper to the sports section. "Make him a egg sandwich to eat on the way. He'll need something on his stomach."

"Is he sick, Jack?" Rose asked, as she laid strips of bacon in the black skillet. "Should I call the doctor?"

"He'll live," Granjack said. "And he'll learn a lesson today nobody coulda talked into him."

Rose lowered white bread into the toaster and broke two eggs into a skillet. I'll be glad when school starts, she thought. Then things will get back to normal.

Jeff had to scramble to make it onto the back of the truck that was hauling the crew up to the site. He was helped aboard by Cody Hunter, standing tall, laughing and jolly. Cody appeared righteous and rested as a deacon who'd spent the evening in church and retired early to a warm bed. Jeff shook his throbbing head in admiration and prayed he would make it through the day without throwing up or passing out.

After the crew piled off the truck, Jeff knelt next to Cody as he gassed up his chainsaw. "How in hell do you do it?" Jeff whispered desperately.

"Jeff, boy," Cody said quietly, never taking his eyes off his work, "I feel like hell on the hoof. But I ain't gonna let these boys know it. They'll rag your ass off and find lotsa ways to make your job harder. Even worse," he said, as he passed the oil can, "if you start thinkin' about how bad you feel, first thing you know you're feelin' sorry for yourself. That's only a half-step from quittin'."

Cody stood up and mashed the saw's oil button several times to lubricate the chain. Holding the saw in his left hand, he pulled the crank rope viciously with his right. The wicked tool spat smoke and noise into the still, clean air. His machine was the first cranked, and the first to bite wood that day. Cody bent close to Jeff's ear and shouted, "On a day like this, you just gotta grab root and growl." Then he revved up his saw and strode off right manful-like into the forest.

After pushing Jeff and Granjack out the door that August morning, Rose downed her third cup of coffee and retreated to her sanctuary. She locked the door, knelt and reached into the corner of the cabinet under the sink. A tiny smile raised the corners of her mouth as she located and extracted the nearly empty pack, knocking over a can of drain cleaner in her haste. After lowering the seat and the lid, she sat down heavily, pulled out a Chesterfield and lit up.

Only a drowning person could have appreciated a lungful of air as much as Rose did at that moment. Jeff's condition had shaken her to the core. Liquor had been a hated and feared part of her life since childhood, and she had prayed since Jeff's birth he would avoid the curse that had cost Rose the love of her father and the life of her husband.

Rose's father, Abel Dance, had been the eldest son of a family that had owned and tilled the same land in eastern North Carolina since King George III sat on the throne of England. The Dance family had once been the most prominent in Corrin County, but after a century and a half of the careless breeding and dissipation that privilege permits, Abel found himself master of a decaying main house and sixty acres of played-out farm land. Abel ceased farming and sold off his legacy lot by lot to subsidize liquor-soaked schemes and fly-by-night investments he hoped would restore in one fell swoop all that had been petered away by six generations.

By the end of the Great Depression, the family estate was reduced to the single acre surrounding their home; their diet consisted primarily of the vegetables the Dance women raised in a small garden. The situation grew so desperate Rose's older sister, Lily, ran off with a traveling salesman and was never heard from again.

Perhaps it was sadly predictable that after burying her father and fleeing to the western end of the state, Rose would fall in love and marry a young man who shared Abel Dance's weakness. Rose believed if she gave William Stuart the love and support her mother had denied her father, the dashing young man could be molded into a stalwart husband.

Leaning back against the cool porcelain water tank and exhaling a long stream of smoke, she thought about little Jeffie, a child born in the midst of one of the periodic polio epidemics that seemed to mothers of that sad era to rage constantly. Eleven children in the county had contracted infantile paralysis by the time Jeff was two years old, and she had driven herself nearly crazy worrying about the boy's every sneeze and cough. The child was only a year old when her husband Will drove his car off a narrow bridge into the river. Grief and fear drove her to cling to the child with a possessiveness that alarmed all who knew her.

It was only when Jeffie started the first grade and was greeted with taunts of "sissy" and "mama's boy" did she see the price a child pays for such protection. Thank God his grandfather had started taking the boy to the lumberyard, the general store, and to ball games where he was exposed to the world of men. The old man taught him to "take up for himself," and it wasn't long before Jeff's athleticism provided him an identity other boys understood and respected.

Rose stubbed out her cigarette and lit a second as she considered her predicament. A big part of the problem, she decided, was "the times." She had read in *Saturday Evening Post* there was an epidemic of teenage delinquency, drinking and drug use, and it was all tied to *that music*. She had known it was only a matter of time before the plague reached Rockton. Sure enough, it had arrived with the morning sun.

Still, Jeff had been such a *good* boy Rose had little experience with disciplining him. He did well enough in school and showed some interest in the lumberyard. Granted, he should be able to see through little Vicky Parrish, but Rose had long recognized the relationship between intelligence and breast size: Large breasts make men dumb.

When she flicked her ashes into the metal bobby pin tray, Rose glanced at her watch. She would have to hurry to make it to the office on time. Jeff, she concluded, had spent the summer working with some of the roughest men found beyond the walls of a prison. In just a few weeks, school and football would take all his time and attention. Surely he had learned a good, hard lesson this morning. If the problem recurred, she would confront the boy head-on.

Rose stowed the last remaining Chesterfield under the sink and left the bathroom feeling decidedly better than when she had entered.

CHAPTER NINE

Jeff loved the first day of school. As he strolled down the oak-shaded sidewalk beside the red brick building, the head cheerleader attached to his right arm, the world embraced and revealed its riches as it does only to those who are young, healthy, and flush with prospect—those who know what they want and feel it within their grasp. Seniors and celebrities, Jeff and Vicky stood mightily astride their small universe of 400 students. Teen-age colossi.

"And then I told Mrs. Baker that *our* uniforms were the ugliest ones in the conference," Vicky railed, disengaging briefly from Jeff, "maybe the *whole state!*" She flung her arms out dramatically to embrace both Atlantic Coast and Appalachian Mountains. The cheerleader often semaphored her gestures, as though playing to the tenth row center rather than an audience of one. The tendency annoyed Jeff, but he ignored it. He'd long since learned when Vicky was in full-rant, he need only nod regularly and make eye contact when her tone implied she had reached a conclusion. Contribution was as unnecessary as contradiction was unwise.

Jeff refused to be dragged into the quagmire of cheerleader politics. Basking under the warm sun of recognition and approval, walking on grounds as familiar as a family estate, Jeff exchanged greetings and noted the changes the summer had wrought in people whom he had known all his life. Those changes seemed to be disproportionately settled upon the bescarved, white-bloused, cinch-belted, dark-skirted, bobby-soxed, penny-loafered coed population. Dressed to the nines for the first day of school, many of the girls defied the late summer heat by stacking starched crinolines under their skirts or layering matching sweater sets, just because they looked so damn good in them.

The great majority of the one hundred fourteen people in the senior class had attended school together since the first grade; they knew each other's parents and what they did for a living, where they lived, all their brothers and sisters. In the ninth grade there had been a small influx of farm kids bussed in from the outlying communities—the booted, blue-jeaned boys surveying the campus with tough, suspicious eyes; the girls, vulnerable and shy, as though entering a party where everyone else had spent eight years getting acquainted. Thereafter, turnover within the student body or the faculty was rare.

The 1955 Homecoming Queen lived on the Mill Hill and, often as not, a boy fresh off the milking stool became football captain or a class officer. There were, and will forever be, the more and less-popular, the have and have-nots, but Rockton High School was about as democratic a place to live out the hormone-plagued adolescent years as one was likely to find. Or so it seemed to Jeff Stuart in September of 1956.

The pair climbed the concrete steps and entered the brick building. The high school, like the junior high and the elementary school, had been erected by the Works Progress Administration in the late 1930's. Granjack had once told Jeff if it weren't for Franklin Roosevelt and the New Deal, the Rockton school system would consist of a string of one-room schoolhouses connected by mud paths.

"What you got now?" Vicky asked, as they sauntered down the crowded hall.

Jeff scanned his schedule. "Business Leadership."

Vicky's eyes grew wide. "What's that?"

"Rose's idea. I've run out of business courses to take. How many different ways can you say balance-your-books, supply-and-demand, buy-low-sell-high, don't-eat-your-seed-corn, over and over." His mother dearest desire was that he attend business college, and Jeff had told everyone but Rose that he would rather stand on his head in a bucket of guts for two years than do so.

The warning bell scattered frantic students in all directions. "I'll see you at football practice," Vicky said.

"Hey, Marty!" Jeff called to the head that bobbed half a foot above the mass. "Wait up."

"What's up, Jeff. Hi, Vicky." Marty said, as he veered across the hallway. Vicky nodded curtly and entered the classroom.

In addition to the natural rivalry between a girl friend and a best friend, Vicky and Marty had nothing in common but Jeff. Marty was not good looking, athletic, or very popular, and, though he took pains to hide it, was widely considered to be a "brain." And he dressed funny.

"You going to Drop/Add?" Jeff asked, as they walked up the hall. Confused kids darted around them, comparing course schedules with room numbers.

"I gotta ditch physical science." Marty said. "Get back into home ec."

"What the hell?" Jeff asked. "What's your angle?"

"No angle," Marty said. "I just figured it was time a sensitive cat like me learned to cook and sew."

"Bullshit!"

As the two strolled down the hall Marty explained his latest scheme to insinuate himself into places where there were so many young girls that, in Marty's words, "the mathematical odds might overwhelm my karma." After vaguely defining "karma," Marty explained that Home Economics was loaded with blooming freshman and sophomore girls. Having been turned down by the cream of the junior/senior crop, Marty was researching the young blood.

"I finally got a copy of that first *Playboy*," Marty whispered, as they entered the office. "Great layout of Marilyn Monroe. You gotta drop by and take a look."

Football practice, both humid morning and torrid afternoon, in the August heat was a snap for Jeff. While his teammates fell to the ground wheezing for breath, or crawled toward the cooler begging for enough water to wash down a handful of salt tablets, Jeff leaned against the blocking sled and chewed on a blade of grass. Ten weeks of running a chain saw had reduced football practice from ordeal to inconvenience.

With two-a-days behind them and the first game looming on Friday, the Rockton Rocks were melding into a team area sports writers predicted would take the conference. Rockton High trailed a long history of football glory. Each year from Labor Day through Thanksgiving, high school football seemed to be the town's sole reason for existence. The team had finished second in 1955, defeated by their arch-rival Richardson Indians, but the Rocks were returning a strong group of lettermen, including their best lineman, Chuck Brady, and top back, Jeff Stuart. Local fans agreed that after a humiliating three year drought, this would be the year Coach Dick Baron would lead the Rocks back into the state playoffs.

"Stuart! Brady! Get your asses over here," Coach Baron shouted.

The two boys veered out of the pack of players who were running laps and double-timed it to the sideline. The short, tubby Baron was standing with a tall, broad, square-headed man with a severe gray crew-cut. Coach "Iron Joe"

Stokowski was known throughout the region as the legendary head coach of Moore-Clayton College in Oak City. Recruited straight out of the coal mines of Pennsylvania by the small Baptist school, Stokowski had made several small college all-American teams at tackle. "Iron Joe" had played *every* down, offense and defense, his senior year. After three years of pro ball and a twice-broken collarbone, Stokowski returned to coach his alma mater and had endured for over thirty years.

One of Stokowski's early recruits had been a short, wiry scat-back from the neighboring town. Dick Baron had set state rushing records at Rockton High School, but his knees gave out in his sophomore year of college. Impressed by the little man's moxie, Coach Stokowski taught him the tactics of the single-wing offense and helped him get his degree in physical education. Baron returned to *his* alma mater to coach, and thereafter the best players from Rockton High were funneled to Moore-Clayton.

"Ya coach tells me you guys might be wortha shit," Stokowski sneered in an accent still covered in coal dust. "Ya think ya good enough to play for me?"

Neither boy could speak, but both nodded assent several times.

"We'll see about that," Stokowski said. The old coach turned and walked off the field. The two boys stood with mouths agape, unsure what to do next.

"You gonna stand there whippin' your willies, or you playin' football," Coach Baron demanded, hooking his thumb toward the line of players still chugging around the field. Neither boy was sure exactly what had just happened, but in the locker room after practice, Chuck boasted that both had been offered football scholarships to Moore-Clayton. Jeff saw no reason to disagree.

CHAPTER TEN

Jeff guided his mother's Plymouth into the gravel parking lot of Woody's Barbecue and cruised the front row, waving to friends. Vicky, sitting so close that the car appeared to be piloted by a single body with two heads, called loudly to kids who had come directly from the Wednesday night pep rally to eat and commune at the drive-in.

Jeff circled the lot and cut the engine, allowing the heavy Plymouth to coast the last twenty yards or so before nuzzling it into a berth in the back row. The car required only the slightest tap on the brake petal to halt within a foot of the rear bumper of the car in front. That particular rear bumper belonged to a cherry-red 1950 Ford.

"Why do you always do that?" Vicky asked, annoyed.

"Coast into a parking place?"

"No. Why do you always park so the speaker is on *my* side?"

A tougher question. Jeff knew if he answered truthfully—that only by forcing Vicky to slide over to use the speaker could he gain a little breathing room—any hope for intimacy later, in private, would be lost.

Jeff shrugged. "It was the closest spot."

"Well, I don't think it's very gentlemanly," Vicky sniffed.

Jeff was saved further discussion when three uniformed cheerleaders appeared in the passenger side window seeking audience with their chief. Although they had just spent the last two hours shouting in unison, there was apparently much to share. When the back seat filled with shrieking cheerleaders and exclamation points, Jeff seized the opportunity.

"Order me a chopped and a cherry-lemon-vanilla Coke. I'll be right back," Jeff said. Before Vicky could protest, he was gone.

The night was warm and humid and the aroma of pork barbecue so lavish that a quarter-mile downwind any freshly-interred resident of the Methodist cemetery was surely salivating. Threading his way through the parked cars, Jeff waved to friends without stopping to talk.

He found Cody and Naomi standing off to the side of the diner talking to a hulking mass of near-humanity sitting astride a Harley-Davidson. Jeff's gaze deserted the biker and leapt to the five-foot frame of Naomi. Very few females in Rockton would venture into public wearing short-shorts, and these shorts, packed as they were, could have scandalized Las Vegas.

To further distract, Naomi wore a striped blouse clasped so tightly around her bosom that her cleavage appeared to descend from her chin. Jeff walked past a gaggle of freshmen boys who were collecting dust on their tongues in admiration.

As he approached, Jeff read the words stitched on the biker's denim jacket: Satan's Helpers—Popeye. Cutting a wide path around the motorcycle, Jeff took a position beside Cody and listened politely. Popeye spoke only an additional sentence before backing his machine up, rocking down viciously on the starter, and departing in a cloud of dust and menace.

Jeff said hello to Naomi and swapped some skin with Cody, lightly brushing the palms of their right hands together and ending with a thumbs-up gesture shoulder-high.

"How's life at Sisboombah High?" Naomi asked.

"Tolerable." Jeff replied, "We've got a football game Friday night. I expect to see you folks in the stands cheerin' for the home team."

Cody shook his head solemnly and popped a fresh toothpick into his mouth. "Yeah, God knows I'd like to, but I struck a deal with the principal the day they eighty-sixed my ass outta there: I swore I'd never again set foot on school property, and he promised to avoid my bootlegger's place." Cody shrugged. "I give him my word."

"I understand," Jeff said gravely. He fell into step between Cody and Naomi as they walked toward the Ford. "You playing any music?"

"I filled in with a country band last week. Played the VFW in Cedar Falls."

"How'd it go?" Jeff asked.

"We escaped with our lives," Naomi snorted.

Cody nodded. "At least I'll never have to play 'Filipino Baby' again."

As the three walked through the parking lot, Jeff felt every set of eyes, male and female, was trained on them. "Gonna be a good rock band down in Winston on Saturday," Cody said, leaning against the hood of the Ford. "Wanna come along?"

"Long trip," Jeff said.

"Not if you drive fast," Cody said.

Jeff hesitated. "It's not gonna be one of those all-night deals, is it? I caught a lot of grief over that."

"No, no." Cody said, shaking his head emphatically. "We'll get you home, twelve—twelve-thirty at the latest."

"I can handle that," Jeff said. He knew better, but what the hell?

Naomi crawled under the wheel. Cody reluctantly assumed the passenger seat. "Want us to come by your house?" he asked, through the open window.

Jeff's mind flashed on the vision of his mother greeting Cody in his "cat" clothes and Naomi in a French tart outfit at the front door. "Oh, no, no!" Jeff said quickly. "Pick me up at the lumberyard. Eight o'clock alright?"

Cody nodded. "Later, alligator," he said, assuming a slouch that left his head resting against the car seat, his eyes dead ahead.

Naomi pulled slowly across the parking lot, but kicked it when she hit the pavement. Heads turned in admiration as the Ford peeled rubber in three gears. When Jeff climbed back into the Plymouth, Vicky dismissed her charges with a wave of her hand. Cheerleaders flushed from the back seat like a covey of quail then bounced and weaved across the lot.

"Who are *they*?" Vicky asked.

"Who?" Jeff replied.

"Those *people* you were just talking to."

"Some folks I met this summer."

"They look like prime greasers to me. Did you see those shorts she was wearing? My daddy would kill me if I went out in public like that."

"I didn't notice."

"I'll bet you didn't," Vicky scoffed. "Somebody oughta tell her she's gettin' too fat to dress like that."

Jeff was relieved to see the carhop approaching. He paid for the order and passed Vicky her food. As he sipped his drink, he considered broaching the subject that he knew might wreck romance for the night. Vicky saved him the trouble.

"Ginger's going to have some kids over for a victory party and cook-out on Saturday night," Vicky said, as she inspected her cheeseburger. "She's going to ask her daddy tonight."

"I've gotta work Saturday night," Jeff said, looking straight ahead. "At the lumber yard. We gotta do inventory."

"Oh, swell," Vicky sighed. "Now I'll have to stay home all night."

"There's no reason you can't go," Jeff protested. "Go to Ginger's and have a good time."

"Girls can't do that. It looks cheap." Vicky attacked the cheeseburger. "Besides, it wouldn't be any fun without you."

Jeff sipped his soda, miserable to the bone. He hated lying; it was dishonorable and gutless. As he bent over his sandwich, he saw Vicky's skirt had ridden up so that the inside of her right thigh, pale and exquisite, was visible. Although unashamed of his lust, Jeff was occasionally disgusted by what he would do to even partially indulge it.

"Oh, well," Vicky said, without looking up from her sandwich, "at least we'll win the ball game Friday night. Kings Valley is always the pits."

Half-time of the Rockton—Kings Valley game. Jeff leaned his sweaty head against the cool metal of the locker in the sweltering, dank locker room. Each fall Jeff learned anew that nothing could prepare the body for the punishment hostile adolescents wield when running full tilt in pursuit of tribal glory. Fortunately, his bruises were fresh and masked by adrenaline and excitement. The real pain would come in the morning.

The clatter of cleats on cement gave way to the sharp crack of half-moon heeltaps on leather-soled shoes striding to the front of the locker room. Every standing player grabbed the closest piece of bench. The last boys to react, the freshmen, were forced to sit up front, next to the fire. After three years of varsity football, Jeff knew the drill. First game: Home, God, and Country.

When Coach Dick Baron cleared his throat, the room fell silent. The short, fat man in the baseball cap bore little resemblance to the lightning-quick wingback that had run wild and free in enemy backfields some twenty-five years back. Two decades of exacting unquestioning obedience from adolescent boys had convinced him he had earned the right to all the pork, cream gravy and Carling Black Label Beer he could pack away. Baron had never married, and still lived with his mother in the house where he'd been born.

"Boys," Baron began, in a voice that rumbled like low thunder over an open grave, "this is a sad day in my life and in the life of this town and this high school. In all my years of coachin', I never seen a sorrier exhibition of panty-waist tacklin' and cream puff blockin' as I seen tonight. The way you boys been jerkin' your gherkin out there makes me believe that you could care less about winnin'! That you're not willin' to pay the price of victory! We oughta be beatin' that buncha Mary Janes by fifty points."

To Jeff, football was more than playing the game in front of a crowd and bringing glory to your town when you won; he would play football regardless of whether anyone watched or kept score. He loved the feeling that flowed through him when he did something exactly *right*. Running, catching, blocking, tackling—he loved it all. The challenge was constant, the results undeniable. Nothing else in his life was so clear-cut, so much *fun*.

As the Coach pointed out that two high school football players, Ike Eisenhower and Dick Nixon, ran the nation, Chuck Brady shook his head and winked at Jeff. Chuck had played a great half on both sides of the ball. He was loose, grimly pleased, and eager to get back on the field and chew up the two skinny kids King's Valley had sacrificed as cannon fodder to the best lineman in the conference.

Chuck couldn't imagine life without football. The months between the final whistle of the last game and the beginning of summer practice were a vast wasteland that he filled with weight lifting, beer drinking, and fistfights. Chuck swore he never went looking for trouble and professed bewilderment as to why he regularly turned up in places where there was no alternative to bruised knuckles and bleeding head cuts. Neither Jeff nor Marty wanted any part of brawling, but Chuck's mother knew that anytime her son left the house alone on a Saturday night, he was liable to come home wearing his own blood or somebody else's.

When Coach Baron raised his voice to what Jeff recognized as the final plateau, the young boys on the front ranks leaned forward to absorb the word and the moment.

"Now you're going to go out there and make up for that disgraceful first half. If you want this team to go down as one of the great Rockton teams, you're gonna take that football and stuff it down their throat. You're gonna kill 'em! You're gonna kill 'em. WHAT ARE YOU GONNA DO?"

"Kill 'em!

"I CAN'T HEAR YOU."

"KILL 'EM!"

"AGAIN!"

"KILL 'EM!"

"DAMN RIGHT!" Baron shouted. "NOW LET US PRAY."

Final Score: Rockton 33 - Kings Valley 6.

CHAPTER ELEVEN

"Yes, sir," Cody said to the doorman, his voice dripping the sincerity of a death bed confession, "he's my little brother, and if he even touches a bottle of beer, I'll break his arm. I promised our Mama that."

"Can the bullshit," the doorman at Alley's Cat Club snarled. "If he's got two dollars, I don't give a shit if it harelips your Mama." The doorman stamped Cody's hand and appraised his outfit from suede shoes to white Panama hat. "Hell, you got guts enough to wear them pants, you can bring anybody in here you want to."

Jeff hastily thrust two dollars out, got his hand stamped and followed Cody and Naomi into the small, crowded club. The music rattled the fillings in his teeth, and his eardrums advised retreat. "Don't worry," Naomi shouted, "you'll get used to it."

Cody's ensemble turned a few heads as he led the expedition across the crowded dance floor, but Naomi's tight sweater and short skirt were the real crowd-pleaser. Every male eye in the joint massaged Naomi as she squeezed between tables and around dancers. Jeff, desiring to remain inconspicuous, had chosen the wrong companions.

Cody chose a table against the wall. "Easier to defend," he explained. The three had barely sat down before the band segued into their break music.

"Thank you, thank you," the front man shouted into the microphone, "We're 'Carl Warlick and the Warlocks,' and we're gonna take a breather right now, but we'll be back shortly to lay some righteous rock'n'roll on you, and have ya dancin' holes in your shoes."

"Great timin'." Naomi said, as the band shuffled off the stage and the house lights were raised.

From halfway across the club, a shrill voice cut through the haze, "Hey, Cody, where'd you get them cat-ass pants?"

Cody was on his feet immediately. He took a step back from the table, and, with arms outstretched, turned in a slow circle. His black checked sport coat and frantic striped shirt were enough to scare the children and stampede the horses, but they were just prelude to the pink pegged slacks with the black stripe up the side. Imported from Richmond and never before modeled south of that city, they soaked up all the light in the dim room and emitted a near-radioactive glow. A low gasp of shock, admiration and envy coursed through the dank haze as the patrons marveled at the breed of man who had the balls to wear such a costume.

"I bought 'em by mistake," Cody shouted across the room. "My Mama gave me some money and sent me to Cox's Department Store to buy some seer-sucker pants, but I went to Sear's and bought me some cock-sucker pants."

Everyone within earshot of Cody's booming baritone—meaning all inside the club and everyone not fighting in the parking lot—howled at the punch line. Throughout the night, Jeff heard the phrase "cock-sucker pants" pass from table to table followed by eruptions of laughter.

Cody turned to Naomi. "Order me a drink, baby, and a beer for Jeff." He shaped and straightened his Panama. "I'll be right back."

Naomi raised her right hand and rubbed her thumb across her finger tips twice. After briefly feigning forgetfulness, Cody forked over two dollar bills and then split. Naomi spotted a waitress—left elbow on a table and right hand on her hip, shooting the breeze with a tableful of men.

"Hey, Toots!" Naomi shouted. "Work some up on ya own time. We're thirsty."

The waitress took her time sauntering over. "What's your pleasure, sister?"

"Gin and tonic, bourbon and seven, and-" Naomi looked over to Jeff.

"Coke?" Jeff offered, unsure of the game plan.

Naomi shook her head. "Give him a beah. Schlitz."

The waitress shrugged and left. Someone pumped change into the jukebox, and the machine responded with Carl Perkins', "Dixie Fried."

While Naomi checked her make-up, Jeff took a look around. The club was bigger than it looked from the parking lot. About sixty people crammed inside, all young, about two-thirds male, a mix of cat-man greasers and country-cowboy types. A dark cloud of cigarette smoke pressed from the low ceiling to shoe-top reducing visibility and breathing air to coal mine standards. Jeff knew that up North the mixing of white and Negro races was viewed as reason enough to stomp the music out before it grew. Not a problem in this club.

After noting the location of the bathroom and the nearest exit, Jeff attempted to make small talk with a woman who both attracted and scared hell out of him. "So..." Jeff said, "how long you known Cody?"

"Three, four months." Naomi said, nodding approval to her mirror before snapping her compact shut.

Jeff pressed on. "Did you know somebody here? I mean...how'd you end up in Rockton?

Naomi laughed loudly. "Beats the shit outa me," she said, shaking her head. "No, I'll tell ya. If you start at the corner of Franklin and St. James Street in Baltimore, Maryland, then Rockton is exactly how far a 1946 Studebaker with a busted piston will take ya."

"How do you like it?"

"It ain't so bad." Naomi shrugged. "But the food bites it."

Jeff's puzzled look drew a barrage of questions from Naomi. "Ya ever eat pizza pie with pepperoni sausage and mushrooms? How about an Italian submarine sandwich? A reuben with sauerkraut? Pastrami and Swiss on rye? Fried scallops? A goddamn bowl of clam chowda?"

Jeff shook his head.

Naomi took a last, long draw off her Kool. "Try swapping crab salad for a fried baloney sandwich."

The waitress ambled over and set the two drinks and the beer on the table. "Dollar-forty," she said, looking at Jeff.

Naomi extended Cody's two bills.

"I'll get mine," Jeff said, whipping out his wallet.

"Better take it, kid," Naomi said firmly. "It's likely the only drink you'll ever get out of Cody."

Naomi pulled two half-pint flasks from her purse and passed one to Jeff. "Drink some off," she pointed toward Cody's bourbon and seven, "then fill it up."

Jeff sipped from the glass then filled it with bourbon. Naomi took a long pull off her drink and filled it to the rim with gin. She knocked it down in three hard gulps. She grabbed Jeff's hand and hauled him to his feet. "Get off ya lame ass and dance,"

Vicky drove slowly down the silent Main Street at twilight cursing the Fates, Small Town Life and that tramp of a sophomore cheerleader, Ginger, who couldn't even crawl through her bedroom window at two o'clock in the morning without waking up everyone in the house. Ginger's daddy had called off the cookout and left the cream of Rockton High society with nothing to do on Saturday night. Except for a tight ring of rowdy greasers whooping it up in front of the poolroom and a short line of kids at the Main Theater, the street was empty. Vicky would never forgive her father and mother for settling in such a small town. Saturday night in Deadsville, USA.

Maybe when she and Jeff got married, they would get rid of that lumberyard and move to Oak City. Jeff could sell insurance or work in a bank—he looked real good in a suit—and she could keep house and shop. A wedding the day after graduation would suit her fine. Of course, her daddy would never stand for it. *They would elope to South Carolina!* But she couldn't give up the wedding—she'd had it planned out since she was in eighth grade.

As she made the left turn onto Clement Street, she steadied her cargo with her right hand. She couldn't resist sticking her finger under the aluminum foil and scraping some icing off the plate. She could smooth it out later. The cake was a peace offering, sort of. She would deliver it and then just go home and watch TV.

Friday night had started so...*magically*. Jeff had scored three touchdowns, the team had crushed Kings Valley, and she and Jeff had nearly gone all the way. The time seemed perfect. But, when she saw Jeff fumbling with that rubber thing, her mother's words—those ugly, bitter, truthful words—filled her head, "They don't buy the cow—." God, she hated that woman. She could still see the look in Jeff's eyes when she pushed him away. It nearly broke her heart.

As Vicky turned into the lot of Stuart Lumber, her stomach turned over and quivered. No lights in the office—no lights in the warehouses. She trained her headlights on the chain link fence that surrounded the lumberyard and got out of the car. Her anger grew with each step. The gate was secured with a Master lock. No lights, no cars, no people!

He was with another girl!

Her mind reeled with names and faces of possible betrayers, including each of her cheerleaders. She jerked the cake off the front seat and arranged her right hand squarely under the center of the plate She pushed off with her right leg while pivoting on her left and launched the cake and plate over the tall fence and a good six feet beyond.

Vicky yielded to neither reason nor regulation as she sped home. Her mind had probably never functioned as efficiently as it did at that moment; she examined Jeff's every word, action, and intimation for the hint that would reveal the identity of the teen-age Jezebel who had slain True Love.

Throughout the evening and well into the night, she burned up the telephone lines in pursuit of the scent of Jeff Stuart and his phantom lover. By midnight, nearly every teen-ager in town was aware of the treachery Vicky Parrish had endured. All that remained to be seen was whether the Head Cheerleader could exact the pound of wingback flesh she swore to all was her due.

Jeff sang "Dixie-Fried" as he unleashed a long-postponed torrent into a grungy urinal at Alley's Cat Club. With nothing to do but watch the chinks of porcelain chip away under the high-pressure assault, he reflected on some of the more profound questions that haunt human consciousness. Questions like: Why did people settle for Perry Como intoning "Hot diggity, dog diggity, boom, what you do to me" when they could hear Little Richard shout, "A wop bop alu bop a wop bam boom!"? Or: Why, oh, why would *anyone* pay a dollar for a 45 rpm record of Pat Boone droning, "Ain't That a Shame?" when that same buck would get you Fats Domino's original? And, crucially: Why would folks, young or old, sit home on Saturday night watching "Your Hit Parade" on TV when they could see and hear real, live, full-sized people sing and play those songs *in person*? Cody had nailed it: "If it ain't live, then you ain't livin'."

Jeff stopped by the table long enough to chug down the last half bottle of warm beer before making his way back to the dance floor. With the passing of midnight, the crowd had boiled down to the hard core. It appeared that everybody in the club still capable of upright posture was either dancing or standing in front of the bandstand. Up there you could feel the music wash over you, pure and undiluted. Jeff's sponsors had cleared out some dancing space for themselves dead-center and had drawn a half-circle of admirers.

He marveled as he watched Cody and Naomi disport with drill team precision *and* savage abandon. Three oily young men stood with their backs to the music and followed Naomi's movement with undisguised lechery. Unfortunately, liquor had robbed them of the sense God gave a billy goat, or they would have known better than to address their remarks to the house.

"Gawdamighty," yelled Shorty, the small fellow flanked by two big ol' boys, "'at's more woman than one man can hannel. She gotta ass like a black widder spider!"

"Damn right," agreed Ugly, "when she hauls ass, it takes two trips and a wheelburrow."

As the three cackled and slapped their thighs, the folks standing nearby edged away. Everyone who has breathed the gamy air of a drinking and dancing club knows that it commonly attracts folks who consider the night unsatisfying and incomplete if forced to take a liquor-soaked body home and put it to bed without first getting it bloody. Best give those folks plenty of room if that is not your desire.

Jeff felt the charge building up in the air and nervously surveyed every dark corner of the club for the broad, surly bouncer who had patrolled the club all night. Nowhere to be found. Of the twenty-five to thirty people in the club, Jeff found none that could be counted as friend.

Naomi and Cody continued their lifts, splits, swings, and through-the-leg-pulls, apparently unmindful of the remarks directed at her anatomy and his manhood. Jeff wanted to leave, but knew Cody had no other ally and likely would need several.

"HOW'D YOU LIKE TO LATCH ON TO ONE A THEM BOOBS AND PRAY FOR LOCKJAW?" shouted Shorty. The gauntlet lay on the barroom floor.

When Cody swung Naomi between his legs and then back out, he released her hands, forcing her to back-pedal furiously to maintain balance. As every eye followed Naomi, Cody wheeled and hit the biggest of the three hecklers with a roundhouse right that lifted the young man right out of his penny loafers and deposited his fat ass on the stage. Skirmishes broke out across the dance floor.

Jeff watched as Cody took a glancing right to the head from Ugly. Unfazed, Cody stepped inside Ugly's roundhouse left and worked over the larger man's body with a series of lethal stomach punches that left Ugly bent and gasping for breath. Cody finished him off with a bolo punch that Kid Gavilan would have been proud of.

The band broke into a solemn version of "Dixie" in hopes that peace and reverence might prevail. Fat chance. The music must have stirred ancestral memories of defeat and humiliation—by the time the Warlocks reached the chorus, even the ladies were swapping punches and pulling hair.

Jeff saw Cody stalk Shorty, who appeared to be involved in a frantic game of pocket-pool in his pants. When Shorty whipped out a knife and engaged the six-inch switchblade, the band fell silent and all but the most distracted of fighters pulled punches and backed away. Cody stopped abruptly at the sight of the knife. The fear in Shorty's face bled into a thin smile. Shorty edged forward, his right foot always in front. His knife made slow tight circles, then jabbed left and right.

Cody backed away, his eyes searching for a beer bottle, a chair, a glass—anything to even the odds against a runt who was doubtless handy with that knife since he had gone to so much trouble to use it. With his back less than four feet from the wall, Cody was fast running out of options.

Then things turned off bad for Cody. No one had paid any attention to Ugly, who lay sprawled on the floor where Cody had knocked his sorry ass. But Ugly arose, darted behind Cody, and pinned his arms; it looked like all that was left of the brawl was the carving and the bleeding.

Cody bucked manfully, but Ugly's hold was secure. Shorty stepped forward to insert his shiv into the tight, vulnerable stomach of the guy who had been a stranger only minutes before. Before he could take that last step, Shorty was blasted from the rear by one hundred-sixty pounds of terrified linebacker. Jeff's right shoulder caught Shorty in the middle of the back. He wrapped his arms around the little man's waist and carried him the three steps to the wall. When Jeff heard the sickening thump of Shorty's head bouncing off the wall, he knew the runt's night was over. Stepping back, Jeff watched the limp body slide slowly, slowly down the wall into a pile and then unfold onto the sticky barroom floor. Only then did Jeff feel the throbbing in his left shoulder.

All the boy could later recall of the next minute or so was the enraged bouncer roaring obscenities as he charged from the men's room holding his pants up with one hand, and the sight of Cody hurdling overturned chairs and tables in pursuit of Ugly.

Approaching police sirens concentrated minds and action as everyone but the bouncer scrambled for one of the two exits. Jeff and Cody chose the rear. As quickly as their shoes hit the gravel parking lot, Naomi slid the Ford broadside into their path. Cody pushed Naomi from under the wheel while Jeff piled into the passenger side. They rode three abreast, Cody dodging men on foot and cops in cars through the lot. He jumped a ditch and straddled a gully, escaping only seconds before the police sealed off the lot.

Cody gunned the Ford down the empty black top road. Nobody spoke a word until the sirens faded to silence. When Cody eased off the accelerator and the needle began a slow descent from ninety-five, Naomi's hands released their death-grip on the dash. She slid back in the seat and exhaled a long slow breath. "You guys alright?" she asked, glancing from Cody to Jeff.

Jeff right hand kneaded his left shoulder. The pain was present but tolerable. "I'm O.K." he said.

Cody steered with his left hand while he stretched and clenched the fingers of his right. "I mighta busted some knuckles. Nothing fatal." As he downshifted to make a turn, Cody's eye flashed wide. "Jesus Christ," he whispered hoarsely, his hand leaping to his head, "My hat!"

Naomi twisted to the right, and reached into the back seat, her bust passing within inches of Jeff's face. She gently placed the Panama on Cody's sweaty head.

"Thank you, Baby," Cody said. He beat out a voodoo rhythm on the steering wheel, "You missed one helluva good fight."

"I didn't miss a thing," said Naomi. "I saw it all."

"Did you see Jeff splatter that filthy redneck all over that nice clean wall?" Cody asked.

"Damn right," Naomi countered. "He sure pulled your ass out of a crack." She turned to Jeff. "That took a lot of balls."

"Hell, yeah." Cody agreed. "And it saved me the trouble of killing that shrimpy sonuvabitch. And when that bigun on my back heard his buddy's head hit that wall—sounded like a ripe cantaloupe dropped on a seement floor—well, he lost his shit and he fell out."

Jeff's stomach quivered as he recalled that sound. "You don't think I killed him, do you?"

"Oh, hell, no, Jeff boy." Cody laughed. "A double-bred, prime-stock, red-neck peckerwood like that—you'd have to beat on his head day and night with a tire iron to *kill* him. He'll probably just have a headache...for the rest of his life." Cody pulled out a cigarette and passed the pack around. Naomi took one. Jeff took one.

Cody dialed across a dozen stations before hitting the right one. The three fugitives sang "Folsom Prison Blues," right along with Johnny Cash. When Naomi squeezed Jeff's thigh during the chorus, all pain fled his mind and body.

CHAPTER TWELVE

The First Baptist Church of Rockton, where Jeff Stuart was sweating out a ferocious hangover in a third row pew, was founded in 1899 by the Rockton Textile Corporation. The church was built on the northeast corner of the mill reservation and charged with the spiritual and moral instruction of the mill workers. The message delivered from the pulpit each Sunday was specific and consistent: Hard work was a cardinal virtue; submission to authority, sacred and temporal, was the path to righteousness; and suffering in this world insured salvation in the next.

Due to stern oversight by company management, the Mill Church was historically one of the more sedate Baptist congregations in town. Those mill workers who wanted to pursue their faith through the medium of "tongues," or the contortions of the "Holy Rollers," were directed to one of the sects outside the town limits where such exhibitions were encouraged. The mill owners accepted the fact that traveling revivals would siphon off a portion of their congregation for short periods of time, particularly in the hot, sordid summer months. But, like the traveling carnival in the fall, revivals generally ran through the citizen's disposable income in less than a week.

After the boom years of the Second World War, the board of Rockton Textile followed the precedent set by the textile giants "down east" and divested itself of the mill houses, the company store and the village church. Deprived of funding and direction, the congregation turned their fate over to a local boy. Billy Ryder had been a successful car salesman in Oak City before "hearing the call" and packing off his wife and two small children to Helms Baptist Bible College. Freshly graduated, Reverend Ryder, who recoiled from the title "Preacher," eagerly returned to a town where he knew there was no shortage of unredeemed souls.

Reverend Ryder spoke: "As you all well know, our culture is under attack on every front—in the trashy books that become best-sellers, in the raving boogie-woogie music our young people listen to, in the smutty television programs that invade our very homes. I had the misfortune to tune into such a program."

At least he's not preaching on Revelations and nuclear holocaust, thought Jeff. Ryder had rode that horse to death. Jeff shifted uncomfortably in the pew and alternately rubbed his aching left shoulder and his throbbing head as Reverend Billy Ryder took a drink of water. Rose Stuart's quick glance conveyed both disapproval and concern. Rose had not been waiting in her armchair when Jeff got home, but he was certain she knew the moment his footstep had crossed the threshold. He folded his arms, his right supporting his left, and his gaze lingered on the glass of water next to the preacher's hand. He craved that water with a lust known only to desert rats and the miserably hung-over.

Church attendance had not been a consideration when he collapsed into bed. After a brief, troubled sleep, Jeff was jerked awake and chased to the medicine cabinet by the agonizing pain in his left shoulder. When he glimpsed his swollen and discolored shoulder in the mirror, he broke into a sweat and slumped onto the toilet seat. A hot shower briefly eased the pain, raising the hope that the injury might fade when treated with rest, aspirin, and Atomic Balm.

Jeff was lying awake, swimming in misery and regret, when Rose called him for breakfast. When his mother asked about the shoulder that he obviously favored, he said he had taken a bad fall in the shower. Although Rose did not mention his late arrival and noisy entrance, he could tell by the grim set of her mouth that the subject would be addressed before day's end. Guilt-ridden, he agreed to church as a possible means of purchasing peace for the Sabbath.

As Reverend Ryder related a tale of lust, greed, adultery, and unpunished criminality that he had mistakenly dialed up on his television, Jeff scanned the congregation. He spotted Marty suffering devoutly on the front pew. Sunday church attendance was the duty demanded of the preacher's boy for the privilege of divorcing himself from all other family life. Marty considered his week a success if he encountered his parents only at meals and for an hour at church.

The minutes dragged by on leaden legs. Finally, the preacher reworked the plot elements as they might have occurred in a Christ-centered society. At the stroke of noon, the preacher had his rehabilitated TV family raising a joyful noise at the Protestant church of their choice. And tithing their asses off, Jeff thought sardonically. One rushed hymn and short prayer later, the restless redeemed were cut loose.

Outside in the bright sunshine, he drank his fill at the fountain and made small talk with the people he had shared Sunday mornings with since birth. Everyone seemed eager to congratulate him on Friday's victory and discuss the possibility of an undefeated season. Jeff appreciated the kind words and responded with modesty and optimism, all the while keeping a close eye on his mother.

Rose was in no hurry to get back to her kitchen and begin the Sunday ritual of fried chicken and mashed potatoes and gravy; it seemed to Jeff that she buttonholed every woman in the congregation, catching up on a week of gossip. He walked toward the car, hoping his mother would take the hint.

"Hidey-Ho, Jeffarenoroo," greeted Marty, as he crossed a stretch of sidewalk where some little kids played Snake in the Gully. "How'd you like that bullshit sermon? The old man lifted the plot straight off 'Alfred Hitchcock.'"

Jeff nodded. "I saw it last Sunday night. Didn't recognize it today."

"Yeah, he butchered the story," Marty said, shaking his head. "That's the way his mind works. It's like he sees all the parts, he just doesn't understand how they fit together . . . what they all add up to."

As the two boys stood in the churchyard discussing favorite episodes of "Alfred Hitchcock Presents," a 1955 Chevrolet station wagon ran a STOP sign on the corner and pulled onto Church Street. The driver was a grim young woman who refused to be deterred by traffic laws or those that govern propriety in a small town.

Heads turned as the station wagon slid to a stop in front of the church. Conversations halted mid-sentence as the parishioners watched the figure in pedal pusher pants and red scarf move as swift, quiet, and intent as a stalking cat across the freshly mowed lawn. Jeff and Marty, oblivious to the hunt, were walking slowly toward the parked cars. When Vicky Parrish spotted Jeff's back in the open churchyard, she felt a thrill akin to that of a big game hunter lining up the cross hairs on trophy-quality prey.

"Stop right there, Jeff Stuart!" Vicky shrieked. Jeff turned and found himself the object of every eye in the churchyard, including the pair that flared wildly at him from a distance of twenty feet and closing. He reflexively raised his right hand in defense. Marty hurriedly backed out of harm's way.

"WHO IS SHE?" Vicky shouted, still advancing. "She's from out of town. I'd know her if she was from here! What have you got to say for yourself?"

"What are you talking about?" Jeff asked quietly. He took a step toward her, hoping that would make shouting unnecessary.

"You weren't at the lumberyard last night," Vicky said, her face growing redder with each sentence. "And you didn't go with Chuck 'cause I asked him. Marty was dating some little freshman, so you weren't with him. Was it that cheerleader from Kings Valley? I saw how you looked at her!"

"I didn't date anyone," Jeff said quietly, moving closer. "Calm down." Jeff placed his good arm on Vicky's shoulder and attempted to guide her away from the eyes and ears of the congregation.

"LET GO OF ME!" Vicky shouted, twisting away so violently she nearly fell down. When Vicky reached quickly into the right front pocket of her pedal pushers, Jeff feared that she might pull out a weapon. Fortunately, her pants were too tight to accommodate anything thicker than two dimes back to back.

"I HATE YOU, AND I NEVER WANT TO SEE YOU AGAIN!" Vicky pulled something from her pocket and threw it at Jeff. The ring hit him squarely between the eyes and fell to the grass. She wheeled around and stomped back to her car.

It took little more than a minute for Vicky to cross the lawn, climb into her car, and peel rubber up the empty street; to Jeff, it was a minute under water, fighting to the surface. Punch-drunk and blind, he had absorbed blows from every direction. Frustration and anger fed on him and filled his mind. Still the center of tightly focused attention, Jeff had no idea what to do. He resisted the urge to kneel down and search for the ring, feeling that would somehow be an admission of guilt.

Rose Stuart knew her part in this tawdry production. She collected her son with a single steely glance and walked directly to her car. As Jeff fell into step behind his mother, the children who had been playing Snake in the Gully gleefully abandoned their game and began searching in the grass for the spurned ring.

The ride was silent except for Rose's announcement that they would have a talk when they got home. They didn't even change out of their church clothes before convening at the kitchen table. Jeff took time only to chase down three aspirin with a glass of water while Rose used a saucepan to reheat coffee salvaged from the morning pot.

"Jeffrey," Rose began, "this talk is long overdue. I've put it off because I realize you're getting older, and I thought you deserved some independence. But things have gotten out of hand."

"I'm sorry about Vicky," Jeff said quickly. "I don't know what she was talking about. I didn't date anyone last night." Jeff knew he had to keep the discussion focused on the morning's incident or he was lost.

"It's not *just* Vicky," Rose said, moving her coffee cup in a tight circle on the Formica tabletop, "not *just* that horrible display she put on this morning. You know I've never understood what you saw in her. She—"

"I agree," Jeff interrupted, "and I'm sorry for what happened. I don't know what she was talking about, but she made it clear we're finished. I don't ever want to see her again."

Rose nodded curtly. "I never made a lot of rules because I always thought I could trust you. But ever since this summer, you've been a different person. You didn't get home till after two o'clock this morning. Where were you?"

"I went to listen to music," Jeff said, his anger growing.

"Did you go to a bar?"

"Yes."

"Did you drink alcohol there?"

"Yes."

Rose released a long, ragged breath. "That's against the law. They could put you in jail just for *being* in a place like that. Who were you with?"

"Some friends."

"Chuck and Marty?"

"No."

"Who?"

"Some people I met this summer."

"On the logging crew?"

"Yes."

Rose raised the coffee cup to her lips and cursed Granjack. All this could have been avoided if she had stood up to that old man. "It's time for me to make some rules," Rose said. "You're going to have to promise me you won't drink or go back into one of those clubs until you're of age. You're too young to be running around with those people. They'll only get you in trouble."

Rose nearly gasped when she saw her son's brows thicken and slide like a black avalanche of rage over his eyes. She had last seen that glare on her husband's face. The fear it had once conveyed revisited her. Confused and angry, she stood up to her son, as she no longer could to his father.

"From now on you have to be in by eleven o'clock on school nights, twelve on Friday and Saturday. If you're late, or if I have any reason to believe you've been drinking, you lose the use of the car, and you—"

The words froze in Rose's throat, when she saw Jeff's face twist into cold defiance. He rose, tossed his car keys on the table and walked out of the room.

CHAPTER THIRTEEN

"Tell me, boy," Doc Bowman asked, as he ordered Jeff through a series of torturous arm motions, "just how fast were you running when you fell in that shower?"

Short, stooped and looking a decade older than his forty-nine years, Doc had mended the wounds of countless domestic disputes and assorted affray in Rockton for over twenty years with little question or comment. Folks appreciated his discretion on matters that could rip the fragile social fabric of a town where everyone shared neighbors and relatives. Doc wasn't discreet; he just didn't give a damn. He was biding his time. As soon as the last of his three worthless sons turned eighteen, Doc planned to break the kid's dinner plate, hand him a hundred dollar bill and a bus ticket to Anywhere, USA and tell him to write when he got work. Then the old man could spend the rest of his life fishing for crappies in the Mill Pond and reading Zane Grey novels. Until then, he would patch up whatever he could and dispense as little non-medical advice as he intended to accept.

"Separated," Doc mumbled through the cirrus of cigarette smoke that saturated his cramped office. "A bad'un. Did you feel it pop out of joint?

Jeff nodded. "But it popped right back in."

"Dislocated. It's gonna take six weeks to heal up, maybe eight." Doc said, lighting a fresh Camel from the butt of the old one. "Either way, son, your football season is over."

On a Monday morning when Elvis Presley's appearance on Ed Sullivan's show should have been the hottest topic on the Rockton campus, the Pelvis ran a poor third. Charting one and two were accusations of unfaithfulness leveled at the Football Captain by the Head Cheerleader, followed dramatically by tragic medical news concerning that same cad. Before the eight-thirty tardy bell had rung, Vicky Parrish had dramatized the showdown at the Baptist Church twice in the girl's bathroom and once in the hall. Solemnly attested to by a chorus of witnesses, the story moved into public domain and spread like contagion across the campus. Vicky's tale was effectively neutered when Jeff showed up at nine-fifteen with his arm, and the destiny of Rockton football, trussed up in a sling.

Within fifteen minutes of Jeff's arrival, every student and teacher knew of his shower accident and its horrific consequence. As he walked from class to class, friends, acquaintances, and kids whom he could not recall ever having seen offered teary condolences and breathlessly asked if it were true that he would miss the whole football season.

"No," Jeff repeated, "I'll be ready to play toward the end of the season." And he believed it. There were eight more games to play, plus playoffs if they won the conference. Doc Bowman said six to eight weeks for recovery, but Jeff heard only the smaller number. He'd ignored Doc's recommendation to get x-rays at the Oak City Hospital assuming that whatever they revealed would only blunt his optimism.

Vicky Parrish declared that Jeff's injury was a fake—a ploy to distract everyone from the humiliation she had inflicted upon him. Nobody listened. For years afterward, Rockton students could remember exactly where they were when they heard the news that Jeff Stuart had been injured and might never play another football game as a Rock.

"Damn idjit!" Jack Stuart shouted out the truck window at the green '51 Mercury sedan that had just blown around him. Jack slowed and let the dust clear before pushing the truck back up to twenty-five miles per hour. Crazy sonsabitches come flittin' around tryin' to kill a body. Stay on paved roads, damn your eyes!

A sour stomach and a troubling mind had chased Jack from the lumberyard. He'd driven off after mumbling a vague intention of checking up on Ab and his crew. Jack figured he was as likely to see an angel in a flaming chariot as he was Ab, but he was damned if he was going to sit around the yard all day. The sun had scarcely passed to the west, and he knew it would be a struggle to keep from pulling the demijohn from under the kitchen sink before five o'clock.

The old man had considered waiting until Jeff came home from school so the boy could do the driving, but it just got too complicated. He didn't know if the boy could drive with that bad arm, or if he just wanted to be left alone. He felt he should talk to the boy but didn't know what to say. Meal times had gotten so tense the old man had taken to loading up a plate and carrying it back to the rock house to eat. He was haunted by the feeling he'd seen this tragedy played out before but could do nothing to change it.

Jack always tried to route himself around clear-cut areas, but that had become tougher every year. The trees in Western North Carolina were falling like stacked dominoes. The nation's demand for everything from toilet paper to telephone poles appeared insatiable. Every new road afforded access to forests that had never been touched by a saw. When he passed the mutilated landscape of slash residue and rutted hillside, the old man saw the accumulated sins of his long life.

On his twelfth birthday, Jack had run away from the choking gloom and seventy-two hour work-weeks at Rockton Textile. Leaving his mother and sisters behind, the boy trekked for five days back into the mountains. He caught on as a cook's helper with one of the big Northern—the direction from which all cash and travail seemed to flow—timber companies that had spread across the Appalachian Mountains faster than chestnut blight. Jack ran his own team of mules when he was fourteen, moved up to straw boss at eighteen, and topped out at foreman at twenty. By then, Jack Stuart's ability to tally lumber was legendary. Loggers claimed he could scan a hillside and estimate the cut so accurately you couldn't salvage more than a week's worth of toothpicks from the overage.

Quickly realizing that money generated by the workingman's sweat ended up on the boss man's hip, Jack branched out briefly into the manufacture and sale of non-tax paid whiskey. In less than five years, liquor profits had built a lumberyard capable of processing all the saw timber and pulpwood his crew could cut. He abandoned boot-legging and ran that yard for over forty years, through the World Wars, the Depression, and two devastating fires that would have destroyed a lesser man. No matter the market, supply appeared endless.

But everything changed. The last time he'd gone back to the old home place, he'd found a paved driveway under a pink Cadillac with Florida plates sitting next to a ticky-tacky gingerbread house. If it hadn't been broad daylight, he'd have burned it down on the spot. He'd always intended to go back there in the winter and take care of that. Maybe the coming winter. When the bastard owner is sun-tanning on a beach. In fuckin' Florida!

An overloaded pulp wood truck skidded around a curve taking his half out of the center. Jack braked quickly and swerved right. He narrowly avoided planting his pick-up into the side ditch. It wasn't one of his trucks—he couldn't fire the driver, damn his eyes.

To hell with it. Time to piss on the fire and call in the dogs—the hunt's over! He turned his truck around in a wide, creeping arc. The mill hands got paid on Thursday. Poker games would be running at the American Legion and VFW. He'd take a drink, talk about old times, draw to a flush.

CHAPTER FOURTEEN

"Hit's them bums that's adoin' it," the old truck driver said. "That's how come you to get weather like this."

"Take a left here, please" Jeff said, pointing across the nose of the one-eyed dog sitting between him and the driver. Jeff was hitchhiking the Saturday morning after Rockton's catastrophic 13-12 loss to Blighton when the old man ("Just call me 'Spud,'") in a rusted-out Chevy truck offered him a ride. When Jeff had opened the door, the smell of the dog nearly knocked him down. He considered riding in the truck bed, but the dark, surly clouds that loomed about fifty feet above the ground had peppered down sleet and rain off and on all morning. Besides, he didn't want to offend the old man or his dog.

Jeff had stood by the bench with his arm in a sling and watched as puny Blighton knocked off Rockton for the first time in eleven years. He'd stalked out of the locker room at half-time when Coach Baron had demanded that any player who intended to get injured oughta do it on the football field instead of "in a shower, doing God-knows-what." He wouldn't set foot on sideline or in locker room until he could make that old son of a bitch eat his words.

That morning, when everybody at the lumberyard, customers and help alike, could talk of nothing but the game, Granjack had mercifully cut the boy loose before lunch. Jeff had hit the road in search of the only folks he knew who would be indifferent, if not oblivious, to the fiasco a local sportswriter referred to as the "Friday Night Massacre."

"You ask your Grandpaw," Spud continued, "he'll tell you there weren't no weather like this till after the Second Worlds War. Once they started blastin' them atumic bums, the weather went to hell and never come back."

Jeff cranked his window down a couple inches and inhaled deeply. The cold wind dried the sweat on his forehead, and cleansed the dog smell from his nose and lungs. He adjusted his sling, but the nagging pain persisted. The old man talked faster but drove slower; the dirt road to Cody's house seemed to stretch on endlessly.

"Now don't get me wrong," Spud continued, "I ain't agin' settin' 'em off entire. Hit confounds me how General MacArthur didn't drop one on Korea straight off insteada pissin' his name in the snow for two years. Like I was tellin' the old woman, hit's all foretold in the Bible—"

"You can pull over right there," Jeff said, pointing toward the two wild cherry trees that flanked Cody's road. Jeff gave the dog a rub and slid out of the truck. "I'm much obliged for the ride," he said.

"Think nothin' of it, son" the old man said, waving off the gratitude with his cigarette hand. "Tell your grandpaw ol' Spud says, 'Howdy'. He'll know who you're talkin' about."

"SONUMABITCH!" Naomi shouted, as she paced the room in her underwear. She threw clothing into a suitcase that lay atop the rumpled bed. She was alone in the house, and when the silence threatened to smother her, she chased it away with profanity. The radio was the first casualty that morning. It took a lethal blow from a poorly aimed jelly glass that missed Cody's head by better than a foot. Naomi was embarrassed by her aim and heartbroken over the loss of the only entertainment in the house.

"CHRIST AMIGHTY!"

Their argument had carried over from the night before, but was part of the long-running dispute that had simmered since she and Cody had fallen into each others clutches. When Naomi emerged from the ladies room of the Hi-Hat Club, she spotted Cody sharing a darkened corner with this skinny, bleach-blonde beanpole. The two of them hadn't gotten around to wandering off into the bushes and bumping uglies, but she knew Cody always had his eye peeled for a little "strange."

Naomi's packing slowed as she recalled their first meeting. After her Studebaker broke down outside of town, a local waitress had steered her to a knitting mill that was hiring. Naomi lied about her experience, got a job, and quickly proved to be inept at the sewing machine. The woman working beside her tried to help, but the shift supervisor had no time for a worker who showed little prospect of ever making production.

Following her first week's piddling output, everyone knew Naomi's sewing days were numbered. Consequently, Mack the fixer, the strutting rooster of a mechanic who kept the machines running, was particularly desperate to "plug" Naomi before she left his barnyard forever. After shift change on Friday, the fixer pressed his suit forcefully on Naomi in the mill parking lot. Naomi's protests caught the ear of the third shift fixer, who was, characteristically, late for work. Cody Hunter needed only one punch to dispatch Mack and steal the heart of the short eye-talian girl. Sort of like a redneck Tony Curtis, she'd decided.

"JESUS, MARY, AND JOSEPH!" shouted Naomi, mad as hell that she had allowed herself to lapse into a memory that elevated Cody above the level of worm. She slammed the lid down on her suitcase, then bounced on it several times till it latched. She rubbed the bruise under her right eye to remind herself why she was leaving; now she had to figure out how.

She stared out the window at the Studebaker parked eternally under the oak tree, the rusting engine hanging from chains above its hood—another of Cody's projects. He claimed he was checking junkyards regularly for one damn part or another, but Naomi knew that in all likelihood Pope Pius XII would invite her to his wedding before the Studebaker would roll across pavement again.

Nothing to do but walk out to the main road and try to catch a ride. She was headed to Florida—her mother had a sister in Miami—when the Studebaker broke down. She *would not* go back to Baltimore. "Christ," she said aloud. "I'll walk across friggin' Georgia on my hands before I go back to the neighborhood. They can all go piss up a rope."

"REDNECK BASTA'D!"

Jeff stopped in his tracks about ten yards from the front porch. He was confused, mightily. When he saw the Ford was gone, he assumed he would have to walk back out to the road and hitchhike home. The alternative, he thought as he approached the house, was that Naomi had taken the Ford and Cody might be home. When Jeff heard the epithet hurled through the open window, he didn't know whether to beat a path out of there or hang around and defend the legitimacy of his conception.

Jeff's appearance awoke ol' Blackjack, the hound sleeping under the porch. The dog hauled himself up on his front legs and bayed once before losing interest and verticality. The door opened and Naomi appeared behind the screen door in her bathrobe. "I didn't hear you drive up," she said.

"I hitched a ride. Is Cody here?"

"No. He took the Ford." Naomi's voice was as flat as a telephone operator's.

"Did he get his license back?"

"No."

"Is he coming back soon?"

"I don't give a shit if he evah comes back," Naomi said coldly. She pushed the screen door open and stepped out onto the porch. "I don't intend to be heah if he does."

Naomi gathered her bathrobe tightly in clenched fists, but Jeff's attention never wandered from her joyless face and the bruise around her eye—not quite a black eye yet, but headed that way. Long moments passed while Jeff searched for words. He expected a question about the sling, but Naomi either didn't notice or didn't care.

"He's probly at his Mama's house." Naomi said. "She'll always take her baby boy in. Good-bye, Jeff." She slammed the screen door off its hinges.

Jeff hitched a ride that took him within a half mile of his destination. As a light rain fell on his bare head, he could find little reason to believe his current mission would raise his spirits. In a town with no shortage of sour and disappointed people, Jeff reckoned that Cody's father, Ira, pegged the needle on the misery gauge. What the hell, he concluded, as he carefully skirted a milo field where two heavily-armed hunters laid in ambush for tiny mourning doves, he had nothing else to do, nowhere to go. And he had questions for Cody; he just didn't know if he wanted to hear the answers.

When Jeff crossed the top of the hill, he could make out two figures working inside a small corral by the barn. The cries of bellowing cattle accompanied Jeff's every step as he crossed the pasture. So intent were father and son, they didn't notice Jeff approaching over open ground until he was within fifty feet of the corral. The pair were trying to maneuver a boisterous young bull into a jury-rigged wooden pen scarcely larger than the bull itself and getting no cooperation. Off to the left in an adjacent lot, two smaller bulls bawled in pain and resentment.

"Yo, Jeff," Cody called hoarsely, as he took off his Army field jacket and threw it across the top rail of the wooden fence. "Glad to see you. We've chased this fella across Hell and half of Georgia."

"Don't know how much help I can be," Jeff said, raising his sling and arm off his stomach briefly. Although he felt little desire to do Cody a favor, he knew he had no choice. That was how he'd been raised.

"Don't need no help." Ira Hunter said sternly, staring at the bull that stood drooling and wrathful in a corner of the pen.

"Like hell we don't," Cody said, defiantly. He lit up a Marlboro. "You pick that up at our tea party?"

"Yeah. No football for six weeks."

"Tough," Cody said. But it didn't sound to Jeff like it broke his heart.

"Here's the deal," Cody said, as Jeff clambered over the fence. "You take my coat here and stand over in the corner there. That's where we keep losing him. Just wave the coat at him and shout and keep squeezin' him toward the pen. We'll pinch in from the back and the other side."

After a couple passes, the three succeeded in penning the bull. While the animal thrashed in frustration, Ira Hunter reached into the right front pocket of his overalls and whipped out a Barlow knife and a whetstone. He sharpened the knife blade with undisguised malice.

"Here," Cody said, handing a heavy wooden yoke over the pen and settling it across the bull's neck. "Don't let him back up." Jeff leaned on the yoke with his right hand and all his weight. "Firm up good," Cody instructed. "'cause this feller is fixin' to get real unhappy."

After a nod from Ira, Cody grabbed the bull's tail close to its source and jerked it up in the air. Cody's action seemed to bewilder and immobilize the animal; the bull's angry snorts and bellows changed to panicky lowing. Ira pulled a small bottle of rubbing alcohol from a hip pocket and splashed some on the knife blade, then bent down behind the animal. Although Jeff had never witnessed the operation before, he could tell what was coming. The boy's legs grew rubbery and his stomach quivered. In a single swift motion, Ira Hunter reached between the bull's legs and slashed the animal's right testicle with the knife.

MAROOOO! MAROOOOOOOO! The bull's protest was a mixture of anger and pain such as Nature should not tolerate. When Jeff's grip on the yoke loosened, Cody shouted: "HOLD ON! It's the second one he really resents."

Ira Hunter made another pass with the knife, then quickly splashed some alcohol on the open wound. The ex-bull tried to buck but was too weak; he staggered against both sides of the corral and rolled his head in a circle with his tongue extended. When Ira dropped the rear gate and Cody released the tail, Jeff pulled the yoke off the steer's neck. The animal reeled backwards out of the pen. He nearly fell to the ground before hobbling off to the farthest corner of the corral.

Jeff looked nearly as sick as the wounded steer.

"Congratulations." Cody said, slapping him on the back. "You just made that animal's life one helluva lot simpler. He'll likely go into church work now."

Ira Hunter pulled out his wallet and handed Cody a ten-dollar bill. Cody stuffed the bill in his pocket.

Ira spoke directly to Cody. "We'd all be better off if someone had done that to you years ago," the old man said.

Cody stared into his father's eye. "Missed your chance," he said. "There ain't enough old men in this town to hold me down now."

Ira Hunter grunted and stalked off toward the house. Jeff turned away and stared out into the open pasture, wishing he had spent the morning in bed instead of striking off in the gloom in pursuit of Cody Hunter. He followed Cody over to a faucet next to the barn, and they washed their hands with Boraxo powder.

"You got the time?" Cody asked.

"Ten to twelve," Jeff said.

"Good deal, Lucille," Cody responded. He grabbed his field jacket off the fence and lit a cigarette. "You can drive us over to Woody's for lunch. My treat." He pulled on his jacket and prepared to leap over the fence.

"Whoa, man," Jeff said, standing in place. "I need to talk to you."

Cody leaned against the fence and nodded. Jeff's head reeled from the events of the whole crazed morning. "Naomi said she was leaving you," he blurted out. Cody nodded but his expression did not change. "Did y'all have a fight?"

"Oh, yeah. We have lotsa fights," Cody said. "Hell, that's what we do best."

Silence.

"Did you hit her?"

Cody inhaled deeply from his cigarette and turned the question over in his mind. "Well...it depends on what you mean by 'hit,'" he said, exhaling words and smoke slowly. "If you mean: did I raise my arms up to stop her from pounding on my head with a flashlight? You betchum. I might have clipped her then. That might be what you're referring to."

"Let's see," Cody continued, stroking his chin, "as I was walking out the door, she caught me in the back of the head with a lamp base." He bent over and displayed a large ugly bump behind his right ear. Dried blood in matted hair surrounded the angry knot.

"No, I chased her, but I didn't get ahold of her after that." Cody threw his cigarette to the ground and stepped on it. Leaning back, he extended both arms across the top rail of the fence. "Now I got a question," he said. "What the fuck business is that of yours?"

"It's none of my business."

"O.K." Cody said pleasantly, "Let's go get some lunch." Standing flat-footed, Cody placed his left hand on the top rail and vaulted over the fence—an impressive feat Jeff would have tried to duplicate if he had been whole. As Jeff clumsily scaled the fence, Cody broke off in a trot toward the house. "Keys are in the car," he called from the porch.

The Ford was warm and the radio tuned when Cody ducked into the shotgun seat. He had a guitar in hand. "You ever play?"

Jeff shook his head, as he backed the car out of the driveway. He draped his left arm across the wheel and tried not to move it as he shifted with his right.

"Wanna learn?" Cody asked.

"Sure."

"This was my first guitar," Cody said as he strummed across the open strings. He tuned a couple strings then played a C chord, followed quickly by an F and a G7. "Still in good shape. The neck's just a *little* warped, so you have to lean on the bass strings, but she still rings true." He ripped off the first verse of "Heartbreak Hotel." "You can pick it up quick if you play everday." He pulled some folded notebook paper from his coat pocket. "Here's some songs with the chords and the fingering. Once you can get from chord to chord without sprainin' your wrist, you can play damn near anything—'Star Spangled Banner' to 'St. Louis Blues'."

"Thanks," Jeff said, amazed by Cody's generosity. "I'll take care of it."

They ate barbecue, then picked up two six-packs, Slim Jims, Moon Pies, and drove, played, sang, and drank until dark. Eventually they found themselves back in the Hunter driveway.

"Where you want me to leave the car?" Jeff asked, as Cody slid out of the passenger seat.

"Park 'er at the lumberyard. Leave the key under the floor mat. I'll get her tomorrow."

"Thanks again for the guitar."

Cody winked. "Practice everday," he said. Cody leaned in the open window and spoke as if in conspiracy. "Uh, man, I wonder if you might could, you know...pump me a few?" Cody's eyes roved from front seat to back, floorboard to roof, but never settled on Jeff's face. "Just till payday, you understand."

"Yeah, sure," Jeff said quickly. He whipped out his wallet. "I got five, ten, twelve bucks," he said, holding the bills out as he counted them.

Cody collected a five and backed away from the car. "I'll get it back to you on Saturday," he said. Jeff nodded, knowing better.

Broke even, thought Jeff, as he drove away. Best I ever made out.

CHAPTER FIFTEEN

The whole injury ordeal had forced one hell of a tough adjustment on Jeff. Since the age of ten, he had defined himself first as an athlete; that was his personal and public identity. If you asked the folks in Rockton who Jeff Stuart was, the mass of townsfolk would first tell you he was the best football player in town—only after that would they get into family and religion. Ever since the first game of his junior year—"STUART RUNS WILD IN ROCKTON ROMP"—Jeff had walked the autumn sidewalks a teen-age, red-clay Achilles bearing Rockton Pride on his back. Following the Blighton defeat, Jeff's presence on Main Street was met primarily with sympathetic nods and averted eyes. But the boy also spotted glances of accusation and betrayal. He quickly established several routes from home to school that bypassed the town which stood squarely between the two.

A social life that had centered around football practice, games, and parties with teammates and cheerleaders had also been dislocated by that crushing tackle at Alley's Cat Club. Now a civilian among warriors, he avoided his old teammates, as they seemed to avoid him. Tarred by his public "humiliation" at Vicky's hands in the most conspicuous arena in town—Sunday, high noon, Baptist Church—Jeff assumed, before a single denial, that rejection would inevitably follow any request for a date. He found himself most comfortable when alone.

After a few evenings of intense restlessness, Jeff made some adjustments to his living space and his attitude that served him well during his recuperation. He bought a good radio at the Western Auto and slapped together a makeshift antenna, replicating the wire hanger, aluminum foil model he had seen at Cody's house. Rock'n'roll was all over the dial, and disc jockey John R. spun the blues nightly from WLAC in Nashville.

When his left arm permitted him to fret the guitar without pain, Jeff pushed his bed into the corner of the room and adopted a cross-legged, back-against-the-wall physical and emotional attitude that suited his situation and the music he craved to play. Once he'd built up the calluses on his fingers and mastered the C chord, he could practice for hours with little regard for hunger, thirst, or the pain he was inflicting on his mother—a lady forced to listen through thin walls to woefully amateurish renderings of music she considered horrible when performed by professionals.

Often on Saturdays or Sundays, Jeff hiked through the woods that stretched for miles behind his home. He had grown up there, playing cowboy or army, sometimes with neighbor kids, sometimes alone. Granjack had taught him to hunt squirrels with a twenty-two caliber rifle there. He'd seen many deer foraging but never felt the urge to shoot one. Once he started high school and took up sports with a passion that permitted no rival, he gave up the forest without thought or regret.

He reclaimed old paths that had grown over and watched the forest age from verdant summer to an autumn gallery so dazzling he could only assume its splendor was unique to 1956, or surely he would never have overlooked it. An early frost, followed by a series of cold nights and warm days, turned the maples, oaks, dogwoods, hickories and beeches into a vibrant gallery of reds, yellows, and copper browns. Each time he entered the forest and was embraced by the cool, damp, fecund odor of decomposition, he found it harder to leave; eventually, only darkness would chase him home. He brought books and food in a backpack and strapped a canteen of water to his webbed army surplus belt. He walked until hungry, ate until full, read until restless, walked.

There was little work for a one-armed man at a lumberyard, and the workers didn't mind telling the boy how useless he'd become. Jeff's relations with his mother had become so strained that Janet, the office girl, could hardly work when he was around; she spent large parts of the day in the bathroom. What with Jeff's moroseness and the normal slowdown for approaching winter, both Rose and Granjack regularly found reasons to keep his workday brief.

Jeff managed to catch Cody at home one crisp early-October Sunday morning. Naomi, Cody explained as he rolled fully-clothed out of bed, was still "coolin' out" with a girlfriend in a trailer outside of town. The men left the house with only two fishing rods, a twenty-two rifle, two large potatoes, two-thirds of a pint of Old Crow, and Cody's assurance that was all they would need for a day on the river. Sure enough, they shot a couple squirrels, dug worms, caught bluegills and dined like kings. That was Cody's gift: he could merrily make do with whatever he had.

And then there was Vicky. Their break-up had left Jeff with a smoldering mountain of lust to deal with, an obstacle he found hard to climb over or see around. During those first weeks following their separation, Jeff's dreams were haunted by those all-but-coital memories. Every softly curved line in nature suggested an aspect of the cheerleader's incomparable form. Jeff knew if he proposed reconciliation, Vicky would likely take him back and reward him with increased freedom and greater access. But even the prospect of free grazing in Vicky's garden could not induce him to climb back into *that* relationship—particularly on terms that would effectively pass the whip hand to a young woman who would use it ruthlessly. The only good thing that had come of his injury, Jeff often reminded himself, was his final, definitive, public break-up with Vicky.

School days were especially tough since Vicky had adopted a wardrobe that indicated she didn't intend to remain uncoupled for long. Audible moans from hormone-addled boys echoed off the metal lockers as the head cheerleader sashayed from class to class. The faculty lounge buzzed with indignation and conjecture over where lines must be drawn—what was too tight, too short, too sexy?

The administration, characteristically, dithered. The most practical solution was proposed by an insightful student who had studied the situation closely. "The least they could do," Marty said to Jeff, as they watched Vicky undulate down the crowded hallway, "is assign a hall monitor with a bucket of cold water to follow her around."

"You understand I can only let you have these for a month," Marty said, as he led Jeff from the parsonage and across the lawn to the bomb shelter. "You can take out five at a time, but no more than two of them can be novels."

"What's the fine if I bring them back late?" Jeff asked facetiously.

"No fine," Marty replied earnestly. "But you lose your privileges for a month. Chuck borrowed 'Tropic of Capricorn' last spring and *never* brought it back. He's blackballed for life."

The two boys had just been in Marty's bedroom examining the prize collection of pornography that he kept beneath a trap door in his cluttered closet. The preacher's boy had to dig through the remnants of dozens of projects begun and cast aside during his youth—a John Gnagy "Learn to Draw" kit, the

Charles Atlas "Dynamic Tension" body-building kit, a battered but "Official—Accept No Substitutes—Arthur Godfrey Ukulele," a case of forty-eight cans of petroleum jelly that ten year-old Marty was supposed to sell to win a pony—a closetful of broken promises, and discarded dreams.

However, the brown paper bag Marty extracted from the secure area beneath the closet floor represented the sole endeavor he would not consider deserting. "Ryder's Classic Crotch Collectibles," as the young curator called his acquisitions, represented a remarkable sampling of erotic literature assembled by a resourceful minor working within a society so horrified by the nude human form that they enforced the ban with public humiliation, arrest and imprisonment. These pieces, Marty explained to Jeff, were for on-premises viewing only. They couldn't be removed from the archive. As the collection had grown Marty had been forced to move the lending library out to the bunker.

"Watch your head," Marty advised. He tapped the low tin overhang that covered the sunken bunker that had once scandalized the town and nearly split the congregation of the First Baptist Church into warring factions. Marty pushed open the door and slowly panned the cement floor and cinder block walls with his flashlight. The walls were bare except for a paint-by-the-numbers reproduction of da Vinci's 'Last Supper' that his mother had given him for Christmas many years back. Marty hadn't finished it either—the three apostles farthest from the Savior toiled in monochrome obscurity—but in this particular gallery it didn't matter. Jeff stowed his sling in his coat pocket as he watched various bugs and roaches scramble for corners and cover. The air in the low-ceilinged 20x15 vault was wet, musty, and catacomb thick.

Marty reached under a short wooden bench and pulled out a Coleman Lantern. After pumping it vigorously, he lit the wick. The room took on an orange-yellow glow. He kicked a steamer trunk labeled "Can Goods" and waited for the multi-legged wildlife to evacuate before opening it.

"OK, in here we got some of the better magazines," Marty said. He sat on a rusty lawn chair and laid his wares out on the bench. "'Adam,' 'Prong,' 'Gent,' most of your standards. Take what you want." He opened another box. "Crotch novels. The classics, 'Lady Chatterley's Lover,' 'Fanny Hill,' 'Crank, The Sailor.' I think you'll find that most conveniently fall open to the 'good parts.'"

Jeff glanced nervously at the door. "Do your folks ever come in here?"

"Are you kidding?" Marty snorted. "You couldn't hold a gun on 'em and get 'em out here. The old man prays every night that the earth will open up and swallow this building."

Jeff nodded. He clearly remembered the uproar back in the winter of 1952 when America, right down to tiny Rockton, was going through one of its periodic atomic bomb scares. The Right Reverend Ryder, after a heavy meal of corned beef and cabbage and a horrifying magazine article illustrating the destructive potential of the new hydrogen bomb, had a dream of such apocalyptic realism that he could barely wait for daylight to contract a bomb shelter from one of the several builders who advertised in the area.

Alas, before the contractor had the floor and walls completed, nearly everyone in town had joined a spirit-filled debate over the propriety of a preacher owning a refuge that might allow him to dodge, or at least delay, the Divine retribution promised in Revelations. All parties found scripture to quote, but as more of the churchmen surveyed the shelter's size and concluded it could house no more than the preacher's family of four—no room even for deacons—Reverend Ryder's position became untenable. Ultimately, the preacher declared the whole incident a misunderstanding. He had a tin roof attached and designated the building a "tornado cellar." That in a region where tornadoes were as common as locust plagues.

Jeff quickly made his selections and Marty slipped them into a brown paper bag. Marty secured his archive and the two boys walked out into the bright daylight.

"Where'd you get all this stuff?" Jeff asked, radiating guilt as he glanced furtively in every direction. He half-expected to see Detective Joe Friday from "Dragnet" charging from the woods to lecture him on the link between filthy pictures and Communism. "I mean, your old man raised so much hell, the drug store stopped carrying 'Confidential' magazine. And that's nothing compared to these."

Jeff pulled his sling from his coat pocket, adjusted it around his neck and arm, and tucked the brown paper bag securely under it. They walked toward the parsonage.

Marty smiled sagely. "I get a lot of it from my sister, Sylvia, in New York City. She sends it to a post office box in Oak City. Syl's living with a bunch of artists, musicians, and writers who are so cool they call themselves 'Beats.' They—"

"Beets?" Jeff interrupted. "Like turnips?"

"No, man. B-e-a-t. Beat. Like beaten down by life, or on the beat, in music. It's kinda hard to explain, I guess, cause every time I ask she just gets more vague. Anyway, they believe American society is crazy and if you get involved in it, it'll make you crazy too."

"How can you help it?" Jeff asked. "It's everywhere."

"Yeah, but they say you just have to make your own music, write your own stories, hang around with other 'Beats.' So you don't get corrupted by materialism...or TV! Golly damn, do they hate television! Syl says television cripples more people than polio ever did." Marty laughed and shrugged as he stopped at his front porch. "You want a ride home?"

"Nah, I'd rather walk," Jeff said, turning to leave.

"Oh, this is the best." Marty said quickly. "They believe in 'free love.' Syl says you can't get hung up with just one person, like husband and wife. You should spread your love around to a lot of different people."

"Sounds good to me," Jeff said. "See you later."

Jeff crossed the street in front of Marty's house and angled across the field behind the Baptist Church. The idea of "free love" sounded great to a seventeen year-old with a libido that never winked, much less slept, but he knew it couldn't be that simple. Love, Jeff figured, might be "free," but sex was bound to cost you.

CHAPTER SIXTEEN

"This is crazy, I know it is," Rose muttered, as she steered her station wagon out of town. "And now I'm talking to myself." She shook her head and bit her lower lip, regretting dearly that she had forgotten her pack of Chesterfields.

If I only had someone to talk to, she thought, making an effort not to move her lips. When she thought about the friends she and Will had when they were first married, and all the women she had confided in when Jeffie was young, it made her sad. Mothers of young children bond easily, but as the children grow, the mothers drift apart. There was no time for friends anymore.

Of course, a friend would likely give her the same advice as the *Reader's Digest*: Consult your clergyman. "Right," Rose said loudly, then bit her lip again. Good advice if your clergyman was Reverend Billy Graham, but *not* Reverend Billy Ryder. She might as well take out a full page in the *Rockton Messenger* and advertise her troubles. Reverend Billy might try to keep her secret, but his wife, Alma, would worm it out of him before supper was half-eaten and serve it up like desert for the girls at the beauty parlor on Wednesday.

Even in the best of times, Rose had always found plenty to worry about. Several years back she had grown so distracted that Doc Bowman had prescribed the new tranquilizer everyone was talking about. Rose took the Miltown pills for nearly a month and hated every minute of it. Throughout the therapy, she knew there were things out there that *needed* to be worried about, but that damn "peace pill" kept getting in the way.

Rose was lost in memory when the sign leaped from behind a stand of high grass. She slammed on her brakes and jerked the steering wheel hard right onto the dirt road, nearly clipping the plywood sign:

MADAM LA'MOOR
PALMIST & MENTALIST
CRYSTAL READINGS

Madam La'Moor moved quickly to her window when she heard the squeal of tires on pavement. She saw the brown station wagon righting itself before stopping on the dirt road. Just someone turning around, she figured. When the station wagon began rolling slowly toward her, the prophetess was first elated then alarmed. She pulled the curtains shut, lit an oil lamp and tossed a pellet of incense into it.

Madam ran to her bedroom and changed into her black gown. She jerked the midnight blue turban with the ruby brooch off the dresser and pulled it snugly over her ears. She would have preferred more time to prepare her parlor—she certainly needed to replace the crystal ball that the cursed cat had broken—but she was joyous at the prospect of receiving a customer.

Rose parked next to a black 1950 Buick. She screwed up her courage and climbed out of the car. As she walked toward the old wood frame house, she summoned a well-worn memory for strength. When Rose was sixteen and driven to distraction by her father's drinking, she had spent a precious half dollar to consult Lady Grizelda, a fortuneteller in a traveling carnival. The Gypsy woman had recounted with amazing clarity Rose's sad life. But Lady Grizelda foresaw a brighter future. She predicted Rose's hard work and noble heart would soon be rewarded with travel and the means to escape her wretched lot. She predicted that a financial windfall and freedom would soar like a white bird in Rose's future.

Sure enough, the following spring Abel Dance died, and the last vestige of his family's land was sold off. After the government glommed off the bulk of the estate, enough money remained to stake Rose's mother to a suitcase filled with new clothes and a train ticket back to her family in Wilmington. Rose's share, when combined with a small scholarship award from her high school, was sufficient to pay for one year's room and board at Stallings Secretarial School in Oak City. Far, far from her eastern Carolina home.

That memory impelled Rose up the rickety steps and across the uneven plank porch. Now only a faded door stood between her and destiny. She raised her hand slowly and cautiously and tapped her knuckles against the peeling paint.

Madam La'Moor heard the tentative knock as she spread a clean red cloth on the round table in her parlor. "Psst, psst, Caliban. Come here, kitty," she hissed desperately. The black cat had wandered up when Madam was moving in and was welcomed as a good omen and an ally against the mice who claimed free run across floors and inside walls. But the tom had proven resistant to responsibility or domestication. Once inside, his first act was to nudge Madam's crystal ball off the table, shattering it. Cats, just like Men and the Law, Madam La'Moor thought: sneaky, disloyal and never around when you needed them.

At the second more determined knock, Madam La'Moor gave up on the wampus and snuck a peek out the side of the curtain for a cold reading on her client: tall white woman, nice suit, neat. Wearing a wedding ring, appears physically sound. Pretty face, but a worrier. Money problems were unlikely, the seer concluded, but looks like she could use a roll in the hay.

Madam La'Moor opened the door abruptly, and Rose took a startled step backward—the desired effect. "I am Madam La'Moor," the mentalist intoned in a languorous English accent. "How may I assist you?"

"Er, I, uh..." Rose explained.

"You have questions that need answers, problems that beg for solutions. That is my gift. Please enter," Madam La'Moor said. She spoke in tones as rich and pearly as an Elizabethan actress, but less clipped, more musical. Madam La'Moor's training had been classical; she had studied under the estimable "Bird Man," an emaciated sideshow dwarf who could recite entire scenes, all characters in dialect, of select Shakespearean tragedies. No comedies.

Rose stood stunned, unable to believe her eyes or ears. She had expected a shriveled, white woman speaking in the rolling, middle-European cadences she'd heard in the Wolf Man and Vampire movies—like Lady Grizelda. Certainly not a chocolate-colored Negress, who looked and sounded like Winston Churchill in drag.

"You have been brought to me by the Guiding Hand," Madam La'Moor said. "You may leave if you wish, but you will take back with you the crushing burden of worry and indecision that can only be relieved by one who can peer into the past and gaze into the future."

Rose stepped inside the shadowy, sweet-smelling room. "I would like a consultation, please," Rose said.

The prophetess smiled and nodded. No speech impediment, limp or obvious affliction, she noted gratefully. Madam La'Moor lifted the aromatic oil lamp from the table and led the white woman through a bead curtain into her parlor. She motioned for Rose to take a seat at the small round table.

Although the room was dim, Rose was reassured by what she saw. On the wall above the mantle hung an expansive and dramatic painting of the zodiac. A poster with a large dissected palm was pinned to the wall on her right.

"I, uh," Rose began hesitantly, "think we need to—

"My fee is five dollars," the fortuneteller interrupted. "But you pay only when you are satisfied you have received help with your problem." Madam La'Moor sat down and inverted the small hourglass on the table. "When the sand runs out, our encounter will be complete."

"I would like a crystal reading," Rose said.

"Oh no, my dear," Madam La'Moor cooed gently, while mentally drawing and quartering her cat. "I can see your entire life and all that is to come resides in those beautiful hands." She gently raised Rose's right palm for examination. "Many people do not understand that the hand clearly reflects the hopes and fears of our lives, as well as the past and future. They reside here, waiting to be read like the pages of a book," Madam spoke so softly Rose had to lean forward to hear.

"I can see you are a very kind woman who takes the worries of others on your shoulder while ignoring your own desires and needs." Madam traced a line in her client's hand while gazing intently into her face. "You are having trouble with a relationship." Rose's eyes widened in confirmation, and the prophetess continued. "Many women are burdened with husbands who do not recognize the bonds of marriage," (frown), "but this is not your problem. And there are those men who are not capable of keeping up their husbandly duties," (hand jerk), "but your palm indicates clearly this is not your situation. Your problem does not concern a romantic involvement. That is a side of your life you have mastery over," (nod).

Madam La'Moor navigated swiftly through the corridors of her client's life guided unerringly by facial tics, breathing changes, hand pressure—the countless involuntary reactions more telling than words.

"When a woman reaches maturity," Madam continued, "it is often our children who rule over our happiness," (eyes widen). "A young girl who is eager to forsake the rules of home and church can bring great sorrow to her mother," (no response), "but that is not your burden, and thankfully so. More often it is a son's behavior." (long exhale-Jackpot!) "When a son, who has always been a good boy, falls under the influence of a bad crowd, (gasp) he can bring great sorrow to his mother. And when his mother has no husband to help her," (eyes tear, hand squeeze), "then she may feel the weight of the world on her shoulders."

Rose's left hand moved from beneath the table, and she embraced the soft brown hand gently between hers. She had been determined not to confide her troubles, even disclose her name, until she was convinced the fortuneteller was not a fake. Madam La'Moor had pinpointed her problem without a word from Rose's lips. She was so relieved she nearly cried while pouring out her concerns, objections, and fears in a torrent of words and emotion. Football, Vicky, late hours, alcohol, new and dangerous friends, "that music," all were cited before Rose concluded: "But the worst thing is we can't talk to each other any more. I need to know what I can do about that, and if it's going to get any better."

Madam peered once again at the palm. "Eventually communication will improve," Madam said slowly, "but first it is likely to get worse." Lord knows it always does.

The air left Rose's body in a rush. "How long before it gets better?"

"It will be between three and five seasons duration before your hearts will understand each other again." That should pay some bills.

"As much as a year?" Rose whispered. "What can I do?"

There was a pause as Madam La'Moor considered the question. The silence was interrupted by the sound of a cat's sharp cry somewhere in the house, then the sound of scurrying paws.

"You must show patience and understanding with your son. If you press too hard he will flee from you. But when you make a rule, you must enforce it without fail." Madam La'Moor had hardly finished her counsel when the sound of the cat, growling, running, and bouncing off the kitchen walls again intruded.

Rose glanced distractedly toward the bead curtain, but her gaze quickly returned to the swift-running sands of the hourglass. "Is there anything else I should know?" she asked anxiously.

Madam La'Moor patted Rose's hand gently. As she searched for counsel, she detected movement near the doorway. Caliban, the wampus cat, strutted proudly through the bead curtain and considered the scene. He decided against presenting his trophy to the woman who sometimes fed, but more often bedeviled him. He walked directly to the stranger and growled as well as he could with a full mouth. Rose glanced down, but the light on the floor was dim. When she bent over, she was greeted with the vision of two sets of eyes—one belonging to a proud cat, the other to a terrified mouse—staring back at her. Rose's scream was short, but effective; the cat was out of the room before Rose's body hit the floor.

When Rose awoke in Madam La'Moor's arms, she felt so calm and peaceful that she chose not to speak. The Negress carried her client into the front room and laid her on the couch.

The prophetess placed a pillow under Rose's head, then bustled off into the kitchen to make tea. Madam's mother, a native of the West Indies, had imbued her daughter with the British belief in the restorative powers of herbs. Her client's fragile state persuaded Madam that a high-test blend would be appropriate. Sorting through her cupboard, she extracted a tea with sedative properties, a bottle of blackberry brandy, and a tin of ground hemp. She measured the ingredients into the hot water simmering atop her wood stove.

"I'm sorry to be so much trouble," Rose called from the living room. "I grew up in a house where mice were so common we had names for most of them. But this little fellow, he just looked so...helpless."

"Do you have these spells often?" Madam called from the kitchen.

"Oh, no," Rose said. "I can't remember the last time I fainted. Many, many years ago."

Madam breathed a sigh of relief. If her first mark at the new location were physically crippled or mentally afflicted, the portent would have been so ominous she would have to consider fleeing the town.

When Madam La'Moor returned with the tea and cream, Rose sat up to receive the dainty porcelain cup and saucer. Her hostess sat across from her in a worn armchair. The two ladies sipped their tea quickly as they made small talk about the weather and the arrival of beautiful fall colors. By the second cup of tea, both women were feeling much looser. Madam, who had two grown children of her own, had conceded that motherhood was not an easy lot even for the spiritually-endowed.

"And so, Miss Rose," Madam summarized over the third cup, "your son has ceased to play the football that frightened you so badly you couldn't watch, and he has given up the girl friend who was no good for him, and he spends a great deal of time in his room playing a musical instrument. You suspect he is drinking beer and has new friends rather than the one you never liked anyway. Is that what you consider to be the grave problem?"

Granted, Rose thought, when you say it like that, it doesn't sound so terrible. And, at the moment it didn't feel so terrible either. Rose fought the temptation to succumb to optimism. As she drank the last of her tea—and reminded herself that she must really get the recipe—several objections sprang to mind. Before she could voice them, Madam La'Moor had collected her cup and was walking to the kitchen. It was clearly time to leave.

As she reached for her purse, Rose checked her watch and attempted to cipher the quarter hours in five dollar increments. Her mind, normally quick and precise as an adding machine, resisted either calculating or worrying about the amount.

"The charge for this consultation is five dollars," Madam said.. "Shall I reserve an appointment next week for the same time?"

"Oh, yes, certainly." Rose said, handing over a wrinkled five dollar bill.

Madam La'Moor took Rose's elbow lightly and led her to the door. "I would like for you to contemplate one question before you return. That is: What do you consider to be the gravest problem you face in regard to your son?"

Rose stopped at the door and summoned her courage. She wanted one personal admission from Madam La'Moor—something to balance the mountain of confession she had placed at the seer's feet. "Would you," Rose asked, "tell me what *you* considered a grave problem you had with your son?"

Madam La'Moor cocked her head and smiled slowly. "A grave problem, Miss Rose, is when your fifteen year-old son falls into the clutches of the 'Spider Lady,' a contortionist who consorts with 'Ivan-The Man of Steel,' a brute of low intellect and great passion." The fortuneteller's quiet laughter escorted Rose out the door and into the cool night. "All survived," were Madam's parting words.

As Rose walked to her car, she was confronted by two overpowering urges: the first, a craving for chocolate chip cookies such as she could never recall; the second, a desperate need to get to a filling station, no matter how untidy, and, in a phrase she had overheard at the lumberyard, "piss like a race horse."

CHAPTER SEVENTEEN

"Could ya step on it," Naomi complained. She sat in the front seat of the Ford between Jeff and Cody. "If my butt ain't in that chair at two o'clock, they'll give my appointment to someone else."

"Just ride with the tide, baby," Cody said. "Jeff'll slide you in there on time."

Jeff and Cody had been playing guitars on the front porch when Naomi announced she needed to go to the beautician's. The couple had been back together for several weeks, but Jeff could see that both were still walking on eggs. Cody, bored and beerless, jumped at the opportunity to do his woman a small favor *and* get off the plantation.

When Jeff turned onto Main Street, he saw Rockton sidewalks bustling as they did only on warm spring or crisp fall Saturdays. Cheery clerks rolled wheelbarrows and toted leaf rakes and yard tools out of the hardware store for sidewalk display. Down the block, men in oil-stained blue jeans hustled out of the Western Auto fondling inexpensive parts that promised to boost car performance dramatically. Neighbors remarked on the azure sky and the nippy breeze, but separated quickly to attack chores put aside throughout the long idle summer. If a Rocktonite was ever going to strike a lick of work in his sorry life, apparently that particular October Saturday was *the day* to do it.

Jeff stopped at the light across from the tiny town park. He nodded to the half-dozen relentlessly lazy men who sat on the concrete benches and lied about how much work they *used* to do. He'd just cleared the intersection when the black and white cruiser whipped in behind him. The whirring red light and screaming siren turned Jeff's blood to ice water and his stomach into a heavy round stone rolled off a cliff. He pulled the Ford over in front of the appliance store, close to dead-center of the town.

Chief Parrish cut the siren but left the red light spinning as he crawled out of the squad car. He waved to the sidewalk throng as he ambled up to the Ford. Shoppers and talkers craned their necks and speculated on the crime and criminals.

Parrish leaned in and scanned the passengers, the floor board, the back seat. Cody smiled and touched two fingers to his forehead in the boy scout salute. Naomi scowled.

"License and registration," the Chief growled.

Cody fished the crumpled registration out of the dash and handed it to Jeff. "Why'd you stop me?" Jeff asked. He felt anger creep across his neck and into his face. His hand shook slightly.

"I stopped you cause of that loud muffler and ona count of 'suspicion,'" Parrish drawled. He checked out the paperwork.

"Suspicion of what?" Jeff asked.

"I suspect," the Chief said, smiling, "that if you spend time with these two, you're going to see a lot more of me than you want to." He handed back the papers. "You get a warning this time. Get that muffler fixed."

As the Chief pulled away from the window, Cody leaned forward. "I'm lookin' forward to us havin' another race soon," Cody said amiably.

When Jeff saw Parrish's face flush purple, he pulled slowly away from the curb. "I reckon me and you must be the Chief's favorite people in the whole world," Cody said with a chuckle. "What with you plowin' his daughter and all."

Jeff was too angry and distracted to admit that he had plowed nary a furrow. "What is it with you and Parrish?" Jeff asked.

"Let's get Miss Naomi to the beauty shop, then we'll go drink us a beer and talk about it."

"If one a them old biddy's says a word about me bein' late," Naomi threatened, "I'll tear the joint apart."

"Ata girl," Cody said, and hugged his chick.

"Man, I don't know about this," Jeff said warily. He shuffled his feet as he stood behind Cody on the small porch of the cinder block building. "Couldn't we just pick up a six-pack and ride down to the lake."

With an hour to kill while Naomi got her hair done, Cody would accept no alternative to a stop at the Rockton American Legion Post. Cody pressed the buzzer and allowed himself to be identified through the one-way mirror. When the buzzer replied, the lock on the door handle released. Cody and Jeff stepped inside.

"Hey, Lester," Cody called to the bartender, "this here's my guest. I'll vouch for him."

Lester shrugged. Rockton was a dry town in a dry county, so the Legion Post and the VFW hut were the only places in eleven miles a man could buy a beer or a drink of whiskey across a bar. Although supposedly restricted to those men who had served their country in uniformed military duty, the policy at the Legion was to admit anybody over twenty-one the bartender recognized except law officers and known troublemakers. Jeff, however, was the first teen-age boy to breathe that heady air since Cody, himself, had crossed the threshold with his Uncle Dolman some six years back. Jeff took a seat in the corner, under the "Buy War Bonds" sign, while Cody walked to the bar.

Gloomy as a crypt and reeking of spilled beer, cigarette smoke, and pickled pigs feet, the room looked, felt, and smelled like quarter past midnight in the afternoon. About a dozen men, all looking middle-aged and morose, were scattered around the room. Several wars had been fought since the floor had been mopped, and no state agency had ever, or *could* ever, sanction the sanitary conditions behind the bar or beyond the door that housed the toilet. There was a tale, widely verified, of a veteran of World War One trench warfare—a doughboy who had spent miserable months ankle-deep in mud, blood, and vermin—who had once opened the door of the john and reeled back in horror.

Cody spread beers, pickled eggs, and polish sausages in pairs across the tables. "Here's the deal," he said, as he sat down. "Lester said you can drink three beers so long as you didn't cause no trouble. If your grandpa shows up, god forbid, your ass goes out the bathroom window." Cody washed down an egg with a half-can of Bud. "Think you can drink three beers without startin' a fight?"

"Done it before," Jeff said. "Ok, what's the deal with Parrish?"

"I reckon it all goes back to my misspent youth," Cody began wistfully. He unraveled a tale of small-town misdemeanor and petty vandalism escalating to felony status when the seventeen year-old Cody started hauling five gallon "jimmyjohns" of white liquor to Nashville.

"Drove a 1940 Ford with a bored-out Elgin block engine—custom-made in Atlanta. Fast as any car ever been on the road. I modified ever part of that car—tires, wheel bearings, reinforced the springs. I braced the hydraulic shocks sideways against the axles and chassis so she wouldn't flip on me when she was loaded. Rigged up booster-brakes and a cluster transmission— gave me six gears. If

I wasn't haulin', I was workin' on that car. It was my whole life there for awhile.

"I ran a hundred and forty miles an hour straightaway. The law couldn't touch me, and after awhile they quit tryin'. Everbody in the county knew I was runnin' liquor—wasn't a thing they could do about it. It really galled their ass. That went on for better'n a year and a half, until..." he took a long pull off the beer and shook his head, "one night I was just parked on this dirt road, mindin' my own business layin' on top of this ol' girl, when a police car roars up with the siren and the light. It's my ol' buddy, Ray. Well this ol' girl, she was kinda confused and excited, bein' naked and all, but she blurted out it wasn't her fault since she was only fifteen years-old. Which was news to me. So right away you got your statutory rape, or delinquintin' a minor, or some such. They poked around and found lessen a pint of white liquor, and the next thing I know I was standing in court with cops and lawyers talkin' about which prison they wanted to stick my ass *under*.

"But I got lucky. The judge was an old doughboy, and he believed the Army could straighten *anybody* out. A week later I was on a bus to Fort Jackson for basic trainin'. Spent two years in a motor pool in Kansas." Cody tapped his empty can. "Your round."

While Jeff went to the bar, Cody ambled over to the jukebox and played a quarter's worth of music. Most of the records hadn't been changed since Pearl Harbor, and the rest had scratches that dated from the Truman administration. A lot of big band—Glenn Miller, Benny Goodman, Artie Shaw—the rest country songs, weepers and boogies. He punched in his choices, starting with "Pistol Packin' Mama," and sat back down.

"Any Elvis?" Jeff said, as he passed Cody a beer.

Cody touched his finger to his lips. "There'll be a Jap flag flyin' on that pole outside before you hear Elvis on *that* jukebox." Cody ate a Polish sausage and leaned back in his chair. "You wanta know the real reason Parrish hates me?"

Jeff nodded.

"One time back when I was haulin', Parrish pulled in behind me so close I could see his little pig-eyes in my mirror. I took him over sixty miles an hour and he hung on. These was mountain roads, mind you, out of Wilkesboro. Curvy as a black snake. Then I punched it up toward seventy, he started backing off. So I backed off. He got mad and made a run, so I took it back up toward seventy. He still had plenty of car under him, but he was chicken-shit to push it. *I* knew it, and *he* knew it. And I had a load of liquor sloshin' around. Fuckin' coward."

Jeff nodded grimly. If a man had that on me, I'd hate him, too.

"Your shoulder botherin' you?" Cody asked.

"Nah," Jeff said, realizing that he'd been rubbing it. "Sometimes it does when I sleep on it, or if I raise my arm too quick. It's gettin' better."

"You gonna try to play football again?"

"I don't know," Jeff said. That was the first time he'd admitted any doubt, even to himself. "Man, I ache to play. I have dreams about it. But I didn't miss getting yelled at and treated like a dog."

Cody shrugged. "Make sure it's *your* decision. There's a lot of people in this town that wouldn't give a damn if you ended up in a body cast so long as it helped them win a football game." Cody raised his empty bottle. "Ready?"

Jeff shook his head. "I've gotta drive through town again."

"Yeah," Cody said. "We need to get back anyway." Cody pushed himself up from the table and stretched. "Naomi don't like waitin' at the curb."

CHAPTER EIGHTEEN

"Hey, Stuart, hold up there, boy!"

The raspy voice crackled across the quiet school campus and clipped Jeff between the shoulder blades just as he and Marty were walking into the cafeteria.

"Save me a place," Jeff said. Marty nodded but made no effort to conceal his contempt for the man who was waddling quickly toward them. Coach Baron and Marty Ryder were enemies as elemental as owls and crows. Marty had been forced to take the Coach's ninth grade Health/P.E. class—no male freshman escaped the ordeal—and Baron found reasons on a near-daily basis to unleash his ventilated oak paddle on Marty's skinny butt. Sophomore year, Marty had taken Baron's U.S. History course and studied with rabbinical diligence, specifically to needle the coach with questions and challenges that befuddled and angered the old man.

Jeff's right hand rose instinctively to his left shoulder as he waited for Baron. "How's the old wing coming along?" Baron shouted, as he puffed up the sidewalk. "Bindin' right up, I expect."

"It's better than it was," Jeff said flatly.

"Son," Baron said, "I know you may not be one hundred percent yet, and that'd be fine if this was the middle of the summer and you didn't have nothing to do but lay around and tug at the one-eyed trouser snake, but I need to know if the team can count on you for the Richardson game next Friday. That would give you four practice days to get back into shape—just runnin', mind you, take a few hand-offs, no contact. Next Friday, you still don't want to play, so be it—God's will be done. The team will understand you gave it your best shot and you came up short."

Jeff did not respond. Baron pressed on. "Now we may not need you. We been playin' good ball lately, but it will mean a lot to the boys just to have you on the sidelines. Whether you ever touch the ball or not. Will you come out and run with us on Monday?"

Jeff stared down at the Coach. This could be the last football game he would ever play—the big game with Richardson. Friday would be six weeks since he busted his shoulder. His target date. Jeff rolled his head in a circle to clear it, then looked directly into Coach Baron's watery brown eyes. "I'll come out and run on Monday," Jeff said.

Baron smiled and slapped Jeff on the shoulder, causing both of them to wince. "Yeah, you'll be alright," Coach Baron said. "You always were a tough kid. Guts! That's what makes a football player."

The coach took three steps before spinning around. "Get yourself a haircut before Monday," he shouted at Jeff's back.

The players were glad to see Jeff at practice. He took a lot of ragging as he pulled on his sweat suit and jogged from the dressing room into the sunny afternoon. A cold wind cut through the light jersey, but he knew within ten minutes the sweat would be rolling down his body and the wind on his face would feel welcome. His body did everything he asked of it, but he knew there would be aches to contend with the next morning. The whistles and catcalls that greeted his decision to forego jumping jacks and push-ups rang with the sweet sound of camaraderie in his ears.

After warm-ups, Jeff ran slow laps around the ball field. He ran until exhausted then fell to the wet grass and wheezed until his breath returned. He ran sprints of twenty, forty, and sixty yards, then shagged punts until bored. By the end of the practice, Jeff was running plays as the first team wingback. No contact, just getting his timing back. Felt like old times.

On Thursday Jeff was excused from practice so he could see the doctor. Although he sometimes felt a prickling sensation when he raised his left arm over his head, he felt better than he had even a week before. He had avoided contact and had yet to take a hit on it. After considerable prodding and rotating, Doc Bowman told him to put his shirt back on.

"Are you figurin' on playin' football again?" Doc asked.

Jeff nodded. "Only if they need me," he said, repeating the coach's promise.

"You can do what you want to, boy," Doc said, through an exhaled cloud of cigarette smoke, "but football's just gonna last a few more weeks. That shoulder's gotta last you the rest of your life."

Jeff stared at the floor. "Can I play?" he asked quietly.

Doc balanced his cigarette on the edge of the sink basin where a long row of brown nicotine stains marred the white porcelain. "It's up to you," Doc said, as he washed his hands.

CHAPTER NINETEEN

The mood in the Rockton locker room was, according to Coach Baron, "tight as Maggie's garters" as the boys pulled on their uniforms for what they knew could be the last time in the 1956 season. If they lost this game against Richardson there would be no playoffs. There was some needling chatter and low-key grab-ass, but the time to rub Ben-Gay in someone's jock, spray his locker with shaving cream, or ridicule the size, shape, or sloppy circumcision of his member had passed. Everyone in the room was a veteran now.

The constant line at the urinals indicated just how important this game was to the Rocks. In the heart of every player resided the belief that a just God—the God reflexively called upon in locker room prayers—would not allow them to be defeated in a game so important. In the visitors locker room, only a thin wall away, similar reasoning yielded the same conclusion.

Jeff forced himself to concentrate on the mundane routine of dressing—arranging and lacing his pads, rubbing Atomic Balm on his left shoulder and sore thigh, placing a folded hand towel under his shoulder pads, rolling his socks to the proper height—rituals that had focused and calmed him throughout his career. During his preparation, he reminded himself that he might not play at all. He might spend the whole game on the sideline, never touch the ball.

Jeff maintained an uneasy mastery over his stomach and was relieved when the coach came in to make his "Biggest Game Of The Year" speech. Halfway through, just when Pearl Harbor was bombed and America was lying on its back, a Japanese sword at its throat, Jeff found himself getting sucked into the whirlpool of emotion that swirled around him.

When he charged onto the field shouting, "ROCKTON NUMBER ONE!" with his teammates, the band greeted the team with the school fight song—a reworked version of "Cheer, Cheer for Old Notre Dame" that half the schools in the conference used. The cheers and shouts that rained down when he and Chuck, co-captains, went out for the coin toss overwhelmed Jeff. Rockton lost the toss. Richardson chose to kick off, placing their faith in the stout defense that had carried the Indian team all year.

Jeff hustled over to the sideline and grabbed a ladle from the water pail. He hoped a long drink might settle his stomach. When he lowered the ladle, he was staring into the squinting brown eyes of Coach Baron.

"You ready to play some football?" the coach shouted at him.

"Yes, sir," Jeff barked.

"Then go out there and run that kickoff back for a touchdown."

Jeff strapped on his helmet and ran to the hard-packed infield dirt Rockton would defend the first quarter. As quickly as his cleats hit the playing field, Jeff lost all awareness of the crowd, the cheerleaders, the coach. Mike Smith slapped him on the back as they trotted down to the twenty yard line. Mike waited on the right side of the field as Jeff moved fifteen yards to his left.

The nervous Richardson kicker shanked his kick. The ball sailed to a height of about fifteen feet before drifting sideways. It bounced on the thirty yard line, then skipped, rolled, and wobbled between the two return men. When Mike moved forward into a blocking position, panic shot through Jeff's body as he chased after the skittering football.

Jeff picked up the ball, pulled it under his good arm, and started up-field into a wave of crimson Richardson jerseys. Mike neatly picked off the first man down-field, and a head fake sent the next defender hurtling past as Jeff angled toward the middle of the field. Sighting a crease to his left, he shifted the ball under his left arm and pivoted. A Richardson player got a handful of jersey, but couldn't hold on. As he neared mid-field, Jeff heart leaped as he saw Chuck Brady throw a devastating block on a gangly Indian defender opening a corridor to the goal line. A red jersey closed quickly from the left, and Jeff used his stutter-step to confuse the defender. The Indian slid in front of him and reached back desperately for a piece of the fleeing ball carrier.

Jeff got a brief, clear look at the goal line and glory before he was blasted from behind by the Richardson kicker. The kicker stuck his helmet in the middle of Jeff's back and lifted him a foot off the ground. Jeff instinctively twisted his body to spare his left shoulder impact with the ground. The boy's body was so distinctly contorted when he hit the turf that everyone in the stadium knew the ball carrier would not walk away unassisted from the collision.

The pain flowed slowly as hot tar from his upper back, through his trunk, to his feet. Lying on his back, unable to move, Jeff focused on controlling his breathing and beat back the panic that threatened to drag him into infantile helplessness. The stadium was silent until the siren of the Rescue Squad ambulance crossed the field toward him.

As Jeff lay amid a forest of legs, he fought back the urge to scream. He desperately wanted to remove his helmet but could not raise his arms. Were they pinned under his body? A new wave of panic spread through his chest. Someone kneeled beside him and eased his helmet off. Hushed, indecisive voices swirled above him. "You're gonna be alright," someone said, in a tone so dismal it terrified him. The three rescue squad men huddled, argued, but could not agree on whether or how to move him. For a long, long time, no one did anything.

Perhaps it was the light rain that prodded the white-shirted attendants into action. Jeff breathed a prayer of thanks when he was finally lifted clumsily onto the stretcher and loaded into the ambulance.

Jeff lay on his back in his jock strap atop a cold metal table and stared into a blinding yellow light. The staff at the emergency room—a doctor, two nurses—had carefully cut and stripped Jeff's uniform off him, but every movement sent flashes of pain through the boy's body. "You should be glad you're feeling that pain," the doctor said.

Jeff was soaked in sweat and shivered as a cold breeze blew across his nearly-naked body. He wondered if the whole experience—the bumbling ambulance crew, the gothic emergency room, the three masked strangers who spoke occasionally in medical code but mostly about an *I Love Lucy* episode—might just be a horrible dream.

The three took turns pressing and pricking his legs and toes. Jeff had no trouble making a fist when told to do so, and felt like using it when instructed to raise his right leg off the table. He raised the leg several inches, before the searing pain ended the experiment. The feat seemed to cheer his three antagonists, and that relieved him. The emergency room doors sprang apart and another patient was wheeled in—car wreck, heavy bleeding. A nurse mercifully threw a sheet over Jeff stomach and legs as he was wheeled out of the emergency room.

Rose Stuart was waiting in the hallway and fell upon Jeff with a warm and gentle embrace and reassuring words. She spoke calmly to the nurse, who informed her that Jeff had sustained an injury to his back, but there was no indication of paralysis. He would be given a shot for the pain and to help him sleep. They would take x-rays, and a doctor would examine him the next morning. Then she rushed back into the emergency room.

Only then did Rose break down in tears of thanksgiving. She hugged her child and spoke to him of the blessing that God had bestowed upon them both. Jeff's eyes filled with tears as well. He felt an injection in his right arm, and within seconds he surrendered gratefully to pain-free sleep.

"You my football player?" the doctor said, entering the examination room. He was tall, well-built with dark hair and an impatient manner. The name tag on his white coat read: Dr. Casey. He had a large envelope under his arm.

Jeff nodded. He was wearing a hospital gown and his left arm was in a sling. He was leaning against a wall beside a colored chart of the human skeleton.

"Have a seat," Dr. Casey said.

"Standing is easier," Jeff said. Climbing out of bed had been a five minute ordeal, and sitting in a chair were nearly as bad.

"We'll give you some muscle relaxants and pain medication for your back. The pain should ease in a few days. You'll want to sleep on a thin mattress on the floor for awhile." He pulled two x-rays from the folder and attached them to the lighted panel on the wall. "The good new is the x-rays on your back were negative,"

"That's good?"

"Negative means no fractures. You're back pain is muscular. If it were skeletal, we'd likely be talking about paralysis now. What happened? Did you get gang-tackled and twisted around?"

"I got blasted from behind, and I rolled my body so I wouldn't land on my bad shoulder." Jeff winced at the memory.

"I'm not going to ask you why you were playing football with a separated shoulder and a torn rotator cuff," The doctor said as he tapped the x-ray with his finger. "If you were forty or fifty years old, say, and you got banged up like this in a car wreck, I'd likely go right in and operate. But you're young, and I'd like to give you a chance to avoid surgery." He stuck the x-rays back in the folder, obviously in a hurry to leave. "Keep your arm in the sling, keep an ice pack on it, and take the pills. If it's still keeping you awake in two weeks, come see me. Otherwise, make an appointment for a month from now."

The doctor had his hand on the doorknob when Jeff asked the question he didn't want to know the answer to. "Can I ever play football again?"

The doctor looked at Jeff as though he were the most hopelessly stupid piece of human flesh that ever drew breath. "Son, let's hope we can get you to the point where you can raise your arm over your head before you try to destroy it."

"Jeff," Rose said, staring straight down the road, "I think we need to talk about your future."

"Can it wait," Jeff said stonily. He cracked the window and stared out at the rolling farmland. "I don't have a future."

"That's why we need to talk about it," Rose said. Her eyes did not waver from the centerline.

Rose had raised the subject repeatedly in the past year, and in each instance the discussion had been short and bitter. Jeff knew his mother wanted him to commute eight miles to Oak City Business College, study quietly in his room at night, graduate in two years and take over the lumberyard. Then marriage, children, grave. How complicated was that?

Up until twelve hours back, Jeff's plan, so much as he had one, was to play football at Moore-Clayton College. He didn't really want to spend another four years in classrooms, but if that were part of the package, he would study whatever football players studied. He would live in a dormitory. Drink beer, chase cheerleaders, raise as much hell as possible.

As Jeff watched the telephone poles flash past, he hoped his mother would not speak. He knew, if pressed, he would attack everything she held dear.

As Jeff stared out the window, Rose took measure of her will and found it lacking. The issue had to be resolved, but not then. Jeff would need time to recover. Time to re-think his future. Time. If only he knew how fast his life would flash past—how important *this* decision was. How little time there was.

CHAPTER TWENTY

Rain, rain, rain. The first half of November, normally a season of beauty and moderation in Western North Carolina, was being washed away by a Canadian cold front and sheets of rain falling from clouds as gray and dirty as cotton mill sweepings. Beautiful autumn foliage that usually clung to the hardwood trees for another month rode the crest of waves that channeled them from gully to creek to river. No blighted soul could design weather more suited for burying a friend or mourning a lost dream.

When Jeff arose from his mattress on the floor Monday morning, his back was sore enough that he had no qualms about telling his mother school was an impossibility. He spent that day, as he had the past two, holed up in his room taking pain pills, sleeping, and silently raging against Coach Baron for destroying his life. On Tuesday, he spent the day cursing himself for not telling the coach to go to hell when Baron asked him to practice, or when he had sent him in on the first play of the game. Jeff used Wednesday trying to figure out why he dreaded facing his classmates.

He felt no guilt over the Richardson defeat; he knew no single player could make the difference in a twenty-one point loss. He knew some students would likely interpret his attempt to play while injured as heroism, and he especially dreaded talking to them. When he returned to school on Thursday, he slept through three of his classes and cut the other two.

When the sun dropped behind the hills to the west, Madam La'Moor released the two workmen into the cold November night. The pair had spent two days foreclosing drafts that had enjoyed free access through walls and around windows and doors. As the seer wearily sat down to her meal of pork chops, beans and rice, she gratefully noted the absence of the snaky wind that had blown out a table candle the night before.

Finding men capable of doing the variety of carpentry, plumbing, and electrical work had not been easy. White carpenters would not work for her, and the leaders of the Colored Baptist Church, where she asked for referrals, were as leery of the new prophetess as she was of them. Consequently, she had to find men who were not only skilled, but independent enough to ignore the church's disapproval. The ones she had found could be termed, in the words of her late, lamented husband, "slow as smoke off shit."

Worse still, her plumber walked with a pronounced limp. While gigging a mark for all his money at one time, or "punk robbing" from children was recognized as bad business, the oldest and sternest of carnival strictures demanded the merciful treatment of gimps and loonies. While Madam La'Moor scoffed openly at many of the superstitions that governed carny life, she adhered to this one. She made sure that she paid her plumber for every minute of his work time.

The seer also had problems buying supplies. While she was relieved that Stuart Lumber welcomed everyone's business, her workmen reported the hardware store in Rockton would not sell to Coloreds. So, every tool or nail purchased required a trip to Oak City. Having spent thirty-five years in a traveling carnival, Madam La'Moor would never have described her life as "sheltered," but nothing had prepared her for the lot of the rural Southern Negro. Bigotry more powerful than the love of money? *That* was unnatural!

Jasmine Kingsley was born in Spanishtown, Jamaica, but moved with her family to New York City when she was six years old. She had been a dreamy girl whose imagination and island lilt separated her from her classmates. When sixteen years-old, she ran off with a carnival "ride monkey." Henry Watkin's soft southern accent fascinated her; he would later confess an identical attraction. They were "married" in the carnival tradition by sitting together through one revolution of the Ferris wheel.

Jasmine was assigned to the cook shack of the rag-bag carny where Henry set-up and broke-down rides. They lived the normal carny life of constant travel, alcohol, drugs and gambling. Eventually, Henry rose through the ranks to head electrician or "juicer," a status rarely conferred upon a Colored man. No matter how drunk, drugged or hung-over, he kept the lights on and the rides rolling.

When Lady Esmerelda was arrested for boosting the wallet that resided in the hip pocket of a police chief's son, an obvious "plant," Jasmine was pulled from the filthy scullery and designated Madam La'Moor—Palm Reader. Traveling through the northeast from spring to fall, Madam learned the secrets of the "mitt camp." There were three rules: First, the marks who came into her tent shared common problems that could be divined by reading cues of appearance, and behavior; Second, the marks dearly *wanted* to believe that she had the answers to those problems; Third, you must always extend hope.

Blessed with a native theatricality and innately crafty, Madam La'Moor quickly learned to spot the "set-ups," as Lady Esmerelda obviously could not, and eventually mastered the pinnacle of carny artistry: She learned to separate a mark from every dollar possible without getting the law involved.

Henry and the Madam spent the succeeding years moving up the circuit from the rag-bags to the majors. They transacted all business in cash, swapped driver's licenses and identities with each new season and kept all forms of government ignorant of their existence. Somewhere between the end of the Second World War and the beginning of the Korean Conflict, Madam lost her taste for the pace and amorality of carny life. She would gladly have passed into an anonymous retirement in southern Florida, but Henry couldn't break the hold of alcohol, amphetamines and casual vice.

On July Fourth, 1956, a heart attack toppled the Juicer from a light tower. Madam La'Moor had him cremated and let him ride in the front seat of their Buick back to his old home place in North Carolina. Madam had merely intended, according to Henry's wishes, to scatter his ashes on the fields he walked as a child. Then she would motor south.

It was land that Henry had talked of lovingly, but his wife had never seen. Madam felt an immediate affinity for the lush, rolling, musky-smelling land which, left untended, sprouted trees and wildlife. Her in-laws had died or moved off, and Madam discovered twenty-six acres and a ramshackle house could be had for the claim of kinship and payment of back-taxes.

Through her carny friends, Madam received a mailed envelope containing certificates of birth, marriage, death and an attested will; she could just as easily have procured documents declaring her the Queen of England. This paperwork, when presented at the county seat with less cash than she normally took in on a payday weekend outside any Army post, conferred upon Jasmine Watkins the rights of a landed citizen in the unincorporated community of Bookertown. For the first time in her life, she owned something that could not be moved three hundred miles over-night.

As Madam washed her dishes that rainy November night, she spent a moment thinking of her friends, many of whom would be wintering in Florida. Sunshine, cronies united in contempt for the world of suckers, a paid-off constabulary—Utopia for freaks and con artists. In a life stunningly devoid of regret, Madam La'Moor wondered if she had made the right decision.

She had resolved to stick it out for a year before deciding whether to retire to Florida's eternal summer, pick up with another carny or remain in "Boogertown." As she watched the rain turn to sleet in what she knew was only a prelude to a harsh winter, Madam La'Moor had a feeling her future would be populated by palm trees, white beaches and gulf currents.

Madam's reverie was broken by the sound of an approaching car. By the time the seer had dried her hands and walked to the front window, Rose Stuart, two days early for her appointment, was already out of her car and halfway up the new set of steps. At her feet was Caliban, the cat that had been missing for three days. The prophetess was even more surprised to discover that she welcomed the company.

"Things are even *worse* than ever," Rose declared after describing Jeff's injury and the bitter aftermath. Caliban sat next to her on the couch nodding in and out of sleep. "I have to threaten him to even get him to go to school. I can't say anything without him getting mad and stalking off to his room. He's so stubborn! That's the Stuart in him."

"You were not at the football game where he was injured?" Madam asked, as she sipped her tea.

"Oh, no," Rose said, flushing. "I never go"

"Do you think this bothers Jeff."

"No," Rose snapped. "He's never said anything about it." Rose gulped her tea and stroked Caliban fiercely. "That's not the problem. The problem is his attitude and the people he goes out with. He spends his time with a grown man who plays that awful music and lives with a...*tootsie* who he's not even married to, as near as anyone can tell. I just found out about this from my office girl, although *everyone else* in town has known for months! I've taken his car keys. I want to give them back, but he won't promise to act right. What else can I do?"

"Your son is wounded and threatened," Madam counseled, as she poured Rose a second and final cup of tea. She had learned that more than two cupfuls of her "Special-Blend" were counter-productive. Rose would want to settle in. "If you try to tell him who he may or may not see, he will either sneak around or defy you openly. Are you are willing to send him from your house over these friends?

"No," Rose said meekly.

"Then you must draw a line you think is reasonable, and that you can enforce. Beyond that, we must look at ways to help *you* get through this period. You must devise a plan." Madam La'Moor hesitated before committing to a decision that she knew she would likely regret. "Perhaps, I can prescribe an herb. It is not inexpensive, but it might ease your mind and help you sleep in the worst of times."

CHAPTER TWENTY-ONE

Cody Hunter stopped in his tracks and turned to Jeff who was following him through the forest. "Would you explain to me," Cody asked, "why Coach Jerk-off put you in the game in the first place? You weren't fit to play fuckin' hopscotch, much less football."

The forest was silent except for Cody's exclamation, and, although stated quietly, Jeff seemed to hear the words echo around the rolling hills.

"It was *my* decision," Jeff responded.

Cody crossed his arms and cocked his head to one side skeptically. "Bullshit!" he said. "Did *you* chase down that squatty little bastard and tell him you were all healed up and ready to play some football?" Cody waited for an answer, but Jeff couldn't meet his eyes. "Or," Cody continued, "did *he* come lookin' for you talkin' about how ol' Boola Boola High couldn't possibly win the Big Game without you?"

Cody turned and struck off through the woods without waiting for an answer. "Damn, Jeff," Cody called over his shoulder, "you couldn't see through that? By the time I was fifteen years old, I knew all coaches were going to Hell." Three strides. "Man, you gotta learn to avoid all that shit where everyone has to dress alike and do the same shit at the same time."

Jeff had passed up Rose's kind offer to drive him to church that Sunday morning. He'd chosen instead to take advantage of a break in the monsoon season to hitchhike out to Cody's place. After a week of wallowing in the haunted past, he needed a shot of Cody Hunter.

After rousing Cody from a deep sleep, Jeff had stoked the wood stove—attempting to raise the temperature in the drafty house above that of a meat locker—while Cody pulled on his clothes. Cody explained that it was Naomi's mother's birthday, and she had driven the Ford off to Oak City for Mass. "Some kind of Catholic gig," Cody said, shrugging his shoulders.

Cody drank copiously from the kitchen faucet, then grabbed two boiled eggs from the refrigerator and a handful of white bread off the kitchen table. The two struck off hiking behind Cody's house. They were going to see, in Cody's words, "the finest ol' sonuvabitch you ever met in your life." They slogged across a muddy creek bottom while Cody used a finely-honed machete to cut a narrow path through the thicket of multiflora rose, laurel, alder, and scrub pine. When the bottom gave way to hillside, the briars and bushes surrendered to a hardwood forest with a broadleaf canopy that had long ago starved out underbrush.

The forest floor showed little effect from the rain that had fallen constantly the previous two weeks. Only the puddled bottom of a red clay wash testified to the deluge that had strangled the flatlands. The pair marched briskly up the steep hill, along the ridge, and down the other side. They had walked silently for better than a mile before Cody stopped in his tracks and raised his right hand abruptly. He placed his hands together, whistled through them, and produced a credible bobwhite call.

"Doooooley." Cody called, in a slightly raised voice. "It's Cody."

Fifty yards ahead of the boys, a heavy, bearded figure stepped from behind a giant red oak tree. The twelve gauge shotgun that rested in his left hand was pointed, mercifully, toward the ground.

"Cudden be no buddy else," the round man answered, in a voice that could have belonged to a well-trained bear. "The law ain't near so damn clumsy, and they's paid off through the election." Then he smiled.

Dooley led the pair into a small, sunken clearing that Jeff found indistinguishable from the surrounding hillside except for the wafts of smoke that drifted up from a well-concealed forty gallon copper cylinder. After pausing long enough to poke up the fire and toss on a couple oak logs, Dooley led the boys to what appeared to Jeff to be a shallow brush pile on a forty-five degree slant of the hillside. Dooley tossed brush aside until he reached a wooden plank door.

The boys followed the moonshiner into the large subterranean room and waited in the chilly dark while he lit a lantern. A small stove squatted in the center of the room, its pipe rising straight up through the high dirt ceiling. Dooley hung the shotgun on a rack above an army cot. As Cody and Jeff sat on wooden crates, the moonshiner produced three tin cups and a demijohn from under the cot. Dooley handed each guest a cup, then filled it from the demijohn. He extended a tin can toward Jeff. "Have you one a these, son." Jeff and Cody each plucked out a stick of peppermint candy.

Cody took a short drink of the clear whiskey and a long pull off the candy. "Fine as frog hair," Cody admired.

When Jeff swallowed his first sip of non-tax-paid liquor, it was a revelation to his mind and soul. He had expected a potion as ornery as the men who distilled it; he found, instead, a beverage whose taste would hardly alarm the members of the Ladies Aid Society. After one sip of illicit spirits, Jeff understood why grown men would risk their freedom to make, sell, or buy it.

Satisfied that his duty as a host was accomplished, Dooley smiled and filled his cup. After a sip, Dooley reached under his cot and pulled out a lumpy army duffel bag. He extracted a battered six string guitar and handed it to Cody. "Now play me that there 'Careless Love' one time, like you mean it."

"Your grandpap ever tell you about his whiskey days?" Dooley asked, as he strummed the guitar. Cody was outside relieving himself.

The question surprised Jeff. He shook his head.

"Woulda been around nineteen hunerd and...nine or ten. He was my first partner. Onliest one I ever trusted. He never got so drunk he let the fire go out, or went into town for sugar and stayed a week, like many another. He made damn sure bidness was took care of before he'd have his fun. Tough little knot. Take two drinks and go bear huntin' with a switch.

"If he hadn't got serious about your grandmaw, we coulda made us some money. Took his money and went back to sawmillin'." Dooley pulled a pouch of chewing tobacco from his overalls and offered it to the boy. Jeff shook his head. Dooley stuffed a handful in his mouth and talked around it. "I never blamed him for it none. If a man can do ary thing else, he ought to. Whiskey is an unforgiving life."

Jeff and Cody sat with their backs against a fallen beech tree and gazed into a stream as clear and pure as that which flowed through Eden. The late afternoon light reflected joyfully off the smooth rocks and swirling waters and convinced Jeff that he had never felt as contented as he did at that moment.

Dooley had fed them pinto beans, sausage, and cornbread while forcing them to drink water, claiming that only a drunkard or a "furiner" would drink alcohol with his meal. If there had been a Bible handy, Jeff would have sworn upon it that he had never eaten a better meal.

The sun that had lazed across the afternoon sky now appeared to drop like a ball bearing off a tabletop. As the evening chill descended on the forest, Jeff pulled his wadded coat from behind his head and gathered it around himself like a blanket. Although he felt he could happily pass his life watching the water dance and listening to its lilt, a burning concern kept pressing into his consciousness.

"Cody," Jeff said earnestly, "what do you want to do?"

"Uh...have another drink?"

"No, no, man," Jeff laughed. "Well, yeah, but after that. With your life."

"I'm going to Memphis," Cody said quickly. "And I'm gonna be so damn hot that I get to make all the rules. Like Elvis. Then I'm gonna buy Mama a big house on the hill...right next to the damn mayor. And when the sun rises, I'm gonna piss off the front porch and let it flood down the middle of Main Street and watch all those hicks try to swim upstream."

Cody took a sip from the Mason jar and passed it to Jeff. "I want to travel," Jeff said. "Get as far from Rockton as I can get. See the Pacific Ocean, Rocky Mountains, Grand Canyon..."

"What's stoppin' you?"

Jeff shook his head. Everything was stopping him. And nothing.

"Tell you what," Cody said, "if I ain't got a workin' band come summer, me and you'll go to Oregon. I know where we can get us jobs drivin' combines in the wheat harvest. I did it when I got outa the Army. Made good money. And, my god, what mountains! Most beautiful country in the world. I shoulda stayed out there."

"Why'd you leave?"

"Somethin' to do with liquor and a girl that oughta been wearin' a weddin' ring but wasn't."

Jeff gazed up into the darkening sky. His eye attached itself to the slow descent of a red maple leaf as it rocked back and forth, its stem pointing toward the sky. It landed in the stream and sailed off to its destiny. "What's the best thing—" Jeff blurted out, "No. The most *pleasurable* thing you've ever done? Make love?"

"Nah," Cody drawled, "that wears off. It's never as good as you think it's gonna be...and you never get enough. You just stay hungry." Cody paused. "Most pleasurable...plowin' barefoot behind a mule on a warm spring morning."

"What?" Jeff's head jerked to the left so quickly he would have fallen down if he hadn't been lying on his back. He had expected, or hoped, to hear of some obscure and profane sensual release Cody had discovered in a Tijuana brothel or in an ancient Oriental marriage manual.

"It's the truth," Cody said. He too seemed surprised. "Granted: plowin' gets old pretty quick. But that first hour...when the sun's comin' up, and the dirt is cool between your toes..."

Jeff had another question and was just drunk enough to ask it. "What is it that you fear?"

Cody's face twisted into a grim smile. "Not a helluva lot," he began, speaking to the clouds, "and nothin' I'm likely to run into anytime soon. But I can't think of anything much worse'n endin' up fifty-years-old on a barstool talkin' to some stranger about the land I shoulda bought...the woman I shoulda married, you know, the chances I shoulda took, but didn't."

Within minutes the fading sunlight and brook's song seduced them both. That was how Dooley found them: stretched out beside the stream like a pair of wandering monks, exhausted from their unceasing quest for truth, and entrusting their fate to the elements and a benevolent Deity. Either that, or a couple of drunks who got down and couldn't get up.

Dooley carried them into his shelter and placed them atop pallets made from feed sacks stuffed with corn huskings. He tossed a blanket over each of them before walking home under the light of a crescent moon to a warm bed and loving family.

Jeff was more than a mite bewildered when he woke up on the floor of Dooley's cave. He was cold, sore, thirsty, and inside his skull a Mississippi chain gang was chanting about "Miss Liza" and laying that tracka-lacka. When he attempted to stand, his brain spun so wildly he sat down to keep from falling. At that point, he discovered how badly his back and shoulder ached. Jeff's first inclination was to lie down and moan until he either died or felt better, but his aching bladder demanded release.

When he stepped into the grim, crowbar-gray light of pre-dawn, he found the air sharp and unforgiving. Although there was no wind, everything appeared "jumpy," as though his brain trailed his eyes by several seconds. As quickly as he peed, drank greedily from the stream, and washed his face, he began the long trudge through the woods toward the highway.

He knew he would be late for school, if he got there at all, but that was unimportant. In addition to hauling around enough physical pain to populate a trauma ward, Jeff carried a heavier burden. He knew that during the time he had been lying drunk in the bootlegger's cave, his mother had been sitting up, waiting, and worrying about him.

When he burst through the front door, Jeff expected to see his forlorn mother sitting in her housecoat, eyes ringed with the tragic shadows that are the legacy of Eve. He had formed an apology on the long walk to the highway, but he knew damn well he deserved whatever punishment his good Christian mother might choose to mete out. His only salvation might be her relief in seeing him whole and well, albeit raggedy-assed.

But Rose was not sitting in her armchair. That disconcerted Jeff, but when he heard his mother singing in the kitchen, he was sore amazed. He tip-toed through the front room and stood in the hall listening to her shaky soprano warbling "Young At Heart" along with Frank Sinatra on the radio.

When he peeked into the kitchen, he found Rose dressed for work and standing at the stove. Jeff couldn't think of a good way to announce his presence, but he couldn't help but believe that she would be eager to see him.

Rose slid a fried egg from the skillet onto a plate that already held two slices of bacon and a piece of toast. As she turned toward the table, Rose gasped when confronted with the bedraggled figure in the kitchen doorway. He was grimy as a ditch digger, his hair looked capable of fighting off a hayrake, and he needed a shave worse than Richard Nixon. She reined in her surprise and sat down at the table.

"I'm sorry, Mama," Jeff said quickly. "I spent the night in the woods. Camping. I didn't mean to-I mean I didn't plan it—"

"You had better get cleaned up and ready for school. You'll have to walk, I don't have time to take you," Rose said, matter-of-factly. "Your grandfather is going to need help today, so come straight to the yard. They're moving everything out of number four shed until they get the roof fixed."

"I would have called you if I could..." Jeff apologized.

"Of course I was worried," Rose said, refusing to look at the abject figure in her kitchen. "I had no idea where you were, or what had happened to you." She buttered her toast. "If this ever happens again you will have a bed to sleep in, but you will do your own cleaning and laundry. If you want to live like a lodger, you'll have to start paying rent." She paused with knife and fork in hand and stared into eyes that resembled two mashed cherries in a bowl full of buttermilk. "Do you understand?"

"Yes ma'am." Jeff turned and walked to the bathroom, his head swimming with a mixture of relief, puzzlement, hangover and dread. He had been spared wails of anguish and accusations of cruelty, but his mother's reaction was as inexplicable as it was welcome. Jeff was struck with the thought that she might be taking those tranquilizers again.

As Jeff pulled pill bottles from the medicine cabinet, he recalled Rose's experiment with Miltown. It wasn't as though she had changed drastically while on the pills—she was still a "good mother." But she was *somebody else's* good mother. Since his mother worried constantly about being late, Jeff had never had to. Several mornings during her "drug" period, she had called only once to awaken Jeff for school before leaving for work, and the boy ended up straggling out of bed around noon. Sometimes dishes would languish in the sink for the better part of a day before being washed, or a favorite shirt that Jeff had intended to wear on a Saturday night would hang sad and unstarched in his closet. Life had been, not tough, but unpredictable.

Especially bad were the times when his mother had forgotten she had taken her pill and had double-dosed herself. That was undoubtedly what had happened the day that Jeff had opened his lunch box at school and found only one large turnip and a saltshaker.

And his mother had not seemed particularly "tranquil" during that period. Rose would often sit in front of the television and leaf through a magazine distractedly, inert but unrelaxed. Granjack had said that Rose resembled an old fire horse that had grown deaf and now imagined fire bells ringing continually; there were fires raging, wagons to be hauled, but she didn't know where.

Jeff swallowed two of the blessed pain pills and a muscle relaxer and chased them with a cupped handful of tap water. Now that the anxiety of confronting his mother had faded, he was left only with the prospect of facing a full school day—including an algebra test at ten o'clock—and a long evening of work at the lumberyard. Why his legs should ache was a mystery to him, but they always did when he drank too much. His lower back felt as though he'd taken a blow from a nine-pound hammer on the tail bone, and his shoulder burned with the fire that spread from his neck to his elbow. His stomach begged for food but threatened to reject anything offered. And, with every heartbeat, Jeff could feel the skin of his forehead distend from the impact of fierce, rushing blood.

Taken in total, not the best way to start a Monday.

As Rose scrubbed the egg yolk from her plate, she reviewed the results of her new approach to parenting. Refusing to worry about Jeff's day-long absence, she'd made herself a large cup of tea from Madam La'Moor's blend and gone to bed right after "The Ed Sullivan Show." She'd fallen asleep quickly, using the noise of an electric fan blowing into her closet so she would not lie awake listening for Jeff's arrival. She'd slept surprisingly well.

Dawn had not awakened her, so Rose rushed through her shower, dressing, and breakfast preparation. She assumed that she still had a good fifteen minutes of privacy before waking Jeff when the boy presented himself like a tramp in the rain. As near as she could tell, she had managed to conceal the shock she felt upon seeing her boy filthy, tired, and apologetic. She'd resisted the impulse to comfort him and coldly stated the new House Rules she'd formulated at Madam La'Moor's. Just having a plan, Rose decided, had made all the difference. Still, she couldn't help feeling guilty about not worrying any more than she had about a child who had apparently spent the night in a side ditch.

"Boy out all night?"

Rose jumped at the sound of Granjack's voice. How could that clumsy old man move around so quietly.

"Yes," Rose said.

"You read him the 'Riot Act'?" Granjack asked. He poured himself a cup of coffee.

"I told him if it happened again, he'll do his own cleaning and laundry, and he'll pay rent."

Granjack nodded. The old man took his coffee to the table and opened the newspaper. "Tough times," he said.

Damn right, Rose thought.

CHAPTER TWENTY-TWO

Jeff sat in the chair, staring first at the black telephone, then at the five numbers he'd scrawled on a scrap of paper. After waiting for over an hour for his mother to leave the house, Jeff was wracked by indecision and second thoughts. He snatched up the receiver and dialed before he had a chance to chicken out.

"Hello," a female voice responded.

Jeff stated the line that he had rehearsed. "May I speak to Arlene, please?" Idiot, *that's* Arlene!

"This is Arlene."

"Yeah, I know, uh, this is Jeff...Stuart. How you doin'?"

"I'm fine, Jeff. How are you doing?"

"I'm fine, too. I was just wondering...I heard you broke up with Stan, and if you're not doin' anything better next Saturday, maybe you could double-date with Marty and his girl...and me, of course, and maybe see a movie...or something?"

"Well, gosh, Jeff, I'd really like to, *but*-

Jeff's extended his neck over the telephone table and waited for the ax to fall.

"You see, its kind of a bad time. My mom and dad have sorta talked to me... about *you*. You see, they were at church that time Vicky yelled and threw the ring at you...and they say you've been hanging around with a bad crowd."

"I see," Jeff said. He wanted to say something more, defend himself, but all he could think about was the beautiful auburn hair that framed Arlene's porcelain skin. Hair that bobbed with every step, swung uniformly when she turned her head, and shimmered like spun copper in the sunlight.

"But I still want to be your friend," Arlene continued. "I don't care what anyone says. Is that OK?"

Jeff could not vanquish the memory of Arlene's lithe body cloaked in a red sweater and white skirt. He shook his head to clear it.

"Sure, Arlene. I'll see you at school."

By the time Jeff had hung up the telephone, he had fallen madly in love with a girl who he had never been particularly eager to date. The experience would have been even more painful if he weren't growing accustomed to it. Little more than two months had passed since he and Vicky had broken up and Rose had revoked his driving privileges; in that time he had gone from Big Man on Campus to Untouchable. Every couple weeks, he would ratchet up his courage and ask a girl out. He'd found no takers. After years of cruising in the passing lane of Rockton High social life, Jeff had crashed headlong into two unalterable small town verities. There are no secrets. Nothing is forgotten.

"Now let me get this straight," Jeff said, as he paced the debris-covered floor of Marty's bedroom, "*you're* offering to get *me* a date."

Marty smiled benignly as he lay on his unmade bed, his size-thirteen feet flat on the bedspread, his knees skewed awkwardly toward opposing walls. Marty was the only person Jeff had ever known who could look clumsy while lying down. The previous summer the sight of his shirtless friend in baggy madras Bermuda shorts had so shaken Jeff that he questioned the basic tenets of Darwinism. Millions of years of evolution for *that*?

"Your trouble," Marty counseled, placing both hands behind his head, crossing his ankles, and forming an arthritic "V" with his knees, "is you're spoiled. You've been the star athlete for so long, you've lost touch with reality. You're like the homecoming queen who got caught in the back seat with her drawers wrapped around her shoes. People don't look at you the same now. The men blame you for the lousy football season, and the women think you're some kind of crazed rock'n'roll delinquent trying to corrupt their daughters."

Jeff leaned against Marty's dresser and considered the accusation. "I can't say I give a damn what the men think, and the women ain't that far wrong, but damned if I can see how I'm any different than I was last summer. Or last year."

"You may not feel different, but when you drive Cody Hunter and his round, firm, and fully-packed, boogie-woogie baby down the middle of Main Street in that red hot rod, it scares the bejesus out of Mr. and Mrs. Jones coming home from church. Hunter's the closest thing to Elvis Presley these folks have seen close up, and you appear to be his first disciple. You're sort of like...an apprentice to the Anti-Christ." Marty brightened, pleased with his turn of phrase.

Jeff was well aware of the outrage that followed Elvis's appearance on Ed Sullivan, still—"Are you telling me that the people in this town got nothing better to do than to worry about what kind of music a high school kid listens to? Or who he listens to it with?"

Marty laughed sardonically. "It's a lot bigger than the music," he added, with a note of triumph. "When you were playing football, didn't you ever wonder why those folks had nothing better to do than to gamble their happiness on whether the kids of *this* town could knock down and run over the kids from *that* town?" Marty sat up and swung his legs over the edge of his bed. "*That's* some seriously crazy shit. You're lucky you got out of that racket with your body in one piece."

"I might get back into that racket next year," Jeff said, testily. He was surprised to hear himself admit that the dream endured. He'd worked hard not to think about it.

"Are you shittin' me?" Marty gasped, dismayed. "They wreck your shoulder and your back, and you've had a bum knee since you were a freshman. Christ, Jeff, do they have to cripple you to make you understand. You were a *good* high school running back when everything was working, but college players are gonna be bigger and faster than *anybody* you played against."

"I can play against anybody," Jeff responded, angrily. "I made all-conference last year."

"*Second* team, all-conference," Marty corrected, "and you ran behind the best line in the district. Chuck opened up holes that *I* coulda run through."

"That's big talk from a kid that lasted one day in junior varsity tryouts," Jeff spat back.

"I'm no athlete, and I never will be," Marty admitted. "But you can see things when you stand on the outside that you can't—"

"You've been on the outside all your life," Jeff said, jerking open the door. "Maybe when you get off your ass and *do* something, people will pay some attention to you."

When Jeff closed the door to Marty's bedroom, he assumed he would never open it again. He had been betrayed by his oldest friend, his blood-brother. He had always suspected that Marty envied him, but he'd never imagined his best friend would revel in his downfall.

Marty had little trouble rationalizing his position as the bearer of unwelcome news to a friend. Somebody had to tell him, he concluded, as he lay back down. But he chose not to acknowledge the satisfaction he felt when delivering that news.

CHAPTER TWENTY-THREE

"It struck me," Rose said, concluding a summary of discontent that spanned her life from first consciousness to her latest sip of tea, "right after Thanksgiving dinner. I was watching the parades. Everyone looked so joyous. Christmas is coming...it's the most wonderful time of the year, everyone knows that. I know I shouldn't complain," she said, quietly, "I have so much."

Indeed, you do, thought Madam La'Moor, trying not to project her impatience. The two sat wordlessly for several long minutes. Rose was ready to grab her coat and flee the room when Madam finally spoke.

"It seems, Miss Rose, that when you were young, you felt happiness would come when you left your childhood home. But it didn't. Then happiness required that you be married and settled. After that, financial security was necessary. When your son was young, you felt he was too timid. He has since become too independent. Now, you say your happiness depends on *his* contentment." Madam paused to allow Rose to consider her predicament. "No doubt Jeff's life will prove as complicated as yours or mine or any other. Miss Rose, I see no end of obstacles to your 'happiness'."

Madam La'Moor's verdict took Rose's breath away. The shiver that ran through Rose's body chased Caliban off her lap and into a corner. It had been disheartening to discover, right in the middle of Macy's parade, that she had never been happy; it was devastating to be told that she never would be.

"I just can't believe that," Rose said, shaking her head. She stared at the tea leafs as they jumped around in the bottom of her cup. "If you can't be happy," she whispered, "why would you want to live?"

The prophetess took the teacups into the kitchen, leaving her client to ponder the "$64,000 Question." Rose had visited Madam's house at least once each week since her first consultation, and their sessions had grown increasingly informal. They no longer used the parlor, palm reading or astrology; Rose simply sat on the couch, accepted a cup of tea and started talking. Madam still dressed for Rose's arrival, but often doffed her turban by the second cup of tea. Perhaps, she had allowed the sessions to become too informal. Five dollars just wasn't enough to sit and listen to someone bitch and moan for an hour.

Rose examined "Happiness" as though it were a squirming germ under an unfocused microscope. Song titles, movie scenes and snatches of Hallmark greeting card verses flashed through her mind but none offered even slight solace. Her eyes swept across the ceiling, the door, the spider's web in the corner, unwilling to settle while her mind churned on.

When Madam noisily rattled the dishes in the sink, Rose acknowledged the cue. Snap out of it. Nothing had changed. No one had died, she hadn't lost all her money, and everyone who loved her yesterday, loved her still. She slipped on her shoes, stood and put on her coat.

Rose handed a five-dollar bill to the diviner. "Thank you," Rose said. "You've given me a lot to think about." They walked to the door. "Not that I've ever been short of things to think about," she added, forcing a smile.

"Perhaps there is more to life than capturing the great big 'Happiness'," Madam La'Moor said, ushering her client into the evening. "If you have lived without it thus far, how necessary can it be?"

The cold wind from the west invigorated Rose. She paused at the bottom of the porch steps to admire the setting sun. It appeared to be balanced comfortably atop the trees behind her car. The sun's slanted rays provoked the most startling reds and yellows from the oaks and maples that grew beside Madam's house, and Rose leaned against her car to admire them. The leaves had peaked in color weeks before, but she hadn't noticed. This moment was Rose's autumn.

Squirrels leaped frantically from hickory to oak to poplar, working double-time to haul food to the nest before the last light enforced a curfew without appeal. Within moments the sun had slipped below the tree line and the wind stiffened.

Rose crossed her arms and pulled her coat tightly to her body. She knew that she should drive home immediately, get home before dark. But she didn't move. Why, she wondered, do I spend my life shut up in an office, haunted by work that will never be finished? I get up before daylight, why don't I watch the sun rise? Would it matter if the supper dishes waited while I watched a sunset?

Eventually Rose climbed into her car, entrusting the night to the crescent moon that had risen in the east. At the end of Madam's long driveway, she turned the station wagon toward Oak City. Lighting a Chesterfield, she plotted the course to the Twin Circle Grill. She was going to eat her first double-cheeseburger in nearly twenty years—her first since her husband died. With a vanilla shake. And a side of onion rings. Nothing to lose.

"Gotta order a new blade for number two," Granjack said, as he hobbled out of the falling sleet and into the office. "That bunch of peckerwoods brought in that load of hardwood this morning didn't notice the barb wire in it."

Janet, sensing unpleasantness, deserted the filing cabinet and bee-lined to the bathroom. Rose looked up wearily from her paperwork. "What'd they say when you told them they'd have to pay for it?"

"Oh, they said they'd pay," Granjack said, pulling up a chair next to the oil heater to warm his feet. "Didn't have the money on 'em, of course."

"So they had to take the lumber back and sell it to pay for the saw blade," Rose said wearily. She reached into the file drawer and pulled out a folder.

"Yep," Granjack said. "Swore on their mother's grave they'd bring it back before Christmas."

"I'll plan my holidays around that," Rose said drily. "Red didn't notice the wire before he ran it through?"

"Claims it was buried in there," Granjack said. "Red can't see blood on a white rag anymore. Gettin' old."

"Aren't we all," Rose said? She ran her finger along the line of figures. "Blades have gone up again."

"Gonna be a slim year," Granjack said. He watched the steam rise off his boots. Needed a new pair.

When Rose merely shrugged, Granjack's suspicion was confirmed. He'd grown accustomed to seeing Rose flinch every time a board split or a nail bent. A ruined saw blade would chase her to the adding machine for hours searching for corners to cut. Concerned, and in no hurry to return to the frigid yard, Jack forced himself to ask, "Somethin' botherin' you?"

Rose tossed the file on her desk with an indifference that implied it could just as easily go into the trashcan. She pushed her oak chair away from the desk and leaned back, her fingers laced and resting in her lap. The eyes that rarely strayed from the bottom line, lost their focus and settled somewhere over Jack's head in the corner of the office.

"Jack," she said slowly, "do you ever wonder why we do this?"

"Do what?"

"Come to work at seven-thirty, leave at five-thirty. Half-day on Saturday. Day after day, year after year?"

"It's our work." Jack hoped all the questions would be that easy.

Rose nodded slowly. "But even when we're not here, it's what we talk about and think about. Pretty soon it will be Jeff's whole life too."

"Been a pretty damn good life. We got a place to live, plenty to eat. Somethin' in the bank. Lotta folks be real thankful of that."

"You know where I came from, Jack," Rose said. She lowered her eyes to engage his. "I appreciate your work, and all you've done. Just sometimes I feel like I could do something . . . more."

"What is it you wanna do?" Jack asked, trying not to sound irritated.

"I don't know," Rose said. "Sometimes I remember when I took piano lessons. Before Daddy got so bad, and I had to quit. I played for nearly two years, and my teacher said I had *real* talent—" Rose stopped abruptly. She had gone too far.

"Can't see how you're gonna make a livin' playin' the piany," Jack said, "but if you want one, go out and buy it." Sweet Jesus, this is what happens in a country where people make a hero out of that Liberace fellow. It made his skin crawl every time he walked into Rose's house and saw him on TV.

"I didn't intend to make money at it," Rose said stiffly. "It's just something I could have done. For pleasure. It's too late now."

"Ain't too late. Buy it," Jack said, standing up. "No reason to save every penny you make. If Jeff's worth a damn, he'll make his own way. Inherited money will ruin a man quicker'n liquor."

Rose bristled from the several sore points prodded in Jack's short response. Before she could reply, the office door swung open and freed them from a wistful conversation turned into a train wreck.

Jeff leaned in and the December wind carried his words across the room. "Red wants to know if he can take the rest of the day off."

"I'll talk to that sonuvabitch about a day off," Granjack snorted. As he stomped out the door, Rose motioned Jeff inside.

While Jeff warmed his hands at the heater, Rose reached into her desk drawer. She tossed a set of Plymouth keys to the edge of her desk. "You need to be in by eleven on weekdays, midnight on Friday and Saturday."

Jeff waited for the additional conditions: no alcohol, no music clubs, no "shady" friends. "Is that all?" he asked, finally.

Rose nodded. Jeff picked up the keys. "Deal," he said, and walked out the door.

CHAPTER TWENTY-FOUR

"Christ on a rubber crutch," Cody complained, as Jeff navigated the Plymouth off the premises of Alley's Cat Club, "why does every rock band in the world gotta play the same ten songs? Can't them boys figure outa little different way to put three chords together? Maybe give 'Rock Around The Clock' just one night off? That damn song's the worst thing that ever happened to rock'n'roll!" Cody pulled an open bottle of beer from the inside pocket of his coat, swallowed half of it, and offered it to Jeff.

Jeff shook his head. Cody had been alternating bourbon and beer all night but seemed little the worse for it—just a shade looser of lip and limb. Jeff had nursed three beers for nearly three hours. "If that band was so bad," Jeff said, "how come I damn near had to pull a gun to get you outa there?"

"I didn't say they weren't better than no band at all," Cody protested. "I's hopin' they'd play somethin' we never heard, slip in a new lick. They didn't— but they coulda. Anyways, there was still a lot of liquor needed drinkin' before it was time to take it home and put it to bed."

"Don't you have to work in the morning?"

"Don't have to be in till noon."

"Banker's hours."

"Nah. Sometimes I work all night."

"Doin' what?"

"Fixin' cars. It's a damn body shop."

"In the middle of the night?"

"Yeah, well . . . some folks want 'em first thing in the morning."

For Jeff, the first night of his Christmas vacation had been an education in how charmless a bunch of drunks could be when you were sober. He'd met Cody and Naomi at the club, but Naomi had a job interview at a beauty parlor the next morning, so she'd split early with the Ford. Jeff was left to listen to a bad band having an off-night without the alcohol buffer that might have raised their performance to tolerable. The audience found diversion in a series of scuffles that proved no more entertaining than the band.

"Hell, me and Sam and Bo could play covers all night, but damned if I'll do it," Cody ranted. "You ain't gonna play 'Dixie Fried' better'n Carl Perkins, I don't give a damn how hard you try. If you can't play your own stuff, you might as well pantogoddamnmime the whole thing."

The wailing December wind threatened to push the Plymouth off the narrow blacktop and into the side ditch. Jeff glanced at his watch as Cody fiddled with the radio. He could make the midnight curfew, but with little to spare. As they waited for the car's balky heater to kick in, Jeff broached a subject that had dwelled pleasantly in his mind since the afternoon at Dooley's cave. "Were you serious about taking a trip out West this summer?"

"Hell, yes," Cody said, continuing his slow roll across the AM dial. "By June I'll be ready to tell Rockton to kiss my ass good-bye. Out there, you can get all the work you can bear and make enough money in one season to last you till spring. Work peas and wheat then apples." Cody tossed off the name of a man who would employ them as quickly as they walked in his office door in Pendleton, Oregon. Jeff filed away the information.

"It ain't near tough as loggin'," Cody reassured, "and on Saturday night, those folks really know how to pitch a bitch." For the next ten miles Cody spun off tales of hard work, hard play, hard cash. As he rambled on about the Rocky Mountains, he sounded ready to buy a couple six-packs, fill the Plymouth with gas and roll west that night.

Satisfied with the radio station, Cody leaned back in his seat and knocked down the last of his beer. The talk of travel emboldened him. "There's a club just opened in Richardson called Fat Daddy's," he said. "They're lookin' for bands to play. I got half a mind to check it out. I'm tired of payin' good money to hear shitty music."

"You guys can kick ass on that bunch we heard tonight," Jeff said.

"I'll talk to the boys about it tomorrow," Cody declared. "What have we got to lose?"

Jeff deposited Cody at his doorstep but turned down his generous offer to come inside for a nightcap. On the drive home, he grimly set his mind to figuring out, once and for all, the urge that drove him from his warm, secure home into the hostile world of drunks, bouncers, cops, and sporadic violence. When he reflected upon the damnable price that he'd paid since wandering into the Hitching Post six months back, he couldn't fathom what he'd found so all-fired attractive about the Night Life.

As he lay in bed, he slowly rolled across the radio dial hoping to find a song or two that might ease him into an untroubled sleep. His hand froze when he heard a voice so primitive he couldn't believe a radio station would air it. The signal was faint, the record scratchy. He pressed his ear to the speaker but couldn't tell what the song was about—if it was about anything. Something to do with a train, and a bad woman who had stayed out all night. The Black man sang in a bass so dark and low it sounded as if it were covered with six feet of dirt, then howled in a voice that would break up a Klan rally.

Long after the last wail faded away, that voice prowled through the boy's head. Jeff pulled out his guitar and attempted to pick out the song. He sang the words he remembered and quietly growled through the rest. When sleep finally dragged him under, he knew the first thing he'd do in the morning was mail off a dollar to Ernie's Record Shop in Gallatin, Tennessee.

"Smokestack Lightnin'." Howlin' Wolf.

CHAPTER TWENTY-FIVE

"It's early," Jeff yelled to Naomi, as they sat in near-isolation in Big Daddy's Ballroom. "Nobody shows up early for rock'n'roll." He had to shout to be heard over Cody's band blasting away at their front row table. Jeff nearly dropped his beer as an earsplitting explosion of feedback leaped from the speakers. Kitty, girlfriend of Bo the bass man, had passed out in the chair across from Jeff. She had sized up the potential for disaster and had quickly chased three shots of bourbon with three beers; nothing short of a building fire was going to rouse her.

"Yeah," Naomi agreed, sipping nervously at her gin and tonic, "and a Wednesday night, three days after Christmas. Nobody's got any money left." Of course, the weather was dependably lousy. From mid-December to March, rain and snow turned every unpaved patch in western North Carolina into treacherous, intractable red mud.

"This place hasn't been open a month," Jeff added, pulling a cigarette from Naomi's pack. He needed something to do with his hands. "There's no regulars like you get at Alley's club. Cats who come to hear whoever's playing."

"This is their first gig, for Pete's sake," Naomi said, through a fog of smoke she wished she could disappear into. "You can't expect people to show up. They got no way of knowin' you're worth listenin' to. Damn," she added with a shudder, "that drummer sucks the big red one."

The band staggered to the end of one of Cody's original songs with the drummer finishing in a rush, but still a beat late. Naomi had explained that the regular drummer, Sam, had been locked up the day before—something about a stolen car. Cody, hopped up on the fanciful enthusiasm of amphetamines, hired a new drummer rather than cancel the gig. Cody's pill jag had begun when he found Blackjack, his old hound dog, dead under the porch. And, Naomi confided, she and Cody weren't getting along so good. She wouldn't be at the club at all if this weren't Cody's first gig.

Jeff's head spun in dismay at the catalogue of calamity surrounding him. Naomi's tale sounded like the weekly wrap-up of one of the radio soap operas that Rose and Janet, the secretary, listened to at the office. Even Naomi's outfit, a simple white blouse and navy blue skirt, suggested a night more sober than celebratory. She had come directly from a waitressing job with no time to change. Generally, you could warm your hands at ten paces from the sensuality radiating off her party-rags.

Naomi and Jeff clapped vigorously at the end of the song and were joined by three or four other music lovers in the audience. The other half dozen people scattered about the club continued to talk loudly. Naomi had dragged Jeff out on the dance floor early in the set, but they had retreated to their table after two songs when no one joined them. You could have shot marbles undisturbed on the dance floor since then.

Cody snatched his glass of bourbon off the amplifier and carried it to the microphone. "Thank ye, thank ye, thank ye," he said sarcastically. "You're too kind, and I want you to know we appreciate you ever bit as much. We're gonna break your hearts now by takin' us a short breather. I'd like to remind you this is not our regular drummer. He couldn't make it tonight, so we hired on this guy...don't ask me why...seemed like the thing to do at the time."

The drummer flashed a raised middle finger at Cody's back, and then walked off the bandstand and out the back door.

"PLAY DAVY CROCKETT!" a drunk yelled from the back of the club. He assumed no one had heard him the first three times he'd shouted.

"Yeah, yeah," Cody said mockingly. "You're a couple years late on that one, but you can bet we'll get around to it next set. We wanna send all you pinheads outa here whistlin' your favorite tune." Cody knocked down the bourbon and shook the glass at the surly waitress who was leaning against the bar. "Sweetheart," he shouted, "I need a refill."

The waitress conferred briefly with the bartender then drew a pointed finger across her throat. Cut off.

Cody nodded and smiled. "One of the reasons we enjoy playin' Big Daddy's so much," Cody continued, "is the friendly service. So I'd like to remind you to tip the waitress tonight. She's doin' the best job she can on that wooden leg, and the barkeep told me she's savin' up for a new set of teeth."

"ASSHOLE!" the waitress yelled from the back of the club.

"No need to thank me, Gummy, we all want to help the handicapped." Cody replied graciously.

"DAVY CROCKETT!" the drunk insisted.

Cody shook his head. "Gonna take that break now. You might as well stick around—ain't no roller-derby or midget wrestling on TV tonight."

Cody swaggered off the stage and jerked a chair from another table. He slammed it down next to Jeff, across from Naomi. Bo walked back to the bar gesturing apology, still hoping to get paid, Jeff figured

"Congratulations," Naomi said. "In just one set, you managed to piss off everyone in the house. What's your encore?"

"Hang around, baby," Cody said sharply. "I ain't hardly warmed up. Where's that fuckin' waitress?"

"Forget about her," Naomi said. "She wouldn't bring you air in a jug."

"It might be a good idea to ease back a notch," Jeff advised. "This ain't a big crowd, but they out-number us."

"Fuck 'em," Cody said, so loudly that Jeff winced. "For ten bucks and drinks, I don't have to put up with this shit. I shouldn't be playin' this dump anyway."

Naomi shook her head grimly. "Don't worry about comin' back. Maybe if you'd gotten some sleep insteada poppin' them pills—"

A homicidal glare cut her off mid-sentence. As the table settled into a malicious silence, Jeff plotted his escape. Halfway through the next set, he would plead curfew and slip out.

Cody grabbed Naomi's purse off the table and pulled the flask from it. He swallowed half the gin in one gulp. "I shoulda canceled this gig. When Sam got nailed, I shoulda knowed that was a sign."

"Bo and me tried to tell you," Naomi said, casually sipping her drink. "Cancel or play without a drummer."

"Everbody knows what I shoulda done now," Cody snapped. "What I shoulda done was leave your ass in that cotton mill. I don't fish you out there you'd be sittin' in a house trailer somewhere with a coupla snot-noses watchin' 'Queen For A Day'."

"Oh, you've been a blessin' to me," Naomi said flatly.

Cody's eyes narrowed and his fist clenched on top of the table. "We can have your fat ass on the bus to that houseful of dagos in Baltimore—"

Naomi flung her drink across the table into Cody's face. He shook his head in disbelief then lurched across the table, his right hand raised to slap her. Jeff caught Cody's arm in mid-swing as Naomi slid back from the table. Cody slammed his left fist into Jeff's chest. The boy tumbled backwards in his chair. As Jeff scrambled to his hands and knees, Cody turned the table over, dumping the sleeping Kitty onto the sticky cement floor. He took a step forward, fists clenched, enraged. One more step, Jeff thought, and I'll tackle him, knock him off his feet—

As Jeff prepared to spring at Cody's gut, Bo grabbed Cody from behind in a bear hug. "Get her outa here!" Bo shouted, straining to maintain his hold on the thrashing Cody.

Jeff fought off the urge to throw a punch at Cody's belly. He grabbed Naomi, her face stark white, and pulled her toward the door. Jeff kept an eye on Cody as he bucked and spun, trying to shake off Bo. The last thing the boy heard as he backed out of the club was the clatter of tables and chairs hitting the floor, and a deep, drunken voice:

"Davy, Davy Crockett,
King of the wild frontier."

CHAPTER TWENTY-SIX

"You alright?" Jeff asked. His anger surged as his shaking hand fumbled the key into the ignition.

"Yeah," Naomi answered, breathless. "You?"

"Yeah, but I shoulda hit that bastard—"

"No," Naomi said quickly, "Those pills make him crazy. He could kill you."

The car engine growled in protest before cranking. "Where do you want to go?" Jeff asked. He rolled his window down. Both their coats were soaking up beer on Big Daddy's concrete floor, but neither had missed them yet.

"I gotta get my things. Then maybe you can drop me off at Shirley's." Naomi lit a cigarette with a trembling hand. "She knows about him."

The ride from the club to Cody's house was the retreat of a routed enemy. Despite the frigid temperature and icy wind, sweat poured off Jeff. His hands shook as though palsied as his body continued to pump adrenaline.

Jeff pulled the Plymouth as close to the steps as the muddy ground would permit and followed Naomi into the house. They tracked red clay across wooden floor and cheap linoleum as they walked through the cold, dark house. Naomi lit an oil lamp in the littered bedroom. She pulled a suitcase from the closet and opened it across the unmade bed. She worked intently, sorting and packing clothing, displaying none of the emotion that he felt boiling inside him.

Jeff paced throughout the house but always returned to gaze out the large window in the living room. He waited for the rumbling engine of the '50 Ford turning off the dirt road, expecting to see the glare of headlights pulling up the driveway. At times, he hoped Cody would show up—then his anger would subside, and he wished only that he would never see the bastard again. If Cody showed up, he was ready to do whatever was necessary to protect Naomi.

He wasn't sure if he heard something or felt something, but he left his post at the window to attend to it. He found Naomi sitting on her bed, dropping silent tears into her folded hands. He stared down into her shiny black hair. "Are you alright?" he said.

She seemed to nod, but her head remained bowed. Jeff knelt in front of her. "Can I do anything?" he whispered.

Naomi shook her head and turned away. "Go home," she said.

"You deserve better than this," he said urgently. He caressed her trembling hands.

Naomi looked up, surprised. She studied his face as though assembling a puzzle. "You don't know . . . " she whispered.

"Come with me," Jeff pleaded. "Leave him—"

Naomi jerked her hands away. She pushed the boy so hard he fell backward. "Goddamn it, what do you expect from us?" she demanded. "This is what we are. You can't change anything."

He wanted to crawl away and disappear into the night. He stood and walked to the door.

"Jeff."

When the boy turned around, Naomi rose from the bed and extended her arms. He stepped into a warmth that would haunt him the rest of his life. She kissed him hungrily and unbuttoned his shirt before he realized what was happening. He fumbled her top three buttons open and gazed down upon the breasts that had floated in his consciousness since he had first seen them straining against a halter-top. He tried briefly, clumsily, to unhook her bra before thrusting his hands down inside the fabric, around the outside of each breast. Gently lifting the pair free, he dove between them, pulling her forward until she was bent at the waist, and he was on his knees. He nuzzled deeply, greedily, into their glorious fleshiness.

She placed her hands under his arms and raised him to his feet. She helped him out of his clothes, then stepped out of her skirt. A long kiss led him off on a meandering path across her throat, between her breasts, over her stomach. With a reverence free of haste, he peeled away her panties. He ran his hands over her trembling rear and moved down the backs of her thick, muscular legs. Once again she pulled him to his feet.

Jeff took a step back to view the glorious body he had dreamed of so often, so guiltily. Naomi sat on the bed and edged backwards toward the headboard. She wanted to pull the covers over herself, but the boy would not wait. She barely managed to get entirely on the bed before his hands and mouth were everywhere, ranging over every mound, probing every crease.

Long, hungry kisses made the boy's head swim, but he could not wait to return to the enchantment of those breasts, wondrously large and marvelously pliant, each topped with an irresistible bud. While Naomi moaned in tones just short of pain, he bounced giddily back and forth between nipples.

Eventually, the boy's tongue struck off on a glorious course between the ribs, across the navel and down the inside of the right leg. He had never encountered anything so smooth, so exquisite as the inside of a lady's thigh. He grazed across the lush black down, and completing the arc, found the left thigh as creamily delectable as the right. He greedily kneaded Naomi's sumptuous rear, then gently spread her thighs and gazed upon a sanctum more mysterious and compelling than he'd ever imagined. Well before his curiosity was sated, he was, once more, hauled forward by his shoulders.

Naomi had grown uncomfortable serving as the object of adoration. She knew her emptiness would respond to only one therapy. She shifted the boy's weight to allow a firm grasp and swiftly, deftly introduced him to yet another peak in a night of escalating revelation.

Once guided through the portal divine, Jeff found he had no responsibility beyond hanging in and hanging on. When he attempted to raise his head—to gaze again upon that remarkable body, to kiss her lips—he found himself clamped tightly into place. Her arms squeezed him as though he were salvation itself; her thighs, hardened by gyrations to countless rock rhythms, were wrapped so tightly around his back that movement of any more than slightly less than a half-foot was impossible. He fought fiercely to restrain and prolong the passion that threatened to erupt immediately, but he had little time to consider technique before being swept away by an avalanche that racked his body in an accumulating convulsion.

When the iron bands encircling him relented, Jeff pulled himself up on his elbows. Naomi's head was twisted to the right and her eyes were closed. He kissed her gently on the cheek and tasted the salt of a tear. Suddenly aware of the chill, he reached for a blanket that lay bunched beside them.

The winter's night, previously as silent and indifferent as the vacuum of space, released a sound that paralyzed the boy's soul.

"What?" Naomi said. Her body coiled into a single tense muscle.

The whine of an approaching car on the dirt road sucked all breathable air from the bedroom. The lovers listened in unholy dread, waiting for the car to turn up the driveway and seal their fate. The car seemed to slow, then sloshed away down the muddy road.

But the spell was broken; Naomi was instantly out of the bed and pulling on her clothing. When those glorious breasts disappeared into her brassiere, when her cotton panties rose to conceal the lush forest between her perfect thighs, Jeff felt as though he had witnessed a death. He was seized by the fear that he would never again see anything so wondrous.

They dressed without speaking, avoiding eye contact. Naomi spread the blankets over the bed to cover their tracks. She carried her suitcase to the car as Jeff trailed behind uselessly. A light rain began to fall. The silence in the car was interrupted only by Naomi's curt directions to Shirley's place. By the time he pulled the station wagon into the mobile home park, the rain had turned to sleet. When Jeff pulled up next to the faded green house trailer, Naomi reached over and blew the horn twice. When Jeff cut off the motor, Naomi kissed him on the cheek and whispered, "We can't see each other."

She collected her suitcase from the back seat and walked quickly across the patchy lawn. Jeff watched numbly as Naomi, framed in the halo of his headlights, stood unsteadily on the cinder block step and knocked on the trailer door. A pale young woman with a child in her arms opened the door and let her in.

Jeff stared at the door until his windshield was covered with sleet. He turned the car around and drove away. Sleet and snow obscured his vision and accumulated quickly on the frigid road. The Plymouth wobbled uncertainly in curves, but Jeff was oblivious to everything but the storm that raged inside. Every attempt to impose order on his thoughts was frustrated by his mind's unwavering demand to float off and commingle with Naomi's flesh. The Plymouth found its way home with no conscious help from its driver.

CHAPTER TWENTY-SEVEN

Saturday, 1:15 p.m. Jeff stood at the entrance of the Country Kitchen searching for the courage to walk inside. He hadn't seen Naomi since Wednesday night—she hadn't gone to work, and no one had answered the door at Shirley's trailer when he knocked. But she was inside now; he'd caught a stomach-churning glimpse of her through the diner's window. The previous two days had wreaked a fearful toll on his mind and body, a cost that was apparent to the people entering and leaving the diner.

"Damn, Jeff," Piney, the lumber truck driver said, as he exited the restaurant rubbing his full belly, "you look like you been shot at and missed, shit at and hit." Jeff mumbled something about having the flu and quickly stepped inside the door.

Jeff chose this time to avoid the lunch crush, but wanted the diner to be busy enough so he would not be conspicuous. If Naomi saw him when she emerged from the kitchen with a tray full of plates, he couldn't tell it. The sight of her produced a flush that he felt cross his face and scalp and raise the hair on the back of his neck. He tried to gather his thoughts as she passed out plates to a couple in a booth, then walked toward him.

"What would you like to eat today?" she asked formally, her face as blank as a sleepwalker's.

"I'd like to talk to you."

"Have at it."

"Where you been? I couldn't find you."

"I'm back with Cody."

The words echoed in Jeff's mind without registering, but his body reacted. The sensations that shot through him were those that followed the near-paralyzing tackle at the Richardson game. "Why?" was all he could manage.

Naomi placed both hands on the table, and leaned over so that only inches separated her face from Jeff's. "That's the way it is," she said evenly. "Get used to it."

"It's been weeks and weeks," Rose confided to Madam La'Moor, "and the boy has done nothing but go to school, piddle around the lumberyard, and play that infernal guitar. And the things he plays," she said, as she stroked Caliban vigorously, "let me tell you, Delphina, these are *not* happy songs. Lordy, they sound like slave songs." Rose looked up quickly to see if her remark had offended.

Kvetch, kvetch, kvetch, thought Madam La'Moor, though her face remained placid. The prophetess had spent most of the day driving her limping plumber and his six year-old daughter around Oak City and Richardson in search of a doctor who would attend to the little girl's racking cough. Upon finding an M.D. who would see Coloreds, they had been treated rudely and over-charged. Madam's busted toilet—that had necessitated the plumber, who had pleaded for help for his child—remained unusable. She had known better than to get involved with a cripple!

Worse, the mentalist's stash of ganja was running dangerously low, and no carny was scheduled through the area for months. Consequently, Madam La'Moor could scrape up little sympathy for Rose and her litany of minor problems and anticipated catastrophes.

Rose frowned at her teacup, aware that something was missing. She fretted over whether to broach the subject that was squirming around in her consciousness. It was silly, she knew, and Delphina seemed to be in a bad mood, but she couldn't seem to shake the fear, and there was no one else to talk to. "There's something else!" Rose blurted out, surprising them both.

What now? thought the seer. In the previous two weeks, Rose had related a web of potential tragedy that, if brought to fruition, would have reduced ragged, boil-scarred Biblical Job to sympathetic tears. In addition to her morbid son, her pregnant unwed office girl, Janet, faced a Dickensian future, and Rose's semi-alcoholic father-in-law seemed to have little will to live, and even less to turn a profit. Consequently, the family business was headed for the crapper—a working indoor crapper no doubt, Delphina thought bitterly. The fortuneteller had never seen such an eagerness to "borrow trouble." Perhaps, thought Madam La'Moor, this lady needs a few nights of tramping through the mud and a piercing winter wind to sit in a stinking, spider-infested outhouse with her bare rump hanging over a rotting altar. *That* would provide focus to her life.

"Well, I don't know how to say this," Rose began, as she fingered the buttons on her dress front, "but I had this cousin in Wilmington, down on the coast, and he was just the nicest little boy, but when we were growing up...there came a time when the boys and girls quit playing together, and Danny, my cousin, he still wanted to play with the girls." Rose stopped, hoping she had said enough to make her point.

Madam La'Moor paused, her teacup halfway to her mouth. "And...?" she prodded, trying not to sound impatient.

"Well, you see," Rose continued, slowly, torturously, "Jeff never had a father around, and when he was young he was sort of a...mama's boy. But he got over that," she added quickly. "It's just that he doesn't seem to want to date anyone, and he spends all his time alone. He's let his hair grow way too long. Some people believe that kind of thing runs in families..." Rose trailed off, hoping she had not made a better case than Madam could refute.

"You think Jeff is..." Delphina rejected the half-dozen epithets she recalled from the carny before settling on: "a sissy?"

Rose nodded her bowed head.

"Are you crazy, Woman?" Madam La'Moor asked incredulously.

Rose's chin leaped off her chest, her face set in a curious mask of resentment creased with disbelief. Only after Delphina had broken down into a full, deep laugh, did Rose's anger slowly ebb. Rose's small, almost forced, giggle grew in confidence as it hitched a ride on Madam La'Moor's runaway guffaw. Fool, fool, fool! Rose's laughter mocked her fear. Of course he's not a queer! What were you thinking?

"Jeff is not a homosexual," Delphina stated in a voice bordering on exasperation. She had sought out and observed Jeff from afar on the Rockton streets, studied his carriage and interaction with male and females. Although recognizing that she was still capable of being fooled by the endlessly mutable riddle of sex, Madam would have bet the farm that at the core of Jeff Stuart's misery lay a female.

Reassurance washed over Rose like spring rain over delta cotton. As she luxuriated in the humiliation of her gravest fear, she felt that never again would she worry so much about anything. Having grown suspicious of joy at an early age, Rose was left with only release from pain to provide some measure of contentment to her life.

Delphina was seized by an impulse so strong that she acted without reflection. Time to roll the dice. "I have an exciting revelation for you," she whispered, as she reached over and touched Rose's knee. "It came to me last night during meditation, but I chose to withhold it until you unburdened yourself."

Rose leaned forward. "What?" she asked, her face as open and trusting as a child at Christmas.

Madam glanced left and right, as though to insure that no one else would overhear the remarkable news. "You have a secret admirer," the seer confided.

Rose blinked twice and shook her head like a fighter tagged by a wicked hook. Caliban, frightened, jumped off her lap. "A *man*?" she asked. Her eyebrows collapsed so quickly they threatened to crush her thin nose.

Of course a *man*, the mentalist thought indignantly. What kind of joint do you think I run here?

Once again Madam placed her hand on Rose's knee as she whispered. "He is a man whom you have known for many years. You share many interests, but lately he has begun to look at you with new eyes," the seer concluded, raising her eyebrows suggestively.

"*Who* is it?" Rose demanded. She sounded more irritated than pleased.

The seer had not expected that reaction; she withdrew her hand, leaned back, and spoke to a point above and to the right of Rose's head. "I don't see names," she intoned in a voice that might have emanated from a cloud. "I see the vision and feel the spirit."

"Then what did he look like in the vision?" Rose pressed. She sawed her wedding ring vigorously against a reddening knuckle.

"I can tell you no more," Madam replied flatly. She stared straight ahead, silent and unyielding as the Sphinx. Albeit a somewhat pissed-off Sphinx.

So immersed was Rose in her quandary that for one of the few times in her life, she passed up an opportunity to apologize to someone. Her body trembled like a confused Chihuahua, unsure if she was angry, afraid or excited. Why this, now? she thought, irritated.

Madam La'Moor was a trifle confused as well. She'd tossed out the old "secret admirer" bone many times, but couldn't recall a similar reaction. The "vision" had been offered as a gift—spiritual nourishment to a woman who had been dining out regularly on fabricated misery.

Rose stood up and absently gathered her coat around her shoulders, more for protection than warmth. "Is there anything else you can tell me about this 'man'?" Rose spoke the word as though she doubted that the species even existed.

"Nothing more," Madam said, refusing eye contact. "There is no reason to accept this vision as a burden. You may ignore it entirely, if you choose."

Rose nodded absently, as she reached into her purse and withdrew her payment. She placed it on the coffee table and walked slowly to the door. After stepping onto the porch, Rose turned and said, "I wasn't going to mention it, but lately the tea has not been as good as—"

"Good night," Madam La'Moor said definitively.

As Madam watched the distracted woman walk to her car, she recalled nostalgically the days when she could toss off prophecy with indifference and aplomb, assured that she would soon be leaving town in a fast car with a pocketful of money.

Rose could not have testified whether she passed a single car or a hundred, stopped at one traffic light or fifty on her drive home. Her mind was filled with swarming emotions and stinging questions: Why, she wondered angrily, did Madam La'Moor, supposedly a friend, have to introduce another complication into a life already too complex by half? And, what right did some *man* have admiring you when you didn't want to be admired? And what kind of *man* would go around admiring a thirty-nine year-old widow who had flatly discouraged every *man* who had smiled or nodded at her for nearly two decades? Didn't this *man* have anything better to do with his life than bother a perfectly contented widow?

Tough questions and conflicted emotions hounded her well into the night. Years before, after Will's death, she had received invitations to dinner, movies, even church—she turned them down. Eventually, men quit asking. She'd remained constant to her husband during the long years when body and soul ached for fulfillment; her loyalty persisted until it had become a reflex and an identity.

She recalled a time, back when Jeff had started first grade, when she considered joining a square-dancing class in Oak City. It was to be her first step back into a society that did not revolve around her son. But in mid-September, her sour mother-in-law, Daisy, died. Before a blade of grass sprouted on her grave, Granjack was reputedly wading through the county's abundant crop of widows and frustrated housewives spawned by World War II.

Unfortunately, the high school football team was enduring a disastrous season that year, so there seemed to be little for townsfolk to talk about except who Jack Stuart was plugging that particular week. The more wanton Jack's reputation grew, the more scrupulously Rose was forced to guard hers. She dropped square dancing and doubled up on church. Now, her reputation was such that when she entered the beauty shop every other Thursday, the gossip shifted to subjects other than men and sex. She sensed everyone was relieved to get her permed and out the door.

At the base of the stone wall that she had erected around her heart lay the well-tended grave of William Stuart, a man—no, a boy—that she had known for three years and mourned for seventeen. Why, she wondered as she lay in bed, did the knowledge that some man found her attractive make her feel as though she had betrayed Will.

After hours of thrashing in bed, Rose descended into the sleep that does not refresh. She had a terrifying dream in which her hand melted from the heat of a burning coal. She burst awake, pulled off her wedding ring and flung it across the dark room. Horrified, she cut on the overhead light and searched the floor on her hands and knees. When she found the ring behind her dresser, she studied it as though she'd never seen it before. She slipped it on and off her finger several times before placing it on her nightstand.

She sat up in bed and read her Bible. Eventually, the endless "begats" of Genesis induced a restless half-sleep.

CHAPTER TWENTY-EIGHT

Jeff's eyes burst open in the pitch-black room. All the doubts and fears, guilt and regrets, that he had beaten back before falling asleep emerged and fed on him like impatient ripping ragged pieces of flesh from his gut, boring toward his backbone.

Why did she send me away? How can I live without her?

His mind settled on the memory of that night, and, briefly, he swam in ecstasy. He strained to recall every detail, each curve, crease and swell, the glorious roundness that could surround, nurture, protect. But the salvation he had glimpsed when buried in her flesh now lay moldering, slain by the realization that he would *never* touch her again.

He had finally been cut in on *The Game*—the Game that men and women killed to get in, or stay in, or get out of—allowed to play once, then banished without explanation. Granted, he hadn't played all that well, but he had played with a noble heart. Or as noble a heart as a man could have when plowing his best friend's girl.

Then it was back to the questions that had no answers, the doubt and guilt that could not be salved. He twisted his sheets into knots, desperate to sleep. He avoided looking at the clock; he didn't want to know how little he'd slept, how little he would. Often sleeplessness persisted until dawn, and the boy knew he would spend another day weak, dispirited.

Down the hall, Rose wrestled nightly with her own misery. Up the road, Granjack's drinking cycles acknowledged neither sun nor moon. There were nights that winter when the Stuart homestead hosted fewer hours of restful sleep than a medieval castle under siege.

Jeff went to school because it was easier than staying home. He was glad to have people around, although he had very little to say to anyone. He often ate lunch at a table with six or eight chattering classmates without offering an opinion or comment. His distraction was accepted by friends who had known him since first grade but had given up on understanding him. He made up with Marty because he had neither the will nor the energy to hold a grudge.

The boy attempted to listen in class, but when boredom or despair intruded, he would read one of the books he carried. Most often he retreated to characters and locations that his grandfather had introduced him to years before. Jim Bridger, John Colter, Meriwether Lewis and William Clark led him through virgin forest and over uncharted mountains. Jeff's distraction was so complete that he traveled endless hours in the company of solitary, self-sufficient mountain men without recognizing why he found them so compelling.

He was relieved when there was work at the lumberyard after school, since that meant fewer hours to fill before sleep. After supper, he went to his room because that was easier than deciding where to go, then going. Attracted by an exotic recruiting poster in the window of the post office, he picked up enlistment brochures from the Army and Navy recruiters. At night he studied the color photographs of Europe, the Orient, the Caribbean, all lands where bright-faced young men in heavily starched uniforms found adventure, romance and a fresh start.

Occasionally, the solitude grew so oppressive that it forced him out of his bedroom. He spent one evening tossing fifty-cent pieces across green felt at Snook Carter, the best pool shot in town. He persisted because there was no one else to shoot with and, once out, he couldn't bear the thought of going home. When Marty talked him into going to the drive-in one Saturday night, he drank up the beer so quickly that Marty had to spend hours driving him around with the windows open until he was sober enough to be delivered home. Every night, he dialed past the radio music of frenzied white kids and settled on the weary laments of old black men.

He shared his thoughts with no one. To complain would have been unmanly, to mention Naomi's name would have been ungentlemanly, and—if word got back to Cody—possibly lethal. He avoided proximity to the auto shop where Cody worked and the music clubs. Although Jeff spent the bulk of his time mourning the past, he knew the future might hold danger to more than his mental health.

Something else to worry about.

CHAPTER TWENTY-NINE

"I'm thinkin' it's time we heard some music," Cody said, his mouth full of hamburger steak and mashed potatoes. "We haven't been out—" he stopped abruptly when he recalled their last outing—the disaster at Big Daddy's Ballroom— "hell, since Christ was a corporal. There's a hot bunch comin' to Alley's Saturday night, what say you put on those pink pedal pushers I bought ya, and we'll shag on down there?"

"We got the bread?" Naomi asked.

"We'll have it Saturday."

"Sure, why not," Naomi said, with little enthusiasm. "More gravy?"

Cody shook his head. "I think I'll see if ol' Jeff wants to come along. I'd like to tell him...I don't hold no hard feelin's." He watched Naomi's reaction closely.

"Yeah," Naomi said, rising quickly from the table. She scraped half a plate of food into the garbage can. "He's a good kid." She knew she was being tested.

"Not hungry tonight?" Cody asked.

"I didn't know you were gonna cook," Naomi said, turning toward the sink. "I ate at work."

Cody knew better. There'd been something wrong ever since they had gotten back together. He didn't recall much of what happened during his amphetamine fog, but he knew he'd acted like a horse's ass that night. Bo still wouldn't talk to him. Naomi hadn't demanded the big-time payback he had expected, but she'd sure-as-hell acted differently—often distant, sometimes defensive. And precious little passion had been exchanged between the two.

Maybe, he figured, the relationship was just breaking down. Or, maybe she was hiding something. Either way, he had to find out. Only one woman had ever walked out on him, and rarely a day passed that he didn't curse her memory. None of his women had ever cheated on him; he was sure of that. If Naomi had crossed that line, honor demanded that everyone involved must pay a price.

"It's for you," Rose shouted down the hall. She held the phone while Jeff walked from his room. "I can't tell who it is," she said.

Jeff snatched the phone from her. When Rose lingered in the hallway, Jeff pointedly waited for her to leave before speaking.

"Hello Hello."

"Whatya say, Stud?"

Although Jeff could barely make out the words for the clanging metal in the background, his blood froze at the sound of that voice. "Cody. What's shakin'?"

"Precious little to speak of. Me and the old lady are goin' to Alley's club Saturday night. Think you might be able to shake loose?"

Jeff's head swam in confusion as he felt sweat bead on his forehead. He sank heavily into the chair beside the telephone stand. Was this a test?

"Checkin' your date book?" Cody laughed.

"Yeah, uh, no. Who's playin'," Jeff said, buying time.

"Four piece bunch from Richmond. Two guitars, bass, drums. I forget the name. Lead guitar's supposed to be an ass-kicker." Pause. "That thing at Big Daddy's . . . I was wrecked on pills. I think I owe you a beer. Whatya say."

Jeff's mind froze up. "Yeah, yeah. I think I can swing it," he heard himself say.

"We'll meet you at Alley's. If you get there first, grab us a table."

"Right."

"Keep a cool tool," Cody said, and hung up.

Jeff stared at the phone before hanging it up. Why hadn't he just said he was busy? "Can I use the car on Saturday night?" he called out.

"Sure," Rose responded from the kitchen. She was glad to get him out of the house.

There was a new man at the door of Alley's Cat Club, so Jeff had to show his fake ID to get in. He checked his watch, 9:30. The club advertised their music as starting at nine o'clock, but it was usually an hour later before the band hit its first lick. Rock'n'roll punched no clock.

Stale beer and cigarette smoke filled Jeff's lungs as he walked across the gummy floor and scanned the crowd. He spotted Cody sitting alone. He was jiving with two cats who were standing—actually leaning without support—beside his table. The jukebox was cranked louder than its tinny speakers could handle, so everyone had to shout across a distorted Ike Turner guitar break.

"Take a load off, Jeff," Cody yelled. "You know these ol' boys." Jeff nodded to the two strangers, and they nodded back. Among the cool, introductions were as uncommon as eye contact, good posture or temperance. Jeff ordered a beer while Cody and the ol' boys transacted some business about hubcaps and headers.

"How you been gettin' along?" Jeff asked, after the cats slouched off to their own table.

"Ridin' with the tide," Cody answered, without enthusiasm. "How about you?"

"Stickin' close to home," Jeff replied. "Tryin' to make it through the winter."

They spoke without making eye contact. Both could feel the suspicion, resentment and guilt that swarmed thicker than cigarette smoke above their table. Neither was sure exactly how it all sorted out. Jeff decided to address the obvious. "Naomi gonna make it tonight?"

"Said she has to work late. Said she'd come by later if she ain't wore out." Cody chugged a shot glass of bourbon and turned to face Jeff. "Disappointed?"

"Sure," Jeff said. "She's always good company."

"Yeah," Cody replied, "gooood company."

Cody's tone sounded even more ironic than usual, and Jeff felt the blood rushing to his face. He turned toward the stage where the band was setting up, hoping the lighting was so bleak Cody wouldn't notice.

Jeff drank quickly as he sorted through his thoughts. *Something* was bothering Cody. But if he knew the score, Cody would be more than vaguely insulting; he would be throwing punches in combinations and kicking the body when it hit the floor. Nothing to do but play it cool.

"You got any gigs up?" Jeff asked.

"Are you shittin' me?" Cody sneered. "After that massacree at Big Daddy's, I'll have to change my name and get me some plastic surgery before they'll let me play in this county."

"Sam go to trial yet?" Jeff asked. Cody's ex-drummer had been accused of car theft in a front page newspaper story. Chief Parrish had declared Sam was part of a huge auto theft ring. It was the talk of the town.

"Trial, my ass?" Cody scoffed. "The dumb bastard might as well cut the best deal he can and get on with life in the can." Cody shook his head in disgust and lit a Marlboro.

Cody didn't speak during the band's first set. When Jeff commented on the guitarist's style and the bass player's voice, Cody only nodded. Several semi-attractive chicks danced alone, but Cody put no moves on them. He sat with his legs crossed at the ankles, drinking whiskey and continually lighting a fresh cigarette off the butt of his last. Jeff was tempted to indulge in some two-fisted drinking, but knew better.

When the band finished the set, cats lined up to shove quarters in the juke box. As the Domino's sang "Sixty Minute Man," Cody turned his chair back toward the table and stared across at Jeff. "She ain't comin'."

"What?"

"I knew she wouldn't," Cody said, leaning across the table. "You see, she's been jumpy ever since I set this up. Now, reckon why that would be?"

"Beats me," Jeff said coolly. "Why don't you ask her?"

Cody shook his head. "She won't say. But I got this feelin' you and her been keepin' a secret from me. I wanted us all to get together and have a little talk. See if we could straighten things out. So we could all be friends again."

The edginess Jeff had felt all evening was sliding toward anger as Cody baited him. "If we're all gonna be friends again," Jeff said calmly, "maybe you better start by apologizing for acting like an asshole at Big Daddy's."

Cody blinked quickly and leaned back in his chair. "I reckon I could have been more charmin'," he said, "but what I'm concerned about is what happened after you two left. Naomi won't talk about it, but somethin' happened. She ain't the same, and you ain't the same."

"Maybe if you treated her better, you wouldn't have to—"

Cody sprang forward and unleashed a roundhouse right at Jeff's jaw. The boy tried to duck under it, but it landed above his ear. Dazed, Jeff pushed away from the table and took a step back.

Football had taught Jeff to take a blow, push through the pain, react. His mind processed Cody's movements as if they were in slow motion, even the punches that could not be slipped or blocked. Cody darted around the table and threw another right. Jeff stepped inside the punch and threw a hard left jab that snapped Cody's head back. A right uppercut to Cody's stomach landed with effect—Jeff smelled whisky in the rush of breath from his lungs. Jeff landed a hard right to Cody's nose that sprayed blood widely, then he took a blow to his left eye that immediately filled with blood.

The flurry of punches that followed fell too hard and fast to track or remember. Both men fought on instinct, and skill became less important than rage. Cody fought with the righteousness of a man betrayed. Jeff knew he was "fighting in the wrong." Maybe that was why, when he caught an explosive right hook on the jaw, he felt as though he had finally paid off a debt.

Lying on his back, Jeff rolled his head from side to side and saw an ocean of people swirling around him. Where had they come from? As he rolled over on his side he could hear the scratched record on the juke box blaring, "I rock 'em, roll 'em, all night long," over and over. He pulled himself to his hands and knees and watched his blood spill from his nose and collect in a pool on the floor.

"Stay down," someone shouted.

Jeff pushed off from the floor and balanced unsteadily on his knees. His head rolled in a jerky circle as he waited for the blow that would allow him to lie down and rest.

Cody walked away. As the crowd scrambled out of his path, he stalked out of the bar. Unseen hands helped Jeff into a chair. They placed his coat over his shoulders. A pile of wet paper towels appeared on the table. He wiped the blood from his face. The cool towels masked some of the pain he knew would come later, but nothing could wash away the shame. As soon as he could walk, he left the bar.

Jeff sat in the Plymouth staring at the light in his mother's bedroom window a hundred yards away. Louder than the sound of the engine hum and the rattle of the muffler, the boy listened to the ragged wheeze of his breath as the air fought past dried blood and swollen and displaced tissue.

As the last nine months flashed through his mind like a black and white newsreel—meeting Cody and Naomi, the first bar fight and shoulder injury, the lost football season, his break-up with Vicky, and now a public beating in a barroom—he could see that it had been a long, twisted trail leading to humiliation. He had failed everyone: his mother, his friends, his team, his school, himself.

Jeff concluded suddenly, stunningly, his whole life had been altered by a coin flip in the parking lot of the Hitching Post. If either Chuck's or Marty's coin had completed another half-revolution, he would not have gone into the roadhouse and seen Cody Hunter on the bandstand. All that followed...would not have followed.

Fifteen minutes after Rose turned off her bedroom light, Jeff drove until close enough to cut the motor and coast into the driveway. He snuck into his dark home, a fugitive come to steal back his life.

CHAPTER THIRTY

"Oh, merciful God," Rose moaned, when she saw Jeff's face the following morning. He rushed to her side and lowered her trembling body to the couch. He put his arm around her shoulders and stroked her hands as he reassured her that he looked much worse than he felt. As her tears ran down her cheeks and into her lap, Jeff explained he had been jumped by at least three, maybe four guys after leaving a dance in Oak City. They attacked him, he figured, because he was from Rockton, and he'd been dancing with somebody's girl friend. And, yes, they had been drinking; he could smell it on them.

Twice Rose appeared to collect her emotions, but broke down again when she raised her gaze to the grisly mosaic of bruises that defiled her son's handsome face. Smears of black, blue, and yellow were traversed by open red cuts and broken blood vessel snaking under his skin. Both eyes were swollen nearly shut, and islands of blood tracers floated inside the white. How could this have happened to the happy little child she had held and comforted not so long ago.

Rose's first impulse was to call the police. Jeff protested urgently that he could not identify any of the attackers, that he would rather let the whole matter drop than risk a blood feud between teenagers in the two towns. When he swore to his mother he would never again attend a dance, a party, a club, a revival, *anything* in Oak City, Rose reluctantly agreed not to call in the police.

When Jeff assured his mother that the experience had wrought a change in him she had long desired, his sincerity was obvious. He now understood his place in the family and in the town. The confused and erratic behavior that had upset his mother and ruined his reputation in Rockton was over. For the rest of his life, Jeff swore, he would do everything he was capable of to make his mother proud.

As Jeff retired to his bedroom, he repented of the horrible lies he had just spoken, and swore upon everything he considered holy and honorable he would never, ever utter another untruthful word to his mother.

Doc Bowman raised his gaze slowly from *The Riders of the Purple Sage* and registered no surprise at the grotesquely battered face looking down at him. He stubbed out the last inch of a Camel before speaking. "You been runnin' in that shower again, son?"

Jeff frowned in confusion, before recalling the excuse he'd used back in September. "I got jumped by some guys in Oak City," Jeff said. He was prepared to repeat the whole elaborate lie, but Doc dismissed it with a shrug.

"Take your shirt off," Doc grunted. The old man satisfied himself that the patient's heart was beating and his lungs tolerably clear before studying the collection of cuts, and contusions that covered Jeff's face and upper body like abstract tattoos. When Doc probed the bruises in search of broken, cracked or chipped bones, it was all Jeff could do to avoid crying out. Doc concluded the only permanent damage likely was a loose tooth that might fall out, and a deviated septum that had left a perceptible hump. "Looks like your grandpa's beak now," Doc commented.

After rifling through a desk drawer for several moments, Doc tossed Jeff a leather eye patch. "Wear this," Doc mumbled. "I want to see you on Thursday, and sooner if anything starts botherin' you."

Jeff had scarcely set foot on the campus before the news of his beating at the hands of as many as six Oak City boys was common knowledge. By the end of second period, Chuck Brady had recruited a carload of boys eager to ride the streets of Oak City by cover of night in search of the cowards who had jumped their kinsmen.

At lunch, Jeff talked hard and fast to dissuade his avengers. He swore he's seen nothing of his attackers but bare knuckles and shoe leather. Identification was impossible. Chuck countered that the war party might still be worthwhile to vindicate the reputation of all Rockton youth if not Jeff personally. According to Chuck, if the beating went unanswered, then never again would a Rockton teen feel safe walking an Oak City Street. Consequently, beating up *anybody* in Oak City was better than ignoring the insult. And, Chuck implied, it would certainly be more fun. But the other boys couldn't work up much enthusiasm for picking victims at random, so by the end of the school day the raid had dissipated to random oaths and scattered threats.

All the sympathy that rained down on Jeff's battered head embarrassed the hell out of him. Since his celebrity was based upon receiving a fearful mauling—weakness, humiliation and pain—and then lying about it, all attention was unwanted. And Jeff was particularly amazed at the number of young girls who apparently found him more attractive as a victim and near-cripple than when vital, capable and whole. Taught since birth that a man's worth resided in his strength and accomplishment, Jeff couldn't figure out why women were drawn to vulnerability, even weakness. It confused him further when he heard several admiring comments voiced dreamily by maidens enamored of his eye patch.

Since grammar school, a day had seldom passed when Jeff wasn't confronted with the understanding that he knew nothing about females and likely never would.

CHAPTER THIRTY-ONE

Jeff had little to occupy him during the icy, brutish, and short February days other than school. Granjack would run as many men as he could as far into the winter as rain, snow, ice and mud would allow, but generally both supply and demand reached an equilibrium of near-zero after Christmas. Most of the help were cut loose until spring. The oldest and best workers spent their days repairing equipment, cutting and hauling the odd load of lumber, and filling orders in the cabinet shop. Rose usually put her office helper on half-time from January to April, but Janet had turned up pregnant just before Christmas, so Rose spent much of her energy creating a full day's work for the unwed girl.

To Jeff, the school year that had once seemed to stretch well beyond the horizon now bore down on him like a runaway transfer truck. Even as he attempted to rejoin his class, his fellow seniors could speak of nothing but what they were going to do *after* casting off their shackles. Some had applied to colleges or trade schools, while many more were lining up work that would render a weekly paycheck to be swapped immediately for an automobile. An alarming number of senior girls awaited only their diplomas before marrying that special someone who promised bliss everlasting, or, at least, escape from oppressive parents. The prospect of adventure and a guarantee of manhood lured a virile contingent of senior boys to the military recruiting station in the post office. Everyone seemed to brim with prospects, plans, soaring hopes. But the more certain a senior was of his destiny, the harder it was for Jeff to tolerate his company.

Since Jeff had announced no plan, folks assumed he would join the family business. And they considered him damned lucky to do so. Stuart Lumber was an established company in a town dominated by low-paying jobs in textile mills and furniture factories. He understood why the folks who stumbled numbly from work with lint or wood chips in their hair and black dust fouling their lungs would envy his position. He had been born into a situation that, if managed competently, would provide him security for *his whole life*. From graduation to the grave. In Rockton. Forever.

Jeff took some consolation in Marty's plight. Reverend Ryder had taken advantage of his son's procrastination by securing Marty a place in the freshman class at Helms Baptist College. A recognized center of chastity and Christian rectitude, Helms was conveniently located less than twenty miles from Rockton—close enough that Ma and Pa Ryder could drop in regularly. Billy Ryder's alma mater couldn't turn down an applicant of such sterling bloodline, no matter how dismal his comportment or grades. Marty had stated flatly he would not attend Helms but had yet to arrange an alternative to God's Own Junior College. And time was slip, slip, slipping away.

Chuck Brady was rarin' to start football practice at Moore-Clayton College in the fall. He conceded that, if forced, he would drop in on a class occasionally. Without the bond of football, Jeff found he had little in common with his old friend. Chuck, who had rescued him from a bully in the first grade; who had taught him to swim in the river when Rose, fearing polio, had forbidden Jeff use of the town pool; who had run the Stuart woods wildly, and shared each sport in season—that Chuck was gone. Now he spent most of his time in the company of a select group of mesomorphs who hoisted dead weights in quantities that would have impressed the pyramid builders. When not in the gym, those gents often scoured public gatherings in search of opportunity to test those muscles in combat.

Stripped of dreams of escape and independence, Jeff was forced to consider the most reasonable path, Rose's path: Living at home, commuting to a two-year business school in Oak City, working at the lumberyard. It was while staring at the ceiling of his bedroom in the winter of 1957, that Jeff stumbled on the realization that not getting what you wanted wasn't nearly as bad as not knowing what you wanted.

The sun, a tired pink dot incapable of piercing clouds the color of a deep bruise, appeared ready to surrender as Jeff walked on the high side of the muddy road that led to Granjack's house. The old man had left work in the middle of the afternoon without explanation. The boy knew what he was likely to find if Granjack chose to open the door.

"Leave me be!" was the response to Jeff's knock. He knew Granjack wouldn't be at work the next day, or likely the day after that. Rose would cook and Jeff would deliver meals that would go largely uneaten until the old man was ready to sober up and trudge back to the lumberyard. If the binge lasted more than three or four days, Rose would suggest that he collect Jack's guns while he slept and bring them to her house for storage.

"I can see through my hand," Jack Stuart said aloud. He'd burned himself while stoking his wood stove and had stumbled back to his chair to examine the throbbing wound. As he held his hand in front of the kerosene lamp, he nearly passed out when he discovered that his hand, once brown and callused, then pale and waxy, was now transparent. "Hell," he spoke loudly into the dim, empty room, "I bet I can read the damn newspaper through it!"

Jack considered treating his burn with petroleum jelly, but reached instead for the jug. Transparent skin was added to the catalogue of infirmity that grew daily—all bad shit that would never get better. He lit a cigarette.

He'd never figured on living so long, and he'd come to resent his body's persistence. His folks had both died before reaching fifty, and he'd tried like hell to use up his body before 1940. When that year passed without incident or illness, Jack felt both relieved and betrayed.

Yeah, 1940. Two years before Will was killed. He and Daisy had lost a three year-old girl to diphtheria before Will was born. Any remnant of faith in God or life was buried with the body of his son. Any man who outlived two children and does not rage against God was a gutless sonuvabitch.

If someone had laid a big oak tree on top of me back in 1940, Jack speculated, everyone woulda been better off. God knows there were enough firedsawmen and betrayed-husbands who woulda liked to done it, but lacked the guts. Musta knowed they'd be doin' me a favor.

The pain in his hand drove Jack on an unsteady ramble to the medicine cabinet. He ran cold water over the burn and spread some petroleum jelly on top. Placing his hand on the wall above the toilet, the old man peed in short bursts that frustrated and worried him. "Poor little feller," Jack muttered, in genuine sympathy, "time was you drug me all over this country. Now I drag you around."

Those days were long past. The old man's sex life now consisted of the interval after his first throat full of whiskey when he desperately craved a woman's touch, and his third drink when he decided he didn't care if he ever saw another naked female.

As he lay on his rumpled bed, Jack ignored the soft knock on the door. Feigning sleep, he heard the door creak and the soft clatter of dishes as Jeff exchanged a warm meal for a cold one. He heard the boy toss a log in the stove and leave.

That's a good boy, the old man thought. But if he don't figure out what he wants to do pretty damn quick, he'll find there's lotsa folks ready to tell him what he oughta do. Just like Will.

Desperate to chase those worries off, Jack reached back for the memory of his twenty year-old body planting a double-bladed ax into the massive trunk of a chestnut tree. Soon the feel of cold steel biting soft wood pulsed through his hands, his muscles, his soul. The sound of his ax echoed through the forest as wood chips piled up as his feet.

On the fifth day of Granjack's jag, Jeff knocked, then pushed open the old man's door. The room was cold and smelled of dissolution. He placed the oatmeal and toast on the kitchen table and picked up the supper tray. The food had barely been touched. He stirred the coals of the wood stove and tossed in kindling and two logs. He'd need to haul in wood from the front porch before he left.

Jeff walked quietly to the bedroom door. He wanted to see that the old man's blankets rose and fell with regularity. When Jeff pushed open the creaking door, he found his grandfather lying fully-clothed on top of his bed. His face was gray as wood ash. His eyes were open. Jeff rushed to him and bent down.

"Will?" Granjack whispered. "That you, son?"

CHAPTER THIRTY-TWO

Jeff rode in the ambulance with Granjack while Rose followed in the Plymouth. A medic fitted the old man with an oxygen mask, but Jeff saw that he still struggled for breath. The attendants offered no reassurance on the maddeningly slow drive through the indifferent morning work traffic.

They paced in the waiting room as Arthur Godfrey spieled the virtues of Lipton Tea in cloying detail and made salacious small-talk with the McGuire Sisters. The boy wanted to turn the television off, but his mother found comfort in the familiar voice. Jeff wished he could strangle Arthur with a ukulele string.

Eventually, a short young man in a white uniform and a clipboard walked through the door. "Are you here with Mr. Stuart?" he asked.

Rose nodded.

"I'm Dr. Malone. I need some information," he stated flatly.

"How's he doing," Jeff interrupted.

"Not very well. We're trying to stabilize him." He glanced up at Rose. "How old is your father?"

"He's my father-in-law. He's sixty-four or five, I think. Let's see, he was born—"

"Has he ever had a heart attack before?"

"No. He's been as healthy as a horse-"

"Does Mr. Stuart smoke?"

"Yes," Rose said hesitantly. "But not as much as he used to. Mostly he just lights them and lays them down. Sometimes he'll have two or three going at the same time—"

"Does he drink alcohol?"

"Some," Rose admitted grudgingly, "but I think he's trying to quit."

"What?" Jeff said, astonished. "He smokes a least two packs of Camels a day, and he chews tobacco. The only time he *doesn't* drink is when he has a gout attack, and then he only quits until it's over."

Rose's head snapped to the right to confront her betrayer. The doctor, oblivious to the drama, extracted a sheet of paper from his clipboard and handed it to Rose. "Please fill this out and hand it to the woman at the admissions desk. We'll let you know if there's any change in your father's condition."

"Father-in-law," Rose corrected, as the doctor walked out of the room.

Rose and Jeff, irritated with each other and worried to distraction, sat in the waiting room and thumbed through old copies of torn magazines. They ate a tasteless meal in the hospital cafeteria and then returned quickly to the waiting room. When the afternoon degenerated into a succession of soap operas, Jeff went outside and ran around the hospital grounds until exhausted. Around three o'clock, a nurse informed them Mr. Stuart was resting more easily. They might as well go home.

When Jeff lay in bed that night he knew from that day forward, whether Granjack lived or died, Jeff Stuart didn't have to make any more decisions about his future.

Although his doctors recommended an additional two weeks, Jack Stuart declared ten days of hospitalization to be a gracious plenty. Hospital food, and a roommate who talked to himself all day and moaned all night pushed Granjack to the edge; the discovery of the cost of each day's confinement drove the old man out the door. Few tears were shed by the nursing staff when Jack, clutching a bulging paper bag of pills, was rolled out the hospital exit.

Rose set up a bed in her living room where she could attend to the patient. That arrangement ended by mutual agreement in three days. Jack agreed to have a telephone installed at his home, but only on the condition no one be given the number but Rose and Jeff. Granjack was moved to his own house and bed where he read lurid detective magazines, listened to the radio and slept. Rose's fear of a beckoning whiskey bottle proved unfounded; Jack was too sick and scared to be tempted. He even managed to give up tobacco until an empathetic Doc Bowman suggested that six cigarettes spread over the course of a day wouldn't kill him.

Jeff brought his supper out every evening and often stayed to read or listen to the radio. Although some nights would pass with little conversation, he found that as his grandfather grew stronger, he also grew more talkative. Often

Granjack would start instructing the boy on a facet of the lumber business but would soon find himself wandering through the fields of his youth.

"The first time I laid eyes on this town, hell, it weren't no town. Just a muddy wagon rut with pigs and cows runnin' loose, dogs chasin' chickens through houses. They had the big mill set up on the hill, and the houses was down at the bottom, lined up on either side of this rutted wagon path. Four room, clap-board, set up off the ground on brick piers. Ever house just the same.

"It was a spring day and the smell of the johnny houses lined up in ever backyard was enough to gag a mad dog. Mama had this poster-paper that promised a 'model community.' She kept lookin' at it and turnin' it around in her hands. There we stood in the middle of that path. Mama, my two sisters, and me, all of us carryin' everthin' we could tote in burlap sacks. This woman saw what we was about, and she come out and took Mama by the hand and tole her things wasn't so bad as they looked.

"She took us to the house we was to get, but they was still people in it. A big man in a blue suit was makin' em move all their stuff onto a wagon. There was a man and a woman and about six or seven kids, and ever one but the man was cryin'. 'He's bad to drink,' the woman that brought us said. She took us back to her house to sit on the porch and wait. She give us some water to drink till the other family was moved off.

"By the end of the day we was able to go into the house. That other bunch hadn't bothered to clean it out. Mama and Kate and Jennie set in to cleanin', and I went out to the water pump where there was a buncha kids standin' around. Before the sun was set, I got in three fights. I was nine years-old."

That was the longest uninterrupted utterance Jeff had ever heard from his grandfather. The old man looked worn out from the effort.

"Hard times," Jeff said.

"Never been a good time to be poor," the old man said. He turned over on his side ending conversation.

Jeff balanced the tray of food in his left hand and knocked with his right. When he received an affirmative grunt, he pushed open the door. Granjack tossed aside the weekly *Rockton Messenger* and followed Jeff to the kitchen table. Jeff pulled the cloth napkin off the plate revealing a nutritionally-sound meal of boiled chicken, rice, peas, carrots and dry roll.

"I ain't eatin' this no more," the old man said. He raked the food into the compost pail. After a moment's consideration he reached under the sink and pulled out a gallon jug. He poured two fingers of the clear liquid into a tea glass and downed it in three quick swallows. When he saw the disappointment on his grandson's face, he said, "Get in the truck."

The truck motor groaned in protest but eventually turned over. The icy twilight was not responsible for the chill in Jeff's heart. It had been a little over two months since the attack, and Jeff had wondered just how long Granjack could avoid his vices.

"Town," the old man said, as he gingerly pulled himself into the truck. The truck's heater had just begun to blow warm air when Jeff was directed into the parking lot of Woody's Barbecue. He parked in the back row.

"Eat out here," the old man said. The thought of walking into the crowded grill at suppertime sent a shudder down the old man's frame. For Jack, the hardest part of recovery had been tolerating the affected concern of damn-near everyone he encountered. How many times, he wondered, did you have to assure people that you felt better now than you did back when you nearly died?

Jeff kept the motor running as the curb hop, cold and resentful, scratched down their order: Sliced barbecue, french fries, and vanilla milkshake for Granjack; a chopped and coke for Jeff. The boy had eaten a full meal only thirty minutes before, but the aggressive aroma of roasted pork convinced him he needed dessert.

They had just received their food when the cherry-red '50 Ford pulled into the lot and skidded to a dusty stop on the front row. The two people who Jeff had hoped to never lay eyes on again popped out of the car. Naomi headed directly for the diner, but Cody, ever-vigilant, scanned the parking lot. When Cody's gaze settled on the truck, Jeff's body reacted with a mixture of fear and aggression. The boy's fist clinched and his eyes narrowed as he watched his old friend approach.

Cody walked to the passenger side and tapped lightly on the window. Granjack, immersed in his food, was surprised and annoyed by the interruption. He rolled his window down.

"Somebody tol' me you died," Cody said, smiling. "I tol' 'em they was full of shit. Jack Stuart wasn't goin' nowhere till he was *ready* to go. And we'd all know about it, 'cause ever widder in the county would be mournin', and ever preacher would line up to drive a stake through his heart."

Cody sauntered off, leaving behind only a nod so slight Jeff couldn't really tell if it was aimed at him or not. Granjack chuckled as he rolled up his window. "I reckon he's completely worthless, but you can't help but like him." He took a bite of his sandwich. The whiskey had kicked in, and he felt he owed Jeff some company. "You two do some runnin' around?"

"Yeah."

"He'd sell you a rat's ass for a wedding ring, but he'd be good company out carousin'," the old man muttered through a full mouth. "Things always happenin' around such as him."

"I've heard the same thing said about you."

"I had my moments," Granjack conceded. "Can't say I regret 'em."

"What do you regret?" asked Jeff.

The old man paused, a rare occurrence when food was within reach. "I'da liked to had more children."

"Why didn't you?"

"Weren't my decision."

When they finished their food, Jeff wadded all the paper together and tossed it, left-handed, over the truck and into a trash can.

Granjack nodded appreciatively.

"I shoulda seen more of this country," the old man said, as they pulled out of the lot. "Never been further'n Tennessee. Never seen the Mississippi River. Texas. California...always workin'."

"Maybe you and me will go some time," Jeff said, forcing a smile.

The old man nodded and turned away. Through his window he surveyed a town that had seen its best days. The new highway everyone was so excited about would be the final blow. The bypass would speed people between Oak City and Richardson without running them through Rockton. He knew it wouldn't be long before the businesses moved out to where the traffic was. Shouldn't a town last longer than a man, he wondered?

Jeff parked the truck next to the rock house. "You want some company," he asked, as Granjack climbed the steps.

"I've had all the fun I can stand," the old man said. "I 'spect I'll listen to the radio and go to bed."

As Jeff walked down the icy road, he decided to spare his mother the details of Granjack's "recovery." But he would warn her the old man was likely to be at work bright and early the next morning.

CHAPTER THIRTY-THREE

"Wanna ride over to Oak City for a pick-up?" Marty shouted, his head bobbing above the sea of students in the crowded hall. The final bell had rung on Friday afternoon, and kids were fleeing the building as though it were on fire.

"Nah," Jeff yelled, pushing toward the light at the end of the tunnel. "It's way too pretty to ride, and I got work to do."

"Man, take an hour or two off every week. Even the slaves got that," Marty yelled. "There'll be some good reading on the way back."

Jeff shook his head and charged into the intoxicating sunlight of an early-March day that appeared to have been hijacked from the middle of May. He rolled his shirtsleeves above his elbow to expose skin that longed for warmth and light. There would be frosty nights for the next month, but, to Jeff, *that day* was truly the first day of spring.

The boy dearly needed shelter from the storm. Since Granjack's heart attack, his existence had consisted of little more than school, work at the lumberyard, and spending evenings with the old man. The business that Jeff had assumed could run itself had proven to be remarkably complex. Although they were not yet sending their own crews out, timber arrived every day to be cut, shaped, sorted, and sold.

Instead of walking the railroad tracks, Jeff decided to detour through town. He covered the half-mile in long, bouncing strides and deep breathes that expelled dank air and anxiety stored since the winter solstice. Every storekeep seemed to find reason to be out on the pavement, setting up a sidewalk display, talking baseball, or comparing seed catalogues with eager gardeners. Jeff spoke and nodded to folks as he sauntered down the sunny side of the street.

Kids from the grammar school swarmed the sidewalks, many on their way to the giant candy counter that beckoned in the center aisle of Sharp's Drug Store. Jeff remembered well the thrill of circling the counter with a nickel in his hand, sorting out the old favorites from the promising challengers. That nickel, wisely-spent, could get you all the candy you wanted and some to share.

The second story window of the poolroom vented profanity as Jeff passed underneath. He resisted the urge to shoot a rack before heading home. Granjack, still weak and wan, would be waiting outside the cabinet shop, eager to introduce Jeff to the insidious nature of man, material, or machine gleaned from a half-century of battling each. If the old man tired, Rose would use the rest of the workday to teach her son the subtleties of acquisition and disbursement.

As Jeff passed under the marquee of the Main Theater (*Bus Stop* starring Marilyn Monroe), he heard squealing tires approaching swiftly from behind. He watched in horror and amazement as the familiar green '55 Chevrolet station wagon careened across a lane of traffic. The car slid to a stop less than three feet from Jeff, its front left tire thumping heavily onto the sidewalk curb.

"Wanta ride, big boy," Vicky Parrish said, smiling up at him brightly.

Jeff wouldn't have been more surprised if Fireball Roberts had driven up in his stock car and offered him a lift. Since Vicky had extended nothing but hostility since their break-up, his instinct when seeing her car pointed at him was flight.

"Yeah, sure," he replied, after a moment's hesitation.

"Have you lost weight?" Vicky asked, as he climbed in the passenger side.

"Yeah, I guess so." The winter's misery had shaved pounds from a frame that couldn't spare it. He couldn't help but notice Vicky's skirt was bunched up in her lap displaying the better part of the best legs in Rockton High. Jeff winced as Vicky left a quarter-inch of rubber on the pavement and narrowly avoided cars in each lane as she swerved back onto the road. She pushed the station wagon as though it were both sports car and tank, assuming nobody in that one-horse town had the audacity to hit her.

They rode in a silence so awkward that within a half-mile stretch Jeff had yawned twice. Vicky's agitation was apparent as well.

"Jeff, I'm sorry about...everything," she finally blurted out. "I'm sorry I broke up with you. I was wrong about you seein' another girl—at least you never saw her after that. Did you?"

Jeff was puzzled by the question. All that seemed so long ago. "No," he said, finally.

"I knew it," Vicky said, triumphantly. She looked over at Jeff. He stared straight ahead. "And all this time we've been punishing ourselves over a big mistake. We nearly wasted our whole senior year. Why didn't you just tell me?"

Because I was well rid of you? Jeff thought. As he considered his response, his gaze fell on Vicky's left inner thigh, and he shrugged.

As they approached the lumberyard, Vicky decided to throw the dice. "Jeffy," she said, staring at his profile and ignoring the road, "I was wrong, and I want to make up for it. Let me take you out on Saturday night. I'll pay for everything. I'll pick you up, take you to dinner, and afterwards," she hesitated, loading the dice, "I promise you something...extra-special."

As Vicky spoke, Jeff watched the Chevy wobble over the yellow line. From the corner of his eye he could see Vicky staring at him, waiting for an answer. About sixty yards distant and closing fast, a transfer truck threatened a quick and spectacular conclusion to two teen-age lives. Jeff turned quickly toward Vicky. "Yeah, sure," he said urgently, nodding and pointing toward the road.

"Hooray!" yelled Vicky, throwing her head back, raising her left arm above her head and stretching her legs so her rear rose off the seat. The eighteen-wheeler's foghorn blared and Jeff jerked the steering wheel abruptly to the right, narrowly avoiding twenty tons of on-rushing mortality. Vicky seized the wheel and reached over and squeezed Jeff's thigh with her right hand. "Oh, we're going to be so happy! I've changed a lot, Jeff. You'll see."

Jeff smiled nervously and nodded. "What about your father?"

"You let *me* take care of Daddy," Vicky said confidently.

"Let me out at the gate," Jeff said, as they approached the lumberyard. He hoped his mother wouldn't be gazing out the office window.

Vicky slid over quickly and gave him a quick kiss as he got out of the car. "Seven-thirty, tomorrow night," she shouted, as she fishtailed out of the gravel lot.

Throughout the rest of the day—work, dinner, watching "The Millionaire," with his mother—Jeff weighed the costs and benefits of reconciliation. Only after slipping into bed did he determine that seeing Vicky was worth the ordeal that might follow. As he closed his eyes, the nude form of the short, buxom brunette that had haunted him for months slowly dissolved and re-formed into a lithe blonde.

Friday afternoon was not the best time to pull off the mission, Marty acknowledged as he parked the Buick in the Oak City town square. His preferred modus operandi was to cruise in under cover of darkness and transact his business with a minimum of scrutiny—in and out, unnoticed. As he arranged his sunglasses and tilted his father's felt hat low across his brow, he felt the anxiety and exhilaration that always accompanied a daring, daylight raid. The unseasonable weather would also rob him of the use of his overcoat, a piece of wardrobe he felt conferred age and anonymity.

No problem, Marty reassured himself, as he stuck a toothpick in his mouth and climbed out of Reverend Ryder's Buick. Just another pick-up. He climbed the six stone steps one at a time to avoid any appearance of youth and eagerness. He calmly waited for an elderly woman to exit before stepping inside the double glass doors. Off to his left, Marty noted a grim U.S. Marine Corp recruiter glowering out the window at a slack and ungrateful public.

Here danger lurked. Marty quickly scanned the long line of people waiting impatiently to buy stamps or claim packages. He breathed a sigh of relief when he recognized no one. Only three months back, during the Christmas rush, he'd been spotted by a distant aunt and forced to stand in line and explain to her why he'd driven all the way to Oak City to buy a book of stamps. Marty shuddered when he considered the consequences if that old bag had nailed him leaving the building.

Another dozen unhurried steps carried Marty to his destination. Kneeling, he peered in the bottom row window of post office box 321, registered to Mr. Jim Stark. There was, as he knew there would be, mail awaiting. He dialed up his combination and extracted two magazines in plain brown wrappers along with a letter from his sister in New York. When he placed his eye to the box for a final check, Marty heard, amid the aimless shuffle of feet, the click of determined leather heels walking directly toward him.

"Mr. Stark!"

Marty raised his eyes and discovered, less than three feet away, a short bald man in a tight blue suit. Behind him stood the scowling Marine. Blue Suit held a magazine with the thumb and index finger of each hand as though presenting an item of obvious virulence. The magazine's plain brown mailing wrapper had been torn, revealing a cover photograph of a startlingly robust blonde lady hoisting a double-handful of D-cups.

"Does this belong to you?" Blue Suit asked.

CHAPTER THIRTY-FOUR

Granjack loudly tapped the passenger window with his index finger, a habit that always annoyed Jeff. "The company store sat over there, just this side of where the railroad tracks split. You got paid on Saturday in scrip, nobody else in town would take—"

"Scrip?" Jeff said, abruptly. "What's that?"

"I was tellin' you, damn it," the old man snorted. "The mill paid in scrip, money you had to spend at the company store. They sold food, clothes, medicine . . . bout everthin' but liquor."

"They printed their own money?" Jeff pulled up at the Stop sign at the railroad tracks. "Is that legal?"

"The company told you what the hell was legal." Another tap on the window. "Over yonder's where the mill school used to sit. Just beyond that loadin' dock. Where them trucks is parked."

Jeff glanced briefly and nodded. The old man stared out the truck's windshield and spoke quietly. "Shoulda been better'n fifty kids in school ever day. I can't remember ever seein' more'n a dozen at one time. Six and seven year-olds would work full days at the mill. Just ever onest in awhile come by the school. When you hit eleven or twelve, they'd run you off. Mama taught us three readin' and arithmetic, or we'd never learned. The more you knew, the less use the mill had for you."

Granjack lit a Camel with a shaking hand. "I got to where I couldn't tolerate bein' shut inside with them machines. Weren't long before I proved to be more trouble than the company cared to bear. I got into a scrape with the foreman's son, whipped his ass good. Mama sent me back up the mountain to her brother. Worked as a cook's helper till I was big enough to catch on with a loggin' crew."

Early Saturday morning, and the streets of Rockton were nearly empty. Jeff drove slowly out of town, listening with one ear to memories the old man had hoarded over the years. Repetition was frequent and the boy would tune out until Granjack struck off onto new ground.

Their mission that morning was one that both had long postponed. Timber was a complex and risky business. The fate of Stuart Lumber had always depended on Jack Stuart's ability to assess a plot of land, estimate the value of timber on it, and predict the cost in man and machine hours it would take to cut, haul and process it. That talent, and the guts to repeatedly risk your business on it, separated the boss man from the saw men. Jack had always assumed he'd have several years to teach his grandson the intricacies of cruising timber; his heart attack now threatened to reduce that education to one season.

They were headed to the Richard Mast property, the last site Jeff had worked on the previous summer. Ideally, the two would have gone to a new site, walked it off over the course of a week, and turned in a bid. But with Granjack unable to roam more than a hundred yards from the truck, the best they could do was drive as deeply as they could into a familiar site and discuss it with one foot on the truck bumper.

The Mast land was over a hundred-twenty acres on steep hillside. Jeff had no trouble recognizing the boundaries. As he pulled onto the old logging road, he despaired at the damage the property had accumulated in less than nine months. The land had looked ragged when they'd left it, but summer had helped cover their tracks. Now, scarred landscape and deep gullies separated the cut land from surrounding property. Mud slides had pushed over trees beyond the cut line and smothered the bushes and undergrowth in the bottom land. Much of the creek had filled in and was pooled, scummy and lifeless. Slab piles and sawdust mounds, the refuse of Stuart Lumber's makeshift pulpwood sawmills, loomed high and sprawled wide. No plant life would displace them for a generation or more.

Jeff had seen cut-over acreage all his life, but this was the first time he'd confronted land where he'd held the saw. He drove as far as the truck could climb up the washed-out road and parked it. "You recall," Granjack began, as he clambered out of the truck, "that we cut this in August on accounta the slope and the soil bein' the kinda greasy clay that won't take no more'n a tablespoon of water before it won't allow a truck in. You gotta set up your cuttin' so you got land to work from early spring to late fall.

For better than an hour, the old man hobbled around the truck pointing out variables of topography and soil, importance of access to water, the difficulties and expense of cutting roads to various bases, and getting trucks, skidders, gas sawmills and men into and out of those sites. He spent another hour ranking the quality and value of hickory, walnut, ash, beech and a dozen variety of oaks compared to the softer poplar and pine. The old man attempted to impart a hefty portion of fifty years of experience in a single morning. Both parties knew the task was impossible. Jeff understood about half of Granjack's cryptic instruction and remembered only a portion of that.

"Damn," Jeff said, "I always figured if they had to, Mom and Ab could handle all this."

"Once you tell Ab where to set up, he can run the crew good as any man. Your mama can handle the office, but she can't run the yard. The kinda men we hire ain't gonna listen to a woman unless she's naked or got a knife in her hand." The old man hauled himself up off the running board slowly, in sections. "I'm give out."

"You ever let Ab bid on a site?" Jeff asked, dearly hoping that it happened all the time.

"He never had a feel for it," Granjack said, as he spit out his tobacco. "That's the bossman's job. Two bad bids and you're out of business." When Jeff shook his head and sighed deeply, the old man knew he'd pushed it too far. "We already got two cuttin's lined up this year. One more'll get us by. You'll learn as you go along."

Exhausted, Granjack pulled himself into the truck. Jeff cranked the engine and stared out the windshield at the ravaged landscape. "How long will it take for this to grow back?"

"You won't see nothing but the start of it in your life," Granjack said, his voice sounding as depleted as the land. "We used to just cut off the best and drag it out by mule, or run it down the river in the spring. The big boys showed us how to make it pay. If you're gonna stay in business, this is how you do it."

"Does anyone ever replant?"

"Folks don't generally sell off their timber till their back's to the wall. They don't figure on bein' around for the second cut."

"Does it ever bother you?"

The old man stared out the windshield. Jeff backed the truck out and started the long, wordless trip home.

CHAPTER THIRTY-FIVE

"Will you need the car tonight?" Rose called from outside the cracked bathroom door.

"No," Jeff answered, "somebody's picking me up."

Rose could tell from the waft of Aqua Velva that Jeff had a date. She knew not to ask for a name. Her son had always guarded his privacy like a Mafia don and had grown even more serious and circumspect since Granjack's heart attack. She was proud of the way Jeff had taken to the business but could see it was taking a toll on him. She was glad he was finally getting out.

She felt guilty for even thinking it, but Granjack's heart attack had served a purpose. Although the illness hadn't curtailed the old man's appetite for whiskey and cigarettes entirely, it had slowed him down. And made him a little easier to live with. More importantly, it had shown Jeff that his future lay in Rockton. She knew her son had considered a number of paths that would lead far from home. She had seen Navy brochures, magazine clippings about New Orleans and Memphis and road maps with traced highways leading all the way across the country. There would be time for vacations and such when he was older and had learned the business. He would appreciate it more then anyway.

Rose walked to the living room and turned on the television. She sampled all three stations before settling on "Beat the Clock." Only after sitting down and resting her feet on the ottoman did she remember the task she'd planned for the evening. She couldn't start *that* project until Jeff left anyway.

When Jeff walked into the living room, freshly scrubbed and outfitted in shined penny-loafers, navy blue pants and starched white shirt, pride and love danced in Rose's heart, emotions she knew better than to voice. Mother and son feigned interest in the TV as a contestant with a spoon in his mouth attempted to dig marshmallows out of a mountain of Jello.

"Going to a movie?" Rose asked pleasantly.

"Yeah," Jeff said, his fingers drumming a steady rhythm on the couch arm. "I think we're going to see *Bus Stop* in Oak City."

"Isn't that on uptown?"

Jeff shrugged. Nobody with a car dated in Rockton. The sound of a car horn launched Jeff from his seat, and, after a quick peck on his mother's cheek, through the door. Rose walked quickly to the window. Her heart bounced off her kneecaps when she spotted the Parrish's station wagon. *Damn!* She knew things were going *too* smoothly.

As Rose prepared a cup of her special-blend tea, she counseled herself as she knew Madam would: "If you command him, he will defy you. You must trust that he will figure it out himself." Perhaps it would take only one date to remind Jeff of what a little harpy Vicky Parrish was. At any rate, she had her own problem to work on that night.

She returned to the front room with her cup of tea, sat down and pulled a Big Chief notepad from beneath her chair. Throughout the winter, Rose had struggled with the "Secret Admirer" revealed to her by Madam La'Moor. In the midst of her own soul-searching, Granjack's illness had served as a sharp reminder that *everyone's* days were finite and valuable. The icy wall of denial and guilt she had reflexively erected slowly melted with the advent of spring and the old man's recovery.

Still, she admitted to no more than a clinical interest in fingering the Mystery Man. A devout mystery buff who regretted missing an episode of "Dragnet" as dearly as a Sunday church service, she began a systematic search for the person who was spending a disturbing amount of time thrashing around in her mind. After a quick scan of the small stable of eligible manhood in town failed to turn up an obvious suspect, Rose resorted to scientific methodology.

On page one of her notebook, Rose had written the name of every religious and secular organization she belonged to, as well as the stores and public areas she frequented. The list spilled over the city limits of Rockton into Oak City, Richardson and surrounding towns, and included both business and social groups.

On the second page Rose recopied those institutional headings and wrote the names of every single or widowed man who might conceivably be gazing lovingly from afar. She had labeled a column "Divorced," but so far had been unable to include anyone from that scarlet tribe. As she crossed the room to cut off the television, she resolved to finalize her list that night and move on with the search. She quickly wrote down three names of "justified" divorcées—one who had "good reason" to leave his wife, two who were left by bad women. The most remarkable aspect of the exercise was the discovery of how many men she knew.

Rose modeled her attitude on the dispassionate Joe Friday: "Just the fact's, Ma'am." After eliminating the patently ridiculous and undesirable, Rose was left with five names. Vowing to pursue the investigation without favoritism or prejudice, she resolved to begin her formal inquiry at church the next morning. The congregation of the First Baptist Church contained a couple of suspicious "Johns," one of whom just might be peeping from a distance.

CHAPTER THIRTY-SIX

Neither Jeff nor Vicky would ever forget that Saturday night. After leaving the Stuart home in a cloud of lust, they ate steak at The Embers, saw half of *Bus Stop*, and, with less foreplay than generally attends the coupling of unregistered pets, got it on in the reclined back seat of the Police Chief's car.

Since Vicky had designated time, place, and agenda, she was somewhat burdened by expectation. There was even a moment when she nearly backed out, but neither party believed her slight protest. She might as well have attempted to stop a runaway train by waving a handkerchief.

The experience was "glorious," Vicky decided afterwards, though not quite all she had hoped or expected at the moment. There was pain involved, although less than she had steeled herself for. Oddly, she had felt the experience had been both too short *and* too long. Somehow, there had to be more to it.

Vicky's fear of discovery and haste to get her clothes back on robbed Jeff of the opportunity to redeem himself with a second entry. He fought back the urge to ask her not to "hold that first one against me," knowing it would sound like an apology. Vicky could not be trusted with that kind of leverage.

As Vicky groped for her clothing, Jeff flicked on the dome light. He was rewarded with a vision of resplendent nudity that he knew would grace his final breath.

"The postal guy kept threatening to call the cops in," Marty whispered across the lunchroom table, "talking about how many federal laws I'd broken, and how they could send me to prison *forever.* This huge friggin' Marine stood behind him pounding his fist into his hand like he wanted to beat a confession outa me. They kept accusing me of selling the magazines to other kids. Finally, I told them who my old man was. They called him up, and when he got there, things *really* got crazy. When the Rev saw that stuff, I thought he was gonna have a stroke. He didn't know whether to shit or go blind."

Jeff, with a loaded fork in hand, stared open-mouthed across the table. He'd taken only one bite of his beans and franks when Marty sat down and began unloading his remarkable tale. As classmates passed within a foot of the table, Marty leaned even closer and continued.

"Turns out, the postman and my old man had both served on some church board years ago, so they kinda knew each other. The old man started telling him how a twenty year prison sentence wouldn't really help my morals all that much, and would likely destroy any shot I had at going to Bible College and becoming a preacher. Then the Rev tells him that the scandal would likely kill my mother. I'm sitting there acting sad and repentant while the Marine's scowling at me like he wants to bite my head off and drink my blood.

"That went on for more'n an hour before the mailman decided not to call the feds in. He said that *under no condition* was I to enter Helms Baptist. He was a trustee there and he didn't want *my type* on *his* campus. I damn near gave him an 'Amen' on that, but then this Marine grunts out that there's a gung-ho military school less'n fifty miles away that specialized in straightening out hard cases like me. *Bismarck Academy.*"

Jeff closed his eyes and exhaled fear and dismay. Every kid in the state knew about Bismarck Academy. Comparable only to Stonewall Jackson Training School—a state-run hell-hole for incorrigible throw-away minors—Bismarck had a fearsome reputation for Teutonic devotion to excessive authority and *compulsory* education.

"I nearly browned-out," Marty continued breathlessly. "First thing I knew, all three of 'em were slapping each other on the back, trading secret handshakes and talking about what a great idea that was. By the time we got home the old man was certain that sending me to Bismarck was *his* idea. Quick as we got in the door, he called 'em up, and told 'em to hold a place for me in the fall."

"But they're not going to press charges against you?" Jeff asked.

"Nah. But I had to sacrifice the porno-trunk out in the bunker. Years of research and collecting...gone," Marty moaned, tears forming in the corners of his eyes. "But I've still got the really prime stuff in the closet. I can build the collection back up. None of the bunker stuff was irreplaceable. I'll have to lay low for awhile, but I've still got my contacts. And I've got the rest of my life to work on it."

Jeff watched in amazement as purpose and resolution flowed back into Marty. Fresh from a history exam, Jeff briefly cast his friend as young Adolf Hitler surveying Germany from the ruins of the World War I and envisioning the glory to come in the Third Reich. Nah, Jeff decided. He's just a kid with some tit magazines.

"You're eighteen," Jeff said, taking his second bite of lunch. "Why don't you just tell your old man you won't go to Bismarck."

"Yeah," Marty said, detaching himself from his vision of standing triumphantly atop a mountain of mammaries. "That's what I'm gonna do. But I gotta wait until this post office thing cools off. Right now, I don't have any bargaining position."

Marty checked his watch and stood up. "I've got a sewing project I have to finish or I won't graduate." A grim smile trudged across his face. "Don't that flip your lid? They won't let me in military school unless I pass home economics."

As Jeff finished his cold meal, he puzzled briefly over Marty's situation. Why, he wondered, do good Christian folks think they can teach their sons morality by shipping them off to institutions whose stated purpose is to train those boys to obey orders without question in order to slaughter the boys of other nations?

Strange shit, Bubba.

Jeff and Vicky maintained a hectic and highly stimulated routine throughout the spring. Every Friday and Saturday night, and as many weeknights as they could work out, they would park at a remote location, and jazz, jive, boogie, and rock'n'roll with the joy and sublime conviction that surely no couple had ever done it, or could do it, half so well; if they could, why would anyone ever do anything else?

While the physical release was profound, the ritual and consummation appeased a deeper need in Jeff. The boy, whose movements from breakfast to bed were scripted by the demands of lumberyard and school, discovered that the only time he became an actor in his own life was when settled upon Vicky's delicious form.

Although, for the first time in their long relationship, they were both working toward a common goal—finding time and opportunity to make the-beast-with-two-backs—they still found bones of contention to rag over. Characteristic of the perverse and contradictory nature of young love, the opposition of their parents drove them together when indifference might well have allowed them to part. Vicky, sparing Jeff the possibility of confrontation with her father, always met Jeff's car at the curb; red-clay Romeo waited at the lumberyard when fair Juliet drove. Vicky chose not to tell her boyfriend that the Chief's service revolver always received a spirited cleaning on date nights.

CHAPTER THIRTY-SEVEN

"Grab the bush ax," Granjack shouted from inside his house. "I'll be out presently."

Jeff walked to the shed and pulled the ax from its assigned station. Every tool in its place. He stroked the edge with a file to knock off the sprinkle of rust that had formed over the winter, but the blade was keen. Granjack never put away a tool without sharpening it.

"Where to?" Jeff asked.

"Spring house," the old man said, hobbling off the porch. It was two o'clock on a Sunday afternoon, but Jeff could smell whiskey on the old man's breath.

Jeff rested the bush ax on his shoulder as they crossed the field behind the rock house. The exhilarating May day had summoned all form of wild life. Song birds, crows and hawks eyed each other warily in the dark blue sky, and Jeff nearly stepped on a trembling baby rabbit. The grass field eventually gave way to alder, low brush and scrub around the creek. The kudzu was just gaining a toe-hold that would allow it to rage rampant by mid-summer. Jeff used the bush ax to cut back the ravenous thorns of the multiflora rose that grew like a barbed contagion throughout the field. Granjack had long maintained that, left unchecked, kudzu and multiflora would inherit the earth and kick the meek's ass as well.

"You boys used to keep a deep path wore down from your back door to the spring," Granjack said quietly.

Once he'd breached the thick barrier beside the creek, Jeff 's ax work was done. There was a large clearing around the spring house. The grove of walnut and other hardwoods effectively denied sunlight that underbrush needed. Inside the squat, cinder block, tin-roofed spring house, the pump that provided water to Granjack's house whined quietly. When he stepped inside the cool, serene oasis, Jeff was overcome by the sensation that he was ten years old and might soon be ambushed by Chuck and Marty posing as cowboys or Indians, Germans or GIs.

Granjack lowered himself to his hands and knees and scooped a handful of spring water to his mouth. "Sweetest water in the county," he said, and sampled another.

Jeff cupped both hands and drank deeply. He was surprised at how *uncomplicated* the water tasted. He'd grown used to the chemicals that teemed in the water sanitized to city standards.

"We used to have picnics, Daisy and me, down here. It was beautiful. Seems like there was more rhododendron back then...and mountain laurel. See a deer 'bout ever time we come." The old man sat down on the bank and rested his boots on a rock that jutted from the creek.

Jeff leaped across the narrow stream and rested his foot on a decaying oak tree that had fallen more than a decade before. He'd sat with his back against it many times, cooking hot dogs and marshmallows over a campfire. He stood with his back to the creek, looking for old hiding places and landmarks. The rock cliff looked smaller, less perilous, the distance from the spring to the "big gully" far shorter. The climb to the ridge, once a morning's trip demanding intense planning and careful packing, Jeff figured now to be little more than an hour's hike.

"Damn, that's cold," Granjack said.

When Jeff turned around, he found the old man wiggling his bare toes in the swift, shallow creek. The boy would scarcely have been more surprised had he found his grandfather dancing naked in the window of the Western Auto.

"Sit down," the old man said. He appeared uneasy, even embarrassed.

Jeff sat on the oak log. A shallow wave of discomfort spread from his stomach through his body. He shared his grandfather's aversion to intimacy, perhaps had inherited it from the old man.

"See that walnut tree over there?" The old man pointed to a tall rough-barked tree, about thirty inches in diameter.

"Yeah."

"No branches less'n twelve, thirteen feet off the ground."

Jeff nodded.

"Your daddy could climb a tree like that."

Jeff looked at the tree then at Granjack. He shook his head.

"It's the truth," the old man said, still pointing. "He'd get someone to bet him five dollars he couldn't, and he'd take off his shoes and get a runnin' go at it, and he'd climb it like a damn monkey. I never seen the like of it. He's where you got your runnin' from."

"Did he play sports?"

"When he was a boy. Football, baseball. By the time he got to high school, he wouldn't listen to nobody much. Nobody that yelled at him, for damn sure."

Jeff's knowledge of his father consisted almost entirely of a handful of stories his mother had repeated endlessly. Some were affectionate, more were cautionary, but he knew them all by heart. He'd heard vague, usually indirect comments by older men that his father had been a fast runner and, by all accounts, a good-natured hellion. Once, at the poolroom, after Jeff had made a tough combination shot on the money ball, the rack man had said: "You'll never be the pool shot your daddy was." But Shaky Ben had shuffled off to set a loose rack at another table without explaining the remark.

"There's things you need to hear," Granjack said. "I reckon most of what you know is what your mama's told you. That's well and good. But everone's got their own way of seein' things. Your daddy loved your ma something fierce. I reckon she was the first woman he ever chased that could say 'no' to him. He gave up a lotta high livin' for her. He knew what kinda man she wanted...and deserved.

"Now, when you were born, your daddy was the proudest man alive. He wanted to take you everwhere, show you to everone. That was back durin' the worst of the polio, and your ma was afraid to let you outa the house. That was just one thing they disputed. They saw the world altogether differnt. Will would wrassle a bear if it defied him, and your ma was..." Granjack searched the eddying creek, "she was cautious. If either one of 'em coulda broke over a little, it woulda made things easier. But they got along. They was in love."

The old man pulled a plug of tobacco from his overalls and shaved a piece from it. He wanted to stop talking, go home, take a drink. His voice grew flat and hollow, as though he was trying to keep his distance from the memory. "The way it was...Will went from one day bein' the wildest buck in the woods to bein' married with a baby comin'. That and workin' a fifty—sixty hour week besides. He knew I expected him to take the business. Rose wanted a big family. He saw all that laid out in front of him, and he won't even twenty-one years old.

"You know your daddy died in a car wreck. Your ma always figured he'd been drinkin', but don't nobody know for sure. It was an accident...so much as anything is. If we'd stepped back and studied it, we might coulda seen it comin'. The thing was, everbody did the best they could—did what they *had* to do. Your ma wanted a steady, stay-at-home church-man, and I wanted a son who could take what I started and build on it.

"The difference between me and Will was that nobody ever expected a damn thing from me." Granjack spat and shook his head. "Hell, if I'da had to choose when I was twenty, I'da been a bootlegger and like as not never got married."

Granjack pulled his feet from the water and dried them with his pocket handkerchief. Jeff sorted through the information and his emotions as the old man slowly put on his socks and boots.

"Why are you tellin' me this?" the boy asked.

"Don't know that I ort to," Granjack said, shaking his head. "I don't know what's best for you no more'n anybody else does."

The old man gave up on tying his boots and made a clumsy attempt at standing. Jeff leaped across the creek and helped him up. On the walk back, the boy tried to formulate questions. He couldn't find the words.

When they reached Granjack's door, Jeff asked, "Will you tell me more about my father?"

"When I can," the old man said.

That afternoon, while Rose shopped for groceries, Jeff removed the photo album from the overhead shelf of his mother's closet. Sitting in his room, the boy examined the familiar pictures of his mother and father with new eyes.

Madam La'Moor and Rose Stuart sat in kitchen chairs on the covered front porch and watched the spring rain alternately caress then pound the lush vegetation that had appeared unbidden, at Madam's doorstep. Rose shivered when a westerly breeze carried a fine mist that settled on her face and bare arms. Madam could see that her guest wanted to take their conversation inside. After enduring the longest, coldest winter since her girlhood in Pennsylvania, the seer would not be driven from her porch by anything short of a monsoon.

In Delphina's lap rested copies of "Amusement Business" and "Billboard." She had been scoping the trades for carny openings. Time was running out; most of the majors had secured their palmists already. Still, there were openings. Particularly now that Gypsies had fallen out of fashion. The heading, "Mitt camp, no Gypsies," popped up in both magazines. She had circled several. The longer she waited, the more likely it became that she could catch on only with a rag-bag outfit. A decision had to be made quickly.

"Business has been off this spring," Rose said, breaking a long silence. "Not many people building. If it doesn't get better soon...I don't know what we'll do."

"Have you considered selling the lumberyard?" Madam La'Moor asked innocently. The primal drumbeat on the tin roof demanded she raise her voice.

"Sell it?" Rose sputtered. She nearly dropped her tea cup. "We can't sell it. It's Jeff's security."

"*Se-cur-i-ty.*" Madam tendered the four syllables to the storm and received a roll of distant thunder in reply. "What exactly is *security*?"

"It's protection. Safety," Rose said, annoyed. She hated it when Madam did this.

"And it protects you from...?" Madam asked.

"Danger, fear...anxiety," Rose responded.

"So owning this business has kept *you* free of anxiety?"

"Well, not me," Rose admitted. She laughed nervously. "I'm kind of a lost-cause. It'll be different for Jeff." Lightning flashed over the trees and thunder rattled the tin roof.

Both women stared out into the rain as angry squirrels chattered protest from the trees. They spoke briefly, appreciatively, about the small garden Rose had helped Madam plant just beyond the porch. Six tomato plants, four pole-beans, two mounds of cucumbers, one squash, one cantaloupe. She visited them twice a day to appreciate their growth. For many years, the only vegetable gardens she'd seen had been from the passenger window of a speeding automobile. Madam resisted the urge to speak of the six strong hemp plants that grew wantonly behind the house. Madam was continually discovering the benefits of permanence and home ownership.

"Besides," Rose said, after a full three minute pause, "nobody buys a lumberyard. You either build it up or you're born into it. If you've got enough money to buy one, you'd be crazy to."

Delphina contemplated the swirling clouds and waited for Rose to broach the subject that had chased her into the path of an electrical storm.

"There is something I wanted to ask you, Delphina," Rose said quietly, staring off the side of the porch.

"Please do."

"Do you remember a while back when you said that someone, a man, was paying attention to me? 'A secret admirer,' you called him."

"I remember."

"Is the man in your vision kinda short? You see, I've always been partial to tall men. At least taller than me. And this man," Rose continued, lowering her voice, "well, we have a religious problem."

"A religious problem?"

"He's a Methodist and I'm a Baptist. All my life I've heard these mixed marriages just don't last. I don't want to start something..." Rose's voice trailed off, as she gazed into the storm.

"That description would be consistent with the vision I had," Delphina assured. "Even though he is attracted to you, he is a shy man and may need some slight encouragement."

"I'm certainly not chasing anyone," Rose said indignantly, rocking faster.

"All that is required is a smile, a tilt of the head."

Rose nodded. She didn't like pushy, grabby men anyway.

"Now I have a question," Madam said.

"Yes."

"I have found little green worms on my tomatoes. What can I do about the little beasties?"

CHAPTER THIRTY-EIGHT

CONGRATULATIONS CLASS OF '57

In the festively decorated home of the Rockton Chief of Police, "Love Letters In The Sand" poured like aural treacle over a half-dozen swaying teen couples. Jeff Stuart sat in the kitchen in a rickety folding chair and balanced a silver dollar-sized paper plate of cheese, crackers and tiny sausages in his lap. "If they play one more Pat Boone song," he swore to Chuck Brady, "I'm gonna stomp the damn record player."

Vicky and selected friends had spent hour upon hour of the next-to-last week of school preparing the Parrish home for Saturday night's Big Party. The graduates were provided three rooms, lit for interrogation, with food, games, music and enough fruit punch to float a battleship. Apparently the price of the Chief's absence was Vicky's promise to resolutely patrol the area for beer and ardent spirits. She took on the job with an enthusiasm that was surely genetic; already she had sniffed out a cooler of beer in a car trunk before a church key ever struck tin.

"It's gonna be a long fuckin' night," Chuck groaned. The tackle had brought Sandy, a cheerleader, even though neither cared at all for the other. Vicky had decreed that you had to have a date from the senior class and an invitation to get in the door—there would be no stags, wall-flowers, or underclassmen to drag the gala down.

"They're playin' this game where you have to tell secrets about yourself," Chuck said, peeking into the living room. "You got anything to drink?" he asked urgently.

Jeff shook his head. As the ostensible host of the party, he had pledged to forswear alcohol for the night. The promise, made in the bright, objective light of day, now seemed tragically naive. It would have been so easy, he mourned, to stash a pint of liquor under the front seat of Rose's station wagon. He should have anticipated the smothering gloom that cloaked this party; the colored bunting, posters, and balloons hung throughout the house served as lipstick on a corpse.

When Marty Ryder waltzed through the back door with a full-sized inflatable rubber doll with bright yellow mop-hair, and an "invitation" written on a brown paper bag, Jeff felt the shackles fall from his spirit. Marty blinked as though staring into the Sahara sun as he glanced around the shimmering room full of somber, squeaky-clean couples. "I didn't catch the name of the deceased," he shouted across the room to Jeff. "Anyone I know?"

Marty flipped off the overhead light switch at the door before loping, Groucho Marx-style, across the room. He carried his date under his arm, her body parallel to the floor. Marty introduced "Ruby" around the room and turned to the two desperate faces beside him.

"You got anything to drink?" Jeff whispered.

"I got a fifth of Wild Turkey in the trunk. Would you care for a toot?"

While Cody picked a tune in the living room, and Naomi read *Confidential* magazine in bed, the cops surrounded the house. Cody's place wasn't all that hard to surround, even for four hick cops, since there was only a front and back door, and Blackjack had never been replaced. Chief Parrish and Officer Bradshaw were going to kick in the front while Officers Sigmon and Teague covered the back. If Naomi hadn't turned the radio up so loud, or if Cody hadn't shut the large single pane window to keep out the night air, they likely would have heard the clomping around outside. All they heard was a fierce pounding on the front door and: "OPEN UP, HUNTER! WE GOT A WARRANT!"

Chief Parrish did not wait for an answer to the summons—two kicks and the door flew open. Cody turned toward the back door but froze when he heard glass shatter in the kitchen. He caught a glimpse of Chief Parrish in the hallway, gun drawn.

"HALT! HANDS UP!" Parrish shouted.

Cody wrapped his arms around his face and dove through the window. Chief Parrish squeezed off three shots at Cody's fleeing shadow before he disappeared into the forest.

"And these two guys," Marty related breathlessly, "Sol Paradise and Dean

Moriarty, they don't care where they're going, just so long as they're in a car and moving. But, you see, it's not that it doesn't matter where they go—because they're definitely chasing *something*—it's just they know that that *something* is as likely to be in a truck stop in Iowa as in a jazz club in Oakland, California. The thing is, the more places you look, the more likely you are to bump into it—even though you gotta know that you can't hold it, cause *its* gotta move too. You understand?"

The bulk of Marty's audience, drawn like bored moths to a roman candle, nodded agreement. He'd just received a new book from his sister and had read it straight through. Eager to spread the gospel, he took a quick drink of his spiked punch, and jumped back *On the Road.*

Jeff was pulled away from the narrative by an urgent tugging on his elbow. "Has Marty been drinking?" Vicky asked, as she led Jeff toward the kitchen.

"Highly likely," Jeff said coolly, as he disengaged Vicky's hand. "He's having too much fun to be sober."

"Are *you* drinking?" Vicky demanded.

"Yes," Jeff said. Just not fast enough.

Vicky thrust her arms in the air, palms upward, appealing to an inattentive God. "What if Daddy comes home and finds all this going on?" she asked desperately.

"You said he wouldn't be back before midnight," Jeff said calmly. "At this pace, Marty'll flame out before eleven."

Someone turned over the stack of forty-fives on the record player, cranked up the volume, and Connie Francis begged for attention. Accepting the challenge, Marty reached back into his gene pool and found the voice of three generations of Ryder preachers.

"I saw the best minds of my generation
destroyed by madness, starving hysterical naked,
dragging themselves through the Negro streets at dawn
looking for an angry fix—"

Vicky, who had never been out-shouted in her own house, defended her turf. Pointing at Marty as though he were the villain in a 19th century melodrama, she shouted, "*He*'s not supposed to be here. He wasn't *invited!*"

Marty did not back down:

"—Angel-headed hipsters burning for the
ancient heavenly connection to the starry
dynamo in the machinery of night—"

"MARTY, SHUT UP!" Vicky screamed in a voice that had peeled paint off those walls before. The room fell silent, save for the RIPPPPP of a phonograph needle scraping across a wounded record. Only then did the pounding at the front door echo through the house.

Everyone grabbed a lungful of air and held it as Vicky crossed the room at a trot. She opened the door a cautious six inches and spoke quietly into the spring night. Jeff was lamenting the diminished volume in the Wild Turkey bottle when a shouted, "Jeff Stuart" cleaved the silent room like a curse through Communion. When Vicky tried to shut the door, Naomi pushed her aside like a bratty child and walked directly to Jeff.

"I gotta talk to ya," she whispered urgently. "Let's get outta heah."

Sweat broke out on Jeff's forehead. His throat allowed only quick, inadequate breaths. He took a step forward and found Vicky Parrish, feet widespread, hands on hips, guarding the door. "If you leave with her, Jeffrey Stuart," Vicky said, in a voice that lacked only volume to qualify as hysterical, "I swear I'll never speak to you again."

Marty took a hard look at Naomi, decked out in skin-tight blue jeans and halter top, no bra, and whistled low, "Give *me* that choice," he said loudly.

Jeff placed his hand on Naomi's elbow and walked her out the door. They moved quickly across the street and stood under a tall oak that shielded them from the full moon and a streetlight. Naomi grabbed Jeff's starched shirt with both fists and related in short, clipped bursts the story of the cop's forced entry and Cody's escape. "I heard 'em say he was bleedin'. When all of 'em chased after him, I snuck out to the car," she concluded.

"Why are they after him?" Jeff asked.

"It's gotta be something to do with that car theft thing they nailed Sam on. Sam the drummer. He musta pulled Cody into it."

"Is he guilty?"

"It don't matter, goddamn it." Naomi said, banging her fists against Jeff's chest. "If Parrish catches him, he'll shoot him, or beat him to death."

Jeff felt Naomi's hands slide around to his back. His shirt grew wet with her tears. The voice that drifted up from his chest was plaintive as a prayer. "You gotta help him, Jeff."

Jeff grabbed Naomi by the shoulder, held her at arm's length, and spoke into her face. "What the hell am I supposed to do?"

"Help him," she sobbed.

"Like *he* helped me? Like *you* helped me?"

Tears poured from eyes that could not meet his. "I'm sorry, I'm sorry." Naomi took a deep breath and raised her head. "Jeff," she said, "I'm pregnant."

Jeff's mind spun in confusion. He pushed her away and sat down on the wet grass. "Is it—"

"It's not yours," she said. "It happened after...us."

Jeff stared up at the figure looming over him. "Cody...?"

"He's cool with it. I mean . . . he's coming around." She helped him to his feet.

"What can I do?" Jeff asked. He began to pace. "Do you expect me to go chargin' into those hills...try to pull him out with every cop in town chasin' him? That's crazy! How am I supposed to find—" Jeff's words and movement stopped abruptly.

"What?"

Jeff knew as quickly as the thought struck him that he had no choice. He took two deep breaths. "I know where he is."

CHAPTER THIRTY-NINE

As Jeff raced down the dirt road in Cody's Ford, the flaws in his half-baked rescue plan began exploding like land mines inside his skull. He and Naomi had left the party in opposite directions, as witnessed by several couples making out in cars and on the Parrish lawn, and then swapped cars outside of town. His intention was to distance his mother's car from his grossly illegal mission. He now realized that by driving the Ford, he had forsaken any presumption of innocence if stopped by the police *before* he found Cody. And, if Naomi was spotted in Rose's station wagon, even the local fuzz could figure something was rotten in Rockton.

The exhilaration of once again becoming an active player in his life ebbed quickly. With traffic as scarce as virtue on those back roads, Jeff knew every car the cops spotted would be trailing a dust cloud of guilt. He briefly wondered if the bourbon he'd drunk had influenced his decision to take on this harebrained venture. At that moment, the boy wished he had either taken one drink less or one drink more.

He desperately clung to the hope that the police would decide that tracking a man, even a wounded man, at night through a forest familiar to prey but foreign to hunter would be a waste of time and energy. Surely they could see it was more reasonable to wait until daylight. As the adrenaline that had fueled him faded, Jeff recognized that the Chief, having tasted blood, was as unlikely as a shark to exercise patience.

Gliding quietly without headlights, depending on the full moon for illumination, the Ford sailed like a ghostly galleon between patches of gauzy light as he weaved through the familiar maze of back roads. He cut the wheel abruptly to the right and left to test the car's handling. Crisp. The afternoon rain had not impaired traction and kept his dust trail to a minimum. Having neither seen nor heard another car since leaving the paved road, he prayed that the police would stay bunched around the Hunter homestead.

As Jeff drew within a hundred yards of the old logging trail where he planned to stash the Ford, the hideous shriek of a police siren approaching at pursuit speed bored a hole through his brain and melted his spinal column. Stunned, then panicked, the boy mashed the gas pedal to the floor and charged toward the siren and the logging trail. He nearly ripped the bottom out of the Ford when he whipped the car hard-right over the washed-out red clay ditch then slid it broadside behind a sawdust pile.

The advancing siren was the drone of an army of wasps swarming forth to rip the boy's sweating face off the cool seat cover and carry him straight to Hell. He held his breath as the rumbling machine slid heavily around the sharp curve no more than a stone's throw away. As Doom approached, Jeff closed his eyes and prayed to a loving God to spare him. The police car thundered past, its siren changing pitch as it fled into the night.

Relief washed over his body. When he opened his eyes, he saw amid the clutter on the floorboard, Cody's Panama hat. Once immaculate, the hat looked as though it had been stomped into dirty, misshapen submission then denied a decent burial. The sight bothered him in a way he didn't understand and had no time to consider. He crawled out of the passenger door and submitted to an overwhelming urge to piss.

As he crouched low in the sawdust, his back against the rear tire, Jeff considered driving, or abandoning the car and walking, out of the forest and back home. But he would have to reclaim his mother's car and explain his betrayal to Naomi. His mind spun in confusion and doubt. Ultimately, it was the vision of Cody Hunter shivering and bleeding in the dark that dragged him into the woods.

The full moon could not penetrate the forest canopy. Jeff stumbled over roots and rocks and fell into gullies as he searched for the landmark necessary to continue his odyssey. The dead silence of the forest was interrupted only by an occasional siren, and, finally, the faint sound of water gliding over rocks. He followed the stream uphill until he reached the clearing.

He jerked open the door to Dooley's cave and found himself staring down the business end of a twelve-gauge shotgun. The dim lantern that hung from the ceiling cast an eerie orange glow on Cody's sweating face as he sat on the cot, his bare back against the dirt wall, holding Dooley's shotgun unsteadily against his shoulder. Jeff could not take his eyes off the wavering gun barrel.

"What took you so long?" Cody asked wearily. The shotgun fell heavily across his lap.

Jeff turned up the lantern's wick for more light. "Where'd they hit you?"

"Them lame-dicks couldn't shoot theirselves in the ass if they sat on the gun," Cody snorted bitterly. "But I took a beatin' when I dove through the window." He pointed to the bloody rags wrapped around his left arm.

Cody had torn up his shirt and used the strips to bind his wounds. Jeff gasped when he peeled away the bandages and found two long vertical gashes. They oozed blood so red it looked purple. The boy fought off the dizziness that threatened to bounce his spinning head off the dirt floor. He pulled the demijohn of whiskey from under the cot. "Can you bear this?" he asked, pulling the cork from the jug.

Cody extended his left arm. Jeff poured liquor over the wounds.

"Aieee! Mother Mary and her sister, Maggie!" Cody exhaled the measured scream in a voice that would not carry beyond the cave door. Jeff ripped up the blanket lying on the cot. He soaked it in alcohol, and tied it around the arm as tightly as he felt he could without cutting off circulation. He tied the ends of a three-foot strip and slipped the loop over Cody's head for a sling.

"Water," Cody said quietly, pointing to a canteen on the dirt floor. Jeff held the metal canteen against Cody's mouth, and then took a long drink himself. A police siren shrieked in the distance.

"We gotta get your ass outa here," Jeff said. He looked Cody straight in the eye. "Can you make it?"

"Oh, hell, yeah," Cody said lightly. "I'm up for a little moonlight stroll."

Cody sagged heavily when he stood, but Jeff slipped under the wounded man's good right arm. They had barely staggered out of the cave and into the night when they heard a sound that nearly drove Jeff to his knees in despair.

BAYOOOO! BRUUU! BAYOOOO! BEYO! BEYO! BRUUU!

"Oh, god, no," Jeff moaned, "not dogs."

"Sounds like at least three of 'em," Cody said. "I reckon we better step it up and go."

No time to follow the stream, Jeff thought, as panic drove the fugitives through the dark forest. Cody could manage only a limping trot, and twice they fell to the ground in a tangle. The keening of the hell-hounds pushed them forward. With each step, the dogs grew closer, Cody grew heavier, and Jeff grew more unsure of his bearing. "We're almost there, we're almost there," Jeff chanted, long after he'd stopped believing it.

When the two stepped off a bank and fell four feet into a red clay gully, Cody nearly passed out from pain and fatigue. As he lay on his bare stomach, his throbbing left arm pinned under him, the fugitive knew that everything would work itself out if only he were allowed to rest. The pain, the dogs, the law would all disappear into his dreams.

Jeff's head thumped heavily against the hard, dry clay in the gully. His mind, already reeling from panic and confusion, was stunned into immobility and hopelessness. As he laid in the gully, he realized he had no idea where the road was, where the car was. He could drag Cody no farther. His only hope was putting as much distance as possible between himself and the felon. Parrish isn't looking for me, he reasoned. He doesn't even know I'm out here.

As Jeff climbed up the bank on his hands and knees, the baying of the dogs was joined by a whine so faint that Jeff first thought it was in his mind. But the siren's volume increased so quickly and passed so close that Jeff reflexively flattened himself.

He slid back into the gully. "Get up, Cody, we can make it." Jeff shook Cody into consciousness, got him to his knees and slipped under him. Carrying Cody on his back, Jeff stumbled in the direction where the siren had passed.

The hound's long deep howls turned to excited yips. "They're at the cave," Cody whispered. Seconds later the baying began anew—louder, deeper, and coming on strong. Jeff staggered out of the woods, Cody on his back, less than fifty yards from the Ford. But the dogs gained ground. Moving along the shadow of the tree line, Jeff closed his mind to the pain and forced his legs to move forward.

He unloaded Cody's unconscious body into the passenger's seat, raced around the Ford, and slid under the steering wheel. Slamming the car into reverse, he nearly backed over the lead hound. The dog jumped and wailed outside his window as Jeff popped the clutch and spun onto the dirt road. In the rear view mirror, he saw three shadows charge out of the woods—one unmistakably Police Chief Ray Parrish.

"Able One to all units! Able One to all units! Come in! Over!" Chief Parrish shouted breathlessly into the squad car radio. Immediately after Parrish had stumbled out of the forest, Officer Joe Sigmon rounded the curve, siren wailing. The deputy slid his unit so close to the road's shoulder that men and dogs had to scramble up the bank to avoid being hit. Parrish forced Sigmon out of the driver's seat with a good cussing, and left the dogs and their handlers choking on his dust as he spun the squad car sideways in furious pursuit.

"Hunter's headed south on Duck Creek Road in a 1950 Ford—y'all know the goddamn car." The Chief shouted to be heard over his siren. "He's headed torge the Bowman Road and likely out to Highway Ninety. Block him off, Teague. Over!"

"Gotcha Chief. Over!" Teague replied.

"Oh, hell," Jeff groaned, as the southern breeze delivered the police siren through his open window. Driving with trembling hands and nerves stretched tight as banjo strings, Jeff took advantage of a brief straightaway to snatch the crumpled Panama hat off the floorboard and jam it on his head. Granted, not much of a disguise, but all he had.

He glanced at his passenger, hoping to see signs of life. Cody was wedged between the passenger seat and the door, his head slumped to his chest. His bad arm, blood seeping through the bandage, rested on his stomach. Jeff's eyes wandered over Cody a moment longer than the road allowed. The Ford's left rear tire slid into the ditch, and the fender slammed heavily against the dirt bank. Frantically wrestling the car back onto the road, Jeff's panic was interrupted by a mumble so welcome he couldn't believe he'd heard it. "Cody?"

"Sposed to keep it *between* the ditches," Cody said, in a hoarse whisper. With obvious effort he rolled his head to the right and propped it against the window. "Where are we?" he asked.

"Duck Creek," Jeff replied.

"Tryin' to get to Ninety?"

No time to answer. As Jeff rounded the curve, he cut the wheel hard right onto Bowman Road. As the first glint of moonlight reflected off the squad car pulled broadside and blocking the middle two-thirds of the road struck Jeff's eye, he hit the brake and jerked the wheel sharply to the left.

When Officer Rufe Teague, standing behind his unit, saw the Ford sliding toward him, he abandoned his post. He leaped over the side ditch and didn't turn around until he heard the crunch of metal on metal and shattering glass. The Ford's rear end struck the squad car's front fender a brutal lick—but it kept the Ford out of the side ditch.

There was a moment, just after impact and before Jeff shifted to low and popped the clutch, when the Ford was motionless. Rufe Teague raised his firearm and pointed the barrel at the Ford's driver's side window less than fifty feet away. Teague, the best marksman in the department, considered blowing that silly hat off the driver's head. He decided not to. He thought about shooting out a tire, but decided against that too. If he hit the gas tank the car might blow up. He'd known Cody all his life, shared liquor and poker with him at the

American Legion. Officer Teague watched the Ford fishtail back onto Duck Creek Road spraying gravel, dust and panic. Teague edged his wounded unit off to the side of the road, radioed in the Ford's position and called it a night.

The siren had gained steadily and now sounded to Jeff like it had crawled up his tailpipe. When the Ford reached the end of a forty-yard stretch of straight road, the flashing red light of the patrol car pierced the night and Jeff's heart. Only the Warlick Mill Road remained as a link to Highway Ninety, and he figured Parrish had it blocked off too. His mind searched frantically for another passage—the longer he stayed on the dirt road the worse his odds became of getting off it unshackled.

"Still with me?" Jeff asked.

"Hangin' in like Gunga Din," Cody answered woozily.

"Grab something and hold on," Jeff said, "cause it's gonna get rough."

"If you can't out-drive these guys," Cody said, "we oughta get throwed in jail."

Jeff backed off the accelerator as he approached Warlick Mill Road. As the boy drew within sight of the turnoff, the police car greedily ate up the distance between them. He allowed the Ford to drift to the left, setting up the right turn at maximum speed.

Chief Parrish pushed the squad car within spitting distance of the Ford's bumper. When Jeff jerked his wheel right at the intersection, Parrish fell for the feint and the squad car sailed behind the Ford while Jeff steered hard left and slid sideways past the turnoff. He worked his wheel in controlled jerks trying to keep his skidding rear end out of the side ditch and his nose pointed down Duck Creek Road. The boy had the Ford's rear wheels churning gravel before finishing the power slide. By the time Cody had unwrapped his arms from around his head and removed his feet from the dash, they were squared up and rolling south. The siren behind them grew faint.

"Damn," Cody wheezed breathlessly, "you're gettin' pretty good at that." He stared out the back window and saw exactly what he wanted to see—nothing. "Heard 'em hit the ditch. You let him get so close he couldn't straighten her out," Cody said, wiping the bloody rag on his arm across his sweating brow. "Not bad. Now where you gonna go?"

Back on Warlick Mill Road, Officer Jack Sherrill moved his vehicle out of the road and pulled up to the squad car in the side ditch. He left the motor running and trained the lights on the foundered automobile. Chief Parrish cut his siren and revved the engine to an angry whine, but a rear wheel was suspended above the ditch and spun without effect.

"We might could push it out," Sherrill shouted helpfully.

Chief Parrish shoved his car door viciously, but it opened less than eighteen inches before hanging up on the raised ground. The Chief tore his shirt as he squeezed through the opening like an enraged greased pig. "Get over," he bellowed, sliding under the wheel of Sherrill's squad car.

"I gotta try to take her over the Adair site," Jeff said, sounding as though he wanted to be talked out of it.

"Your call," Cody said, shaking his head. "I got some weight in the trunk. She might make it."

Jeff slowed to make the turn onto the logging road where he and Cody had first worked together. The road had been cleared to last no more than the couple months it would take to log it. Winter snows and spring rains had carved pits and gullies into a piss-poor road barely passable when freshly cut.

Jeff, still running without headlights, slowly threaded his way up the trail. He rolled past the point where the loaded lumber truck had forced him and Granjack off the road the previous summer, and the memory of the humiliating ride backwards to the bottom of the hill sent a shiver down his spine. If he made a mistake now, he would end up in jail. Or worse.

As his motor ran slower, quieter, Jeff leaned his head out the window. "Hear that?" he asked. No siren, but the sound of a speeding automobile approaching. "Parrish," Cody responded. Nothing short of a bullet hole in the heart would stop him.

As the Chief of Police blasted down the dirt road hell-bent to make up lost ground, he nearly broke down and radioed for help. He knew if he told his dispatcher to contact the county police, they would send a couple units pretty damn quick—those county mounties loved a chase. But the Chief would rather eat shit with a splinter than try to explain to those know-it-all SOBs how four cops, three squad cars, and three bloodhounds had managed to lose one wounded man.

Parrish was ready to eat crow, had the radio in his hand, when Sherrill pointed urgently toward a hill off to their right. Sure enough, Parrish spotted a glimmer of light bouncing off chrome about a quarter of the way up. When he reached the logging road, the Chief cut his engine and slid to stop. He was rewarded with the sound of a motor straining in low gear. Malicious glee spread across the Chief's face as he cranked up and pulled onto the trail. "Let's give 'em a thrill," he sneered to Sherrill. He flipped on his red light and siren and charged up the hill.

"Oh, shit," Jeff said, as the siren nailed him like a spear in the back. The tension, excruciating when he was racing down the dirt roads in wild flight, now threatened to break him in two as he inched up a washed-out, rutted path. Any misjudgment could leave him axle-deep in a ditch, immobile and helpless.

When he reached the plateau that had served as the base site for the loggers, Jeff knew that very soon the road would become steeper and more treacherous. He recalled how Cody had driven the loaded pulp wood truck over the ridge when nobody else would challenge it. Jeff would gladly have given up the wheel, but Cody was barely conscious; his ragged breathing scared Jeff as much as the thought of being captured.

Jeff rolled over the relatively flat ground of the base site quickly, building up momentum. His nervous system was connected directly to the Ford's rear axle. He felt every stone and gully his tires rolled over as he picked his way uphill. He made dozens of decisions in the space of a few minutes, all of which had to be correct.

The crest of the ridge, treeless and bathed in moonlight, loomed no more than sixty yards beyond the Ford's hood, when the tormenting siren faded to silence behind him. The squad car's relentless low gear growl was replaced by bursts of high whining engine and spinning tires, alternating with momentary silence.

"Hung up," Cody whispered. "Tryin' to rock her out."

A brief spike of hope flashed through Jeff's heart, but his attention did not waver. He dodged a large rock that had ridden a small mudslide onto the road. When he eased the steering wheel to the right to avoid a deep rut, Jeff clipped the rock with his rear fender.

"Easy on the paint job," Cody muttered, pulling himself up in the seat with his good arm.

KABLAM!

Jeff's rear end rose completely off the seat as the concussion of the pistol shot echoed through the forest like thunder over open water. The Ford shuddered briefly as the pressure on the gas pedal surged, but the driver managed to coax the spinning wheels into slow purposeful motion again.

"JEEEESUUUSS!" Cody shouted, as he covered his head and slid low in the seat. "He's tryin' to kill us!"

Jeff forced himself to focus on the rear wheels and the road that stretched only twenty yards to the ridge. Only two first downs, Jeff thought. Concentrate!

"GIVE UP HUNTER, OR WE'LL SHOOT YA!" Parrish's command boomed from a bullhorn and shook the timber.

Just as the Ford topped the ridge, a second shot passed so close to Jeff's open window that he heard the bullet zing past well before the muzzle blast reached him. Once over the ridge, he had only to control his breathing and contain the urge to let the Ford race down the slope. At the bottom of the hill, Jeff turned onto a silent Highway Ninety. Pinning the needle on fifty miles per hour, Jeff allowed his sweaty back to rest against the seat. He breathed deeply the cool air flowing through his window.

"Two lane blacktop to the Promised Land," Cody said, quietly.

"How you feelin'?" Jeff asked.

"Somebuddy's stickin' ice picks in my arm, and I could use some sleep and a bowl of Wheaties, but I'll make it. Where we headed?"

"The old Rambler's Inn. Naomi's sposed to be there."

"Damn, son, you thoughta everthing," Cody said admiringly.

God, I hope so, Jeff thought. He pulled the Panama hat low over his brow. But he knew that he had scattered dozens of clues over the dirt road, any of which could ruin his life. If Parrish, or anybody else he'd passed on the road, had recognized him, his nightmare was just beginning. The boy assumed each approaching set of headlights was the law. He shuddered as he realized this trip that had lasted for little more than an hour could haunt him the rest of his life.

He was glad Cody did not want to talk. When Cody turned on the radio, Jeff cut it off. After about five miles on Ninety, Jeff turned into the parking lot of an abandoned honky-tonk. As he pulled behind the vandalized roadhouse, his heart leaped at the sight of his mother's Plymouth waiting in the shadows. Naomi jumped from the car and ran toward them as Jeff slumped against the steering wheel and gave thanks.

When Naomi jerked the door open, Cody nearly fell out on the gravel lot. She caught him and smothered him with love and saved-from-the-gallows relief. Cody seemed close to tears as well. As hard as Jeff tried to share their joy, he couldn't. Just go. Go as far and as fast as possible.

As Naomi rewrapped Cody's bandage, Jeff hauled himself out of the driver's seat. Leaning against the car, he closed his eyes and stretched his knotted arms and legs. He filled his lungs with cool night air and listened to the crickets and the rush of water in the stream beyond the parking lot. He took off the Panama and tossed it into the back seat of the Ford, then ran his hands repeatedly through his sweating, itchy scalp.

Naomi ran around the car and hugged Jeff tightly. "You're the best person I ever knew," she said. She pulled his head down and kissed his cheek. "You're my hero." She pressed the keys to the Plymouth into his hand and jumped into the Ford. More gratitude poured from the front seat of the car. Both parties demanded that Jeff visit them in Memphis soon.

Jeff nodded. He knew he'd never see them again. "I'd get offa Ninety as fast as I could," Jeff said. "They've likely got us radioed in." He took the folding money from his wallet and pressed it into Naomi's hand. She wanted to refuse but couldn't afford to.

"I can get us to Tennessee without ever settin' a tire to pavement," Cody called from the passenger side. He extended his right hand, and the boy shook it. Jeff leaned heavily on the door as though trying to push the car out to the road. Just go.

When the Ford pulled out of sight, Jeff climbed into the Plymouth. He tried to insert the key into the ignition, but his hand shook so badly he finally threw the key down in frustration. He bolted from the car as though it were a casket. He ran to the field behind the parking lot and fell to his knees, vomiting.

As he lay on the cool, wet grass, Jeff slowly became aware of a summons that could not be denied. He pulled himself to his feet, and stumbled down the slope and over the broken ground to the creek. He stepped into the rushing water and lowered himself into in the shallow, rocky shoals. He lay on his back while the cold water washed over him and carried his youth downstream to the river, to the ocean.

CHAPTER FORTY

Rose Stuart sat on her front porch in pajamas and robe and listened to the birds merrily chirping their fool heads off. Raising her coffee cup, she chided herself for allowing so many springs to slip past uncelebrated. Years had passed since she had taken the time to re-hang the bird feeders that gathered dust in the shed. She vowed to hang them as soon as she got back from church. She could work in the yard until four o'clock and still have time to fix dinner and get ready for Jeff's seven o'clock baccalaureate service at the high school.

As her wicker rocker creaked reassuringly, Rose allowed her mind to drift back to her date with Larry Hunnicutt only twelve hours before. She had shared spaghetti and a movie in Oak City with the insurance agent; this following a meeting Rose had set up to raise the coverage on her automobile. By the end of the evening, she'd loosened up enough to practically enjoy the experience. The prospect of a good night kiss had haunted her as it might a parochial school girl, but Larry had gallantly chosen to raise her right hand to his lips. He was a gentleman—albeit, a short Methodist one.

She had accepted an invitation to eat Chinese and see a movie in two weeks; she didn't want to appear too eager, so she pleaded a previous commitment the following Saturday. Rose swore to herself she would relax and eat her egg foo yung without continually casing the joint like a Mafia informant expecting someone to blow her cover.

The hedges and bushes need a trimming, Rose thought. She quickly formulated a plan. She would call Jeff for church, figuring he would decline since he had been out late the night before. He would likely be lazing around the house when she returned from preaching, feeling guilty and susceptible to some gentle blackmail. Played properly, that should result in the young man hanging bird feeders and wielding hedge clippers on the overgrown bushes. She smiled and took the last sip of coffee.

Rose had her hand on the doorknob when she heard an automobile skid off the paved road and roar toward her at a speed that, on a Sunday morning, could properly be termed profane. When the dirty, dented police car slid into her driveway, Rose took immediate accounting of her charges. Jeff was sleeping in his room—she'd heard him snoring less than a half-hour before. She walked to the porch railing and looked down the road toward Granjack's house. The old man was standing on his porch peering back at her.

Oh god, she groaned. I know what's happened.

Ray Parrish hauled his bulk out of the front seat with obvious effort. The Chief looked as though he'd spent Saturday night in a foxhole. The face that normally glowed pink now bloomed a dangerous scarlet. He marched up the flagstone path and placed his right foot on the bottom porch step before he spoke a word. "Mornin', Miss Rose. Need to see Jeff," he said. "It's serious."

"Is this about Vicky?" Rose asked, pulling her housecoat tight.

The question seemed to confuse the Chief. He shook his head. "No," he said, irritated.

Rose exhaled a sigh of relief. "Come in," she said, holding the door.

"I'll wait out here."

Rose's mind flooded with jumbled thoughts and jagged fears as she walked through the house. When she opened Jeff's door, she found him clad only in briefs, sprawled face down on top of his sheets. After watching his back rise and fall several times, she walked over and placed her hand on his shoulder. "Wake up, son. Ray Parrish wants to see you."

Granjack was climbing the porch steps when Rose got back. He stared up at Ray Parrish. "What you doin' here?" Granjack asked.

"I got questions for the boy," Parrish said, rubbing the back of his neck.

"You better come in."

"I don't intend to be here that long."

"Nobody's answerin' questions outside," Granjack said. He let the screen door slam behind him. The Chief hesitated but followed. Rose led them into the rarely used formal parlor. The two men sat in armchairs separated by an end table that supported a small lamp and an open Bible. They faced the couch across a low coffee table.

Rose took coffee into the parlor on a silver serving tray and poured it into her best china cups. The three sat stiffly, stirring and sipping coffee in brittle silence. In the tight, airless room, usually reserved for church meetings or visits from salesmen, the ring of a silver spoon slamming against bone china resounded like a klaxon. When Parrish discovered it was his hand shaking erratically, he placed his cup and saucer on the table and ignored it.

"What's going on?" Jeff said, walking into the center of the room. He had pulled on a tee shirt, blue jeans, and shoes without socks. His hair was uncombed.

Parrish stood up. "I need you to come to the station and answer some questions," he said.

"About what?" Jeff asked.

"We can talk about it when we get there," Parrish said. He took a step toward the door. Rose stood up quickly, but Granjack cleared his throat, and all eyes turned toward him.

"Hold on, Ray," the old man said, leaning back in his chair. "Unless you got some papers, I think we'd rather talk here."

Parrish shook his head. "It'd be better if we took care of this at the station—"

"Better for who?" Rose interrupted.

"Sit down, boy," Granjack said. Jeff and Rose sat on the couch.

Parrish stayed on his feet, holding the high ground. He wedged his hat under his left arm and pulled a pad and pencil from his shirt pocket. "What did you do last night between ten o'clock and one in the mornin'?" he asked, with stony formality.

"I went to a party at Vicky's—at your house until a little after ten," Jeff said slowly. "Then I came home and went to bed."

"Did you leave the party with Naomi Costello?"

"No. She left in her car and I left in mine."

"Didn't she come to get you?"

"She came to *talk* to me."

"What did she want?"

"She said the police had busted into her house—her's and Cody Hunter's house—and that Cody had run off somewhere. Then she asked if I could lend her some money, so she could go back to Baltimore. I gave her what I had. Twenty-six dollars."

"Then what happened?"

"She drove off. I came home and went to bed."

"What was she drivin'?"

"Cody's Ford."

"What you pushin' at, Ray?" Granjack asked.

"We're lookin' for Cody Hunter. Somebody helped him get away from us last night. We believe it was Jeff."

"But you ain't sure," Granjack said.

"Sure enough," Parrish snarled. "We can charge him right now with aiding the flight of a fugitive, resisting arrest, failure to stop for a red light and siren, and...lotsa other stuff."

Rose's gasp filled the room, but neither Jeff nor Granjack appeared surprised or discomfited by the threat.

"You didn't bring no papers, Ray," Granjack said flatly.

"I wanted to give the boy a chance to get out from under the heavy charge," Parrish said, staring down at Granjack. He resented the old man's tone and how he kept calling him "Ray." "Alls Jeff's gotta do is tell us where Hunter is. Then we can plead him down. May not have to pull much time at all." Parrish's eyes whipped over to Jeff. "Where is he, son?"

"I don't know," the boy said. "I haven't seen Cody Hunter in months. Hope I never see him again."

Parrish shook his head and placed his pad and pen in his shirt pocket. "Jeff, you can come to the station with me now, or in an hour or two after I get a warrant. It'd go easier on you if you come now."

Jeff and Rose looked to Granjack. "I don't think so, Ray," Granjack said. "I saw the boy come home last night, sommers between ten and eleven. If all this chasin' Cody Hunter happened after that, Jeff couldn'ta had nothin' to do with it."

The Chief's hat, wedged under his arm, fell to the floor. Jeff could see the broken veins in Parrish's marbled face twitch as he bent down. "You know, I'd feel a whole lot better about that alibi if you'd said somethin' about it earlier. Or did it just come to mind?"

Granjack placed his empty cup on the serving tray. "You might say I wanted to hear the whole story laid out," he said. "Don't want to fly off half-cocked. Man get in a lot of trouble that way."

What promised to be a first-class staring match between the old man and the Police Chief broke off when Rose spoke. "I heard Jeff come in early last night," she said, her voice as flat as a carpenter's level. "He went straight to his room and didn't come out. I never go to sleep till he's safe in the house," she said.

Parrish took his last shot. "Jeff, tell me where Hunter is, and we'll work with you. We're gonna find him anyway, and you know he'll give you up. Then you'll be lookin' at hard time on the road."

"I don't know where he is."

"We'll have him by nightfall," Parrish said sharply. He looked from Jeff, to Rose, to Jack. "I'll be back." He spun on the heels of his scuffed black oxfords and walked out the door.

Without a word the three Stuarts walked to the kitchen and assumed their positions at the table. Jeff recounted his tale truthfully from beginning to end, attempting to minimize the dangers, emphasizing the precautions he had taken to avoid being captured or recognized.

"They should be in Tennessee now. I doubt if we'll ever hear of 'em again," Jeff concluded.

"It ain't Cody Hunter's habit to stay outa trouble," Granjack observed, lighting the first cigarette ever publicly smoked in Rose's house. The sight jarred both Jeff and Rose. "I doubt he'll give you up the first time they ask, but you can't tell what a man'll do to save his skin. Then there's the girl."

"She won't talk," Jeff said quickly, with more feeling than he'd cared to share.

Rose stared at the hands that she had wrung to a sickly salmon color. She pointed out the flaws in Jeff's defense. "If anybody saw you driving the Hunter car, you'll go to jail. If anybody saw the girl driving my car, you'll go to jail. If anybody saw you driving my car home at one o'clock in the morning, you'll go to jail." She ran her hands up over her face and through her hair. "Jeff," she said, more in pain than anger, "how could you do something so dangerous...and so *damn* stupid?"

Jeff could only shake his head.

"Seems we got two choices," Granjack said. "We can sit tight and hope Cody Hunter don't get caught, or we can send Jeff outa town till we see which way this thing falls."

Rose shook her head. "He's got graduation in two days. If he's not there, everyone in town will know something's wrong. It'll be the same as admitting he's guilty."

"Parrish'll take it that way," Granjack agreed.

"We could send him down to my mother's people in Wilmington after graduation," Rose offered. "He could stay there for a while."

"I 'spect we better get him outa the state," Granjack said. The old man's shaking hand dropped ashes on the Formica tabletop. "Parrish can likely reach to the coast."

"If I'm leaving town," Jeff interjected, "I want to go further than Wilmington." The thought of holing up with his crazy relatives sent a shiver down his spine. "I want to go to Oregon." He surprised himself with the declaration of a dream he thought he'd buried.

"*Oregon?*" Rose said, in disbelief. "Why would you go to Oregon?"

"Enterprise, Oregon," Jeff said firmly. "I know where I can get work there. There are people I can stay with." He declined to add that all his contacts were supplied by Cody Hunter.

"That's crazy," Rose said, shaking her head. "It's all the way across the country. How would you get there?"

"Chuck's daddy said if I came down to Caldwell Freight, he could set up a ride with a cross-country trucker," Jeff said quickly. "Or I could take a bus or hitchhike."

"Absolutely not!" Rose snapped, angry she had allowed the topic to go that far. "You have a business to learn and little enough time as it is. You can't afford to miss a cutting season."

Granjack stiffened. "You figure I got no more than one season in me?"

"I didn't mean...that," Rose said. But they all knew she did.

Jeff pushed away from the table and stood up. "Look," he said, "I'm sorry you two got involved in this—I didn't want you to. I did what I did, and I'm the one who'll pay for it." He walked out of the kitchen door but discovered he had no place to go. He retreated into the woods.

Rose and Jack found it easier to negotiate the boy's future in his absence. They agreed to go about their lives as though unaffected by Jeff's situation. Rose would go to preaching that morning—it was too late for Sunday school—and would attend the baccalaureate service that night with Jeff. The boy would attend school and graduate on Tuesday night. Wednesday morning, Rose would drive Jeff to Wilmington for a "vacation" of undetermined length.

As Ray Parrish stepped from his bath, he vowed he would take only a short nap and be out of the house before his family returned from church. He knew they would jaw for awhile after preaching, then reassemble with a gaggle of fellow-worshipers at the J&B cafeteria for lunch; he should be able to get a couple of hours of shut-eye before they'd pour through the door on a wave of argument and complaint. Even though he'd missed a night's sleep waiting for a wrecker to pull his patrol car out of the ditch, the Chief wasn't about to wait until Monday morning to get back on the case.

As soon as he walked into his home that morning, his daughter had descended upon him with her tale of cruelty and betrayal at the hands of her monstrous ex-boyfriend. Suddenly, all the pieces of the mystery surrounding

Cody Hunter's escape assembled themselves into an 8x10 wanted poster of Jeff Stuart. Hunter had lost too much blood to run through the woods then drive like a dirt-track racer on those back roads. The girl sure as hell couldn't do it. Jeff Stuart could.

Fatigue and tension melted from the Chief's body as he lay down in his dark, cool bedroom. He considered the pleasure he would feel when he jailed his daughter's boy friend. The Chief had detected a disturbing difference in Vicky since the two had made up that spring. He could see it in the way they looked at each other, the way they moved together. Although Ray hadn't mentioned his discovery to his wife, he could tell she knew as well. The effect on their romantic life had been disastrous. When Vicky's sexuality crept into the house, Ray and Libby's fled out the back door.

The thought of forcing Jack and Rose Stuart to admit that their alibis were lies spread a virulent smile across the Chief's face. His rancor stretched back to childhood sandlot ballgames when he and Will Stuart rarely passed up a chance to swap punches. He resented the Stuart arrogance. Rose had had her snoot in the air ever since she came to Rockton from down east. And that stumpy-ass old fart treated a man in a police uniform like he was no better than anybody else.

Sometimes it takes a long time, Ray thought, as his body dragged his churning mind toward sleep, but the pigeons always come home to roost. He couldn't get a warrant yet. But soon. Jeff Stuart was driving Cody Hunter's Ford Saturday night, and *somebody* had to have seen him. In Rockton, *somebody* sees *everything*.

CHAPTER FORTY-ONE

It was shortly before noon when the sound of churning gravel caused Madam La'Moor to glance up from her worn copy of "Amusement Business." "Run along home, now, child" the Prophetess said gently. The five year-old girl playing on the porch looked up at the station wagon rolling down the dirt road toward the house. She put the jacks and rubber ball into her pocket and stood up.

"Be careful going through the forest," Madam reminded the child.

The girl nodded and smiled. Everyone else called it "woods."

Rose Stuart smiled at the girl as she skipped past. "What a precious child," Rose said, as she climbed the steps. One of the great regrets of her life was never having a little girl to raise.

"Her father sometimes works for me," Madam said, rising from her chair. "He's a good father, an indifferent plumber."

"Can we go inside, Delphina," Rose asked.

"Certainly." From the moment Rose had stepped from her car, Madam noted the rigid set of her carriage. It was not unusual for Rose Stuart to show up at her house in a strained and anxious state. This was clearly different. And more unsettling.

"I'll put on some tea," Delphina said.

"No," Rose said quickly. "I don't have much time."

Madam nodded and sat down in her rocking chair across from Rose on the couch. Caliban the cat curled up on the floor at Madam's right hand and listened intently as Rose dispassionately unfolded the tale of Jeff's felonious auto chase and Chief Parrish's visit. She emphasized the long-standing enmity between Jeff and the Chief and its basis in Vicky. After outlining the grim choices available, Rose revealed her plan.

"Well," Rose said, finally. "What do you think?"

The tale astounded Madam La'Moor. Even more extraordinary was Rose's composure. The lady, so often frantic at the prospect of misfortune, was confronted with a situation far more dire than any she had despaired over, and seemed to be facing it with clarity and reason. Odd, Madam thought: The more specific and immediate the problem, the more focused Rose Stuart became. Apparently, no reality was as terrifying as Rose's fear of the unknown.

Delphina wished that she had a cup of tea, a prop of some sort to justify her hesitation. She reached down and gathered Caliban into her lap. None of her stock responses was appropriate. The All-Seeing-Eye had blinked, then gone blind.

"That is a remarkable story," Delphina said. "You have been thrust into a perilous situation." She absently scratched the cat's head. He purred in appreciation.

"Do you think I made the right decision?" Rose asked, her voice steady.

For the first time since succeeding Lady Esmerelda some four decades ago, Madam La'Moor had no answer to a direct question. She realized any advice was as likely to promote tragedy as contentment. The counsel that had always leapt blithely to her tongue now froze in her throat.

"All things considered," Delphina said slowly, "I believe you made the only decision you could..." Her voice trailed off in uncertainty, an unforgivable failing in the Fraternity of the Omniscient.

Rose displayed no surprise at Madam La'Moor's hedged response. She had decided there was no simple solution. She stood up abruptly. "Thank you, Delphina. I feel better just having talked it out." Rose opened her purse and rummaged in a zippered pocket for her payment.

Madam La'Moor placed her hand gently on Rose's and shook her head. Rose smiled slightly and snapped her purse shut. "Let me know if you have a vision," Rose said, as she walked quickly to the door. But both women knew no vision would be forthcoming.

"Take care," Delphina said, as the screen door slammed. The ex-Prophetess gathered up the dozen or so copies of the carny trade papers, each with circled ads promising riches for picking the pockets of rubes in jerkwater towns. She tossed them in the large trashcan in the kitchen. A year of living with the consequences of her revelations had convinced Jasmine Kingsley that a mark need not demonstrate a limp, stutter, or conspicuous deformity to qualify as a cripple. Why, she wondered, had it never occurred to her that her clientele consisted entirely of the afflicted? For who else walks this sad planet?

It's like living with a head-full of hornets, Jeff thought, as he walked apprehensively toward the auditorium for graduation practice. Although the sun smiled brightly upon pastoral Rockton High that flawless June afternoon, Jeff had spent his penultimate school day expecting the law to swoop down and drag him in chains across the campus.

Inside the stuffy auditorium, his fellow-seniors positively buzzed over the prospect of endless summer following Tuesday night's graduation. Some, like Chuck, focused single-mindedly upon completion of the long overnight drive that would deliver him to Myrtle Beach, South Carolina. There, clothing and inhibition would melt under the coastal sunshine, and Rockton teens would abandon themselves to the wanton pleasures that red clay people assumed were the birthright of sand people. Come Wednesday morning, Jeff, if uncaptured, was committed to a west-to-east trip as well; only his journey would yield a broken-down two-story house filled with loony, pretentious relatives.

When asked about his plans, Jeff was naturally reticent. He felt no urge to share the possibility that a substantial block of his immediate future might include keeping a firm grasp on a bar of soap while taking communal showers with grizzled felons named Turk, Duke, and Blackie.

He hadn't even decided whether he would run when he saw the cops coming.

Rrrrrrrrrrr! Rose sat bolt upright at the sound of the siren. Her head jerked to the left where a conspicuously pregnant Janet froze at the filing cabinet. Janet, who had no idea why the squeaky drawer had alarmed her boss, retreated in tears to the bathroom. Rose decided not to pursue and apologize. Janet was a week beyond her due-date and fragile as a soap bubble. She needs to get out of that house, Rose thought. The girl still lived with her Pentecostal parents who showed no inclination to forgive a wayward daughter or welcome an illegitimate grandchild. Rose had briefly considered taking in the poor girl, but with Jeff's troubles and Granjack's drinking...impossible.

Rose had spent the day alternately plotting Jeff's escape and preparing for his arrest. She had called Aunt Lolly in Wilmington and listened to a convoluted and cheerless monologue. Rose had parried a flurry of protest detailing why this was a particularly bad time to visit, and finally wangled an invitation for Jeff to stay "a while...a *little* while."

She and Jeff would leave Rockton at daybreak on Wednesday and arrive at the creaky home place that night. She would press a check into Aunt Lolly's withered palm securing Jeff's lodging for a month. She did not envy the boy's stay. The house and the wispy, distracted folks who rattled around in it could have been lifted intact from an uninspired Southern-Gothic novel.

Rose had spent the afternoon researching lawyers and calculating the means to pay one. She knew of no one in Oak City competent to handle the fate of her only son. She might have to reach to Winston-Salem, or, God forbid, Charlotte, for a competent attorney.

Justice, she knew, could be purchased, but never cheaply. She could see no recourse to cutting off the timber tract that ran from the spring near Granjack's house up over the south-forty hill and down the other side. No matter how gently Ab's men tried to treat the site, the eroded land and tortured timber would stare down at Rose and Jack every time they walked outside. The runoff would certainly doom the old man's spring; he would have to go to town water. The only other option was to sell the lumberyard and all the equipment at a rock-bottom price. *If* they could find a fool to buy it.

The door swung open and Ab leaned in. "I gotta talk to Jack," he said. His eyes painted the walls and ceiling, but never settled upon Rose. "We startin' the Hawkins' site in the mornin' and gotta know what to take with us."

Rose sighed deeply. "I'll tell him when I see him," Rose said. Ab ducked out.

How could this happen, Rose wondered. Few would dispute that she had lived a good Christian life. She had attended church methodically, worked hard and honestly, and treated others as she wanted to be treated. Not a flawless life, but certainly not a life whose happiness should revolve around the outlaw Cody Hunter avoiding police capture, or, if caught, keeping his damn mouth shut. How did such a well-managed life spin so hopelessly out of control?

Rose could hear Janet's quiet sobs leaking through the thin bathroom wall. Things could be worse, she decided. They *always* could. But they likely would be better if the only person who might help her work through all this weren't off somewhere, probably on a drunk.

Granjack, sober as a judge at the county seat, sat with his feet in the cool spring water and sorted through a past that resembled a busted poker hand. He had built his life and business around hard work and hard decisions. Now that his string was just about played out, he felt like all the rules had been changed up on him. When it came right down to it, all he had was Jeff, Rose, and the lumberyard. And now they were all squared off against each other.

The old man did not hear the birds singing lustily or the squirrels thrashing in the leafy canopy as he drifted in and out of seven decades of random memories. Each time his mind collided anew with his predicament, he shook his head and fingered the pint bottle in his overalls. He was determined to come to a decision before breaking the seal on the pint.

The solution came as revelation. It was dramatic at a time when he often felt incapable of decision or action. It was conclusive in a world where everything seemed to just plug along then peter out. The greatest benefit fell to the one who needed it most, the least to himself. Ah, Nobility. The emotional appeal was so strong that he avoided breaking the plan down into niggling details. That was the Jack Stuart way: Make the decision, push ahead, make it work.

There were grave consequences. He abruptly pulled his feet from the spring, sending the water striders fleeing downstream in the wake. As the old man struggled with his socks and boots, he admitted he could not be certain how the chips would fall. There was potential for catastrophe. But, if he pulled it off, ghosts would be laid to rest, and a sad cycle of Stuart history would end. Time to shit or get off the pot.

Chief Parrish slammed the phone down so hard that tiny silver cracks snaked down the black plastic base. He'd been on the phone constantly for the past two days talking to police in Kentucky and Tennessee, but he'd gotten nowhere with those hillbillies. They wanted everything *in writing*, signed by judges and the like. Chief told them there wasn't time for that by-the-book bullshit, he had a dangerous felon—part of a three state auto-theft ring—on the lam and headed their way. The guy was wounded and likely needed a doctor. Kentucky and Tennessee replied there was no shortage of outlaws in their sovereign states—meaner, slyer, more desperate than any found in North Carolina—but they'd keep an eye out for this Hunter and his moll.

Parrish pushed away from his desk. Hell, he'd always known he'd have to crack the Hunter-Stuart case alone. Of course, it'd likely have been easier if he'd been able to publicize the circumstances. But the Chief could take no special pride in revealing that four cops had allowed a bleeding suspect to escape from his house and then elude three police cars in a dirt road chase. He'd studied it closely and couldn't see how such knowledge would elevate folk's respect for the Rockton Police Department and its leader.

The charges against Hunter now consisted more of offenses committed after the Chief had attempted to serve the warrant than on the original "Accessory to Auto Theft." When the Chief found Sam Langford trapped inside a stolen Pontiac with four wheels pointed toward the stars, he knew he was onto something big. After several months in jail with no court date in sight, Langford agreed to strike a deal. The Chief's first choice of accomplice was Cody Hunter, and after great reluctance, Langford agreed.

If the undependable son-of-a-bitch had shown up for work occasionally they could have arrested him there. The chief had staked out the body shop for two days, but no Hunter. Finally, he'd decided to take down Hunter in his home. It had seemed like a simple procedure and good training for his officers. All the troops had been excited about the chance to do some real police work. No way to know things would go so bollixed up.

Bad luck, he decided. Just plain bad luck.

Of course, if they'd simply arrested Hunter and carted him off to jail, the whole sideshow with Jeff Stuart would never have occurred. He was damn glad it had. The Chief was eager to drive a stake through the heart of a romance that had robbed him of sleep, sex, and proper digestion.

Although Parrish knew bone-deep that Stuart was driving the Ford, he couldn't swear to it in court. Nor could his deputies. In all his years as a cop, he'd never lied outright on the witness stand or asked his men to. But if he got hold of Hunter or the girl, he had no doubt they would toss him Stuart on a silver platter. Or he might be able to break the boy down and find out where Hunter was headed. Either way, he wouldn't rest until Hunter and Stuart were pulling hard time.

CHAPTER FORTY-TWO

As the blue-gowned graduating class of 1957 sat in alphabetical order in the Rockton High auditorium, few could concentrate on the platitudinous bullshit being spouted by their local congressman up on the stage. Overwhelmed by their own memories and emotions, the seniors also had to endure the brutality of a late-spring heat wave that had raised the temperature of the room to a level most had encountered only in a tobacco barn. In the rear of the building, two large electric fans ran full-blast pulling hot air through the open double doors, but to little advantage. All the side windows that hadn't been painted-shut were raised. Down front the doors on each side of the room were wedged open in the hope that a breeze might be coaxed across the stage. The constant rattle of flimsy graduation programs fashioned into homemade fans indicated that none of the climate engineering was working. Everyone in the building was over-dressed, over-heated, and over-wrought.

Jeff had been so busy trying to find an alternative to spending the next few years in the Big House, he had managed to avoid confronting his feelings about leaving an institution that he occasionally compared to a prison. At that moment, weakened by insomnia, sentimentality and fear, he would gladly have traded the limitless horizon he was now being promised for just one more year of security at the bosom of his alma mater, surrounded by those he now recognized as the best friends he'd ever have. As he surveyed the faces of his classmates, he noted none of the eagerness and joy of those about to embark on a boundless adventure—they resembled pirate prisoners lined up to walk the plank.

The lurking presence of Police Chief Ray Parrish did not help. Parrish, wearing a suit of a fashion and fit that indicated the last graduation it attended was his own, had settled with his wife and son directly behind Rose. Jeff was relieved that Granjack had passed up the ceremony. The Devil alone could imagine the trouble that might develop if Jack Stuart, wearing an itchy wool suit in this steam bath, were stuck within swearing distance of Ray Parrish.

"Oh, Lord," Jeff thought, as sweat coursed wild and free under his gown and collected at the waist of his black dress pants, "please silence that windy SOB, so we can get this thing over with." Jeff's patience had survived the presentation of awards and scholarships, the valedictory address and a prayer, but wore thin during the blustery speech of the Oak City cotton mill tycoon cum newly-elected congressman. The lint-head legislator had obviously reworked a campaign speech denouncing Communism and racial integration to include asides about the brilliant and unfettered future awaiting these graduates if they could wrench it away from the pinkos on the US. Supreme Court.

Eventually, the Congressman left the stage to indifferent applause and profound relief. The County Superintendent of Schools, who made but one trip to Rockton High each year, enjoined the seniors to stand up one row at a time and file to the right side of the stage. Mrs. Cagle played "Pomp and Circumstance," while the volume of tears and sweat flowed in rough equilibrium. "Abernathy" through "Farmer" had received diplomas when the blood-chilling sound of sirens of varied pitch traveling in several directions, spread confusion and alarm throughout the auditorium.

If Jeff Stuart had not been sitting down, he would have collapsed. Color fled his face, and strength ebbed from his body. He had figured they would come for him, but why *now*? In front of half the town!

Why so many? How many cops in how many squad cars did it take to haul off one kid? A kid who, at that moment, couldn't stand up, much less run away. Henry Taylor, sitting to his left, stood up with the rest of the row, then shook Jeff roughly. Finally, Henry hauled his classmate to his feet and shoved him down the aisle, toward the stage.

Jeff managed to put one foot in front of the other as he followed the gown in front of him. The procession continued as the sirens competed with the piano's stately march. Jeff could not see Deputy Joe Sigmon walk through the back door and talk to Chief Parrish. As Jeff shuffled toward the steps, Parrish whispered something to Rose. The principal had just begun the "R"s when Jeff felt the heavy hand on his shoulder.

"Come with me, boy," the Chief of Police said.

Jeff was escorted up the aisle, Parrish a pace behind him. Rose stood outside the rear door of the auditorium. Officer Sigmon fidgeted beside her. The boy wanted to hug his mother, apologize again—

"The lumberyard is on fire," Rose said quickly. "Can you drive?"

Jeff did not understand. He glanced at Parrish then back at his mother. Rose grabbed him by the arm and pulled him down the auditorium steps. "Can you drive?" she repeated, directly into his face.

Jeff nodded and followed Rose's fast trot to the parking lot. They piled into the Plymouth. "Follow him," Rose said, pointing to the flashing light of the patrol car. They sped through town behind the keening siren, running red lights and pushing traffic off the road. When they crossed the rise just beyond the Main Theater, Rose pointed to the flames lighting the southern sky. "Oh my God, oh my God," she moaned.

Sirens approached from several directions as they drew within sight of the lumberyard. Cars packed with gawkers clogged the highway and road shoulders, slowing the fire trucks and emergency vehicles. Jeff had to brake quickly and reduce the Plymouth to an agonizing crawl as he drew within a quarter mile of the fire. Officer Jack Sherrill directed traffic with a scattered urgency, trying to wave through volunteer firemen and rescue workers in private cars while culling the rubber-neckers drawn by a calamity that they would talk about for years.

Jeff's mind reeled as a confused farmer with a truck bed full of kids attempted to turn his pickup around in the road, stopping all traffic. Rose shouted curses as the pickup slowly sawed back and forth while her business disappeared in smoke and ash just beyond her influence. Jeff tore off his graduation robe and threw it out the window onto the highway. Enraged, he pulled the Plymouth off the road and planted it in a side ditch. Rose discarded her high heels, and the two ran hand-in-hand the final hundred yards to the lumberyard gate.

They dodged teams of firemen and emergency workers as they charged toward the oppressive heat and smoke. Jeff saw that the cabinet shop, in the southwest corner of the fenced compound, and the two lumber sheds closest to it had been devoured. The Rockton Fire Department was pouring water on the storage building closest to the gate. A west wind had pushed the fire to the stacked rough lumber that stretched from the southern fence line to the middle of the compound. The Lovelady Volunteer Fire Department tried to keep the blaze away from the mounds of sawdust. If ignited they would scatter burning ash in every directions.

Rose shouted at the fireman to keep the flames away from the trucks and skidders. The vehicles were parked inside the fence less than twenty yards from

Rose's office. The Fire Chief ignored her. He was concerned only with containing the blaze within the compound; if it spread to the surrounding woods, fire trucks would be useless. Rose, desperate to save her files, made a run toward the office. The heat and smoke drove her back before she reached the door.

Jeff witnessed the excitement and desperation swirling about him but felt only a vague sense of loss. He knew an important, an irreplaceable, part of his life and ancestry was disappearing in the smoke that billowed up toward the three-quarter moon. The spectacle of fire and concentrated humanity fascinated the boy. The smoke, the heat, the shouts of men who loved their horrible, deadly work—

"Granjack!" Jeff shouted. He searched the lot. He wasn't there, no one had seen him. Jeff tried a shortcut, a footpath that ran along the south perimeter of the lumberyard and cut through the woods to Granjack's house. The smoke and heat turned him back. The boy ran along the highway, dodging parked cars and gawkers. As he ran onto the dirt road that led to his house, the trees on his right filtered out the smoke that had attended his every step. He greedily inhaled the cool, clean air as he ran with abandon. The moon guided him around the potholes in the twisting, rutted driveway.

Just as the boy drew within sight of his house, he saw a shadow, a shape, lying close to the driveway. A cold terror grew with every step he took. Jeff moaned as he fell to his knees beside his grandfather's body. Granjack lay on his stomach, his left hand trapped under his chest. His right hand was extended toward his home, one hundred-fifty yards distant.

Jeff placed his hand on the old man's cheek. Cold. He rolled his grandfather over on his back and unbuttoned his overall bib. He felt for a pulse in the wrist, in the neck. The boy ripped open the white shirt and laid his sweaty head on the old man's chest. He shook the body and listened for a heartbeat again.

Jeff pulled off his sweat-soaked shirt and wrapped it tightly around the body. He rested his right hand on the old man's chest and rocked back and forth, crying quietly.

When he stood to make the walk back, the boy's eye picked up a glint of metal about ten feet away. He walked toward the lumberyard, bent over and picked up a flashlight. Although he felt he might suffocate from grief and fatigue, he knew what must be done. He carefully turned the old man's body around so that the lumberyard lay in front of him, and he placed the flashlight a few feet behind his boots.

Within seconds, an ambulance with siren and flashing red light roared up the driveway and slid to a stop.

CHAPTER FORTY-THREE

The firefighters managed to contain the Stuart fire within the compound, skillfully preventing its spread to the trees that surrounded three sides of the lumberyard. All the saws and woodworking machines were lost, as well as the four trucks and two skidders parked inside. Heat and smoke had ruined Rose's office, but the records in her filing cabinet and desk survived. It was midnight, a good two hours after Jack Stuart had been declared dead at the Oak City Hospital, before the firemen were able to leave the charred remains of the lumberyard. The Fire Chief declared that the fire had started in the cabinet shop, a reservoir of combustible liquids.

A goodly portion of the congregation of the First Baptist Church, as well as assorted Methodists, Lutherans, and Church of Christers appeared at the Stuart house the following day. They brought heart-felt condolences and home-baked casseroles. Rose and Jeff, exhausted but gracious, received sympathy, support and enough food "to feed the thrashers," as Granjack would have said.

Although no griever asked directly, Rose quietly explained that Granjack must have seen the flames from his house or smelled the smoke and attempted to walk to the lumberyard to investigate. No one speculated as to why he didn't drive his truck there, as he did every working day. They assumed the old man panicked, or couldn't find his truck key, or was incapable of driving. The Stuarts had endured a double tragedy; no one at this gathering was inclined to remark on the erratic behavior or drinking problem of the elderly deceased.

When Marty Ryder entered the house with his mother and father, Jeff resisted the urge to embrace him, knowing it would embarrass them both. They shook hands. He led Marty through the gloom-choked house and out the back door. It was a graceful June day with a slight westerly breeze to invigorate the darting birds and insects. A day that you outght to grab your fly rod and stay out till the bluegills quit biting at dark. Jeff couldn't have left the yard if his life depended on it.

Marty shook his head and kicked at the grass. "Man, I don't know what to say—"

"You got a cigarette?" Jeff interrupted.

Marty, surprised, produced a cigarette and match. He hadn't seen Jeff smoke since...hell, he couldn't remember the last time. Maybe at that honky-tonk bar a year back.

Jeff took a long pull and coughed.

"How you holding up," Marty asked softly.

"Hard to say," Jeff wheezed. "I'm so tired I don't know how I feel. I'm afraid to go to sleep."

They walked silently, aimlessly around the backyard. Marty noticed that every time Jeff stopped walking he was facing the old man's rock house.

Marty leaned against the huge red oak where he and Jeff had worn out many tire swings. "You know," he said, "I never felt like your grandfather liked me. I used to want him to, but I don't think he ever did."

"He liked you fine," Jeff said. "God forbid he should ever say it." Jeff, unsatisfied, threw the cigarette down and stepped on it. "You know who he *did* like? Chuck." Both boys shook their heads. "Maybe," Jeff continued, "because Chuck attacked things head-on. Like the old man."

They sat in the grass, their backs against the oak. "What are you gonna do this summer?" Jeff asked. He was desperate to talk about something besides death.

"The Right Rev's got me signed up for a course over at Moore-Clayton. It's a class to teach you *how* to study." Marty laughed. "At least it'll keep me out of the hot sun for a few hours a day. That'll run through August, then—" Marty's right arm shot out abruptly in a Nazi salute, and his accent plunged to low-German, "induction into der Bismarck Academy."

"You ever feel like tellin' the Rev. to go to hell?"

"Every night in bed, I kick his ass till his nose bleeds," Marty stated, maliciously. "But then I wake up hungry."

As they sat under the tree, Jeff's head slowly bent toward sleep. The sound of the screen door banging jerked him back.

"Jeff," Rose called from the back porch. "There's some folks here would like to see you."

Jeff rose and wiped the dirt from his Sunday pants. He went back inside to greet the dear hearts and gentle people who lived and loved in his hometown.

"We'll never be able to eat all that food," Rose said, as she placed reheated dishes on the small table, "so we may as well start with the best." They were eating supper in the kitchen. Rose hoped Granjack's absence would seem less oppressive in the smaller room.

Jeff silently filled his plate with food he had no appetite for. He had spent the time between the reception and dinner walking the woods behind their house. "Is this from Chuck's mama?"

"Yes," Rose said. Molly Brady's chicken-broccoli casserole, like Rose's potato salad, and Sally Reeve's barbecue sauce, was a Rockton delicacy. "Granjack never failed to tell me to bring home a plate of Molly's casserole from church suppers." She turned away from the table to compose herself. She grabbed a wicker basket of home-baked rolls from the stovetop. Who brought them? She'd ask around before sending out notes.

"I didn't see Chuck today. Was he here?"

"No," Jeff said. "He went to the beach."

Just like him, Rose thought. They ate in small bites, chewed deliberately. "I moved the records from the office today," she said. "The fire department had to help get the safe open. We'll pay everyone for a full week. It wasn't their fault the yard burned down." She chose to think Jack would have done the same, but she knew better.

"I talked to Jack's sister, Jennie, in Missouri," Rose continued, fearing silence. "She's not gonna be able to come for the service. She sounded real sorry about it, but she said she'd been practically bed-fast for over a year. Just as well, I guess. We'd have to push back the funeral." Granjack's younger sister, Kate, had died shortly after World War II of a disease no doctor was able, or cared enough, to identify. "Terminal Meaness," Granjack called it. There would be no nieces, nephews or cousins attending.

"We'll receive tomorrow night at seven at the funeral home," Rose said absently. "The funeral will be at two o'clock on Friday. Just a graveside service. I never knew Jack to walk into a church when he was alive, I don't have the right to drag him in there now." She studied the food on the end of her fork. "I'll have Reverend Ryder speak. Short, nothing preachy, no Hell-fire. But people expect something."

Jeff nodded.

"It must have been horrible for you, finding him...like that," Rose said finally. She barely lifted her eyes from her plate.

Jeff nodded.

"Did he say anything?"

"No." Jeff had told her this before, but beneath the cloak of grief and fatigue they shared, neither was sure what had been said, thought, or assumed. "He was dead. I knew it when I saw him lying there. Before I turned him over."

"You turned him over?"

"Yeah. I listened for a heartbeat. He was already . . . cold."

When Rose saw tears fall onto Jeff's plate, she moved quickly around the table. She fell to her knees and embraced her son. "Oh, you poor child," she said.

"Mama, the way he was lying there . . . I could tell he was walking back to his house."

"But they said he was headed to the yard-"

"I turned him around . . . so it looked like that."

Oh, my Lord, Rose thought, that's just like that old man. He built it, he could burn it down.

They succumbed to waves of grief, long postponed. Eventually they staggered to the couch where they cried until exhausted. They fell asleep at opposite ends of the couch as twilight descended on the longest day of the boy's life.

After breakfast on Thursday morning, Rose and Jeff walked to the rock house. Neither had been there since the old man's death, and didn't want to go then, but it was the next task on Rose's grim check list. The funeral parlor needed a suit to display Granjack in. Rose could have done it alone, but she was relieved and grateful when Jeff offered to go along.

While Jeff sorted through piles of newspaper and magazines that flanked Granjack's ragged easy chair in the front room, Rose went into the bedroom. She raised the window to chase out the "old man" smell. The bed was as rumpled and grumpy as the old man had been. Granjack believed in letting a bed "air out" during the day—never made one in his life. Rose stripped the bed, tossed the sheets by the door and folded the blankets.

Opening the doors of the cedar chiffarobe, Rose sorted through the shirts, coats and pants, many of which had witnessed the rise and fall of Prohibition. The dark blue suit, reeking of mothballs and disuse, hung like a sentinel in the far left corner. As she laid the suit across the bed, Rose offered a silent prayer that the funeral home would be able to get the suit dry-cleaned and pressed before the reception that night.

In search of underwear and socks, Rose pulled open the chiffarobe's top drawer. Beneath a pile of boxer shorts, she discovered a gray metal payroll box.

She removed the box with trembling hands and sat on the bed. The lock required no key. Inside, she found newspaper clippings of Jeff's football games, some obituaries, and historical articles. There were two photographs of silent movie star Lillian Gish, an old Barlow knife, two pocket watches, and several tattered Confederate bills. The bottom of the metal box was covered with old coins. Atop all those yellowed documents and worn souvenirs sat a clean white business envelope.

The envelope was not sealed. Rose extracted and unfolded the sheet of lined notebook paper and read the brief, scrawled contents.

"Mom," Jeff called from the next room, "should I take the guns to our house?"

Rose jumped at the sound of his voice. She stuffed the paper back into the envelope and slipped it into the pocket of her housedress.

"Yes," she said, "take them back. We've done enough here."

CHAPTER FORTY-FOUR

"And we must all remember that our lives hang by a slender thread over a fiery pit. Jack Stuart did not know when he charged across that field to defend the business he'd built with his own two hands that he would be meeting his Maker within moments. None of us know when we will be called to defend our lives before Saint Peter. That's why we must dedicate our souls and our lives at *this moment* to the Lord God Almighty."

Rose Stuart cleared her throat loudly from the front row of the graveside service. That was the second time she'd had to restrain the preacher. Reverend Ryder, declaiming before a vulnerable congregation under a funeral tent on a steamy, still day, smelled the blood of the Lamb and couldn't resist taking his shot. It was a reflex.

The restless shifting of sweaty backs and bottoms on unforgiving metal folding chairs and the flutter of funeral home fans convinced the preacher that further exposition was unlikely to yield converts. Reverend Ryder led the assemblage in singing "Onward Christian Soldiers," the casket was lowered, and the service concluded. When he stepped forward to embrace Rose Stuart, the preacher still entertained strong doubts that Jack Stuart was beaming down from above. More likely sweating harder than anyone here.

The mourners stepped forward to extend sympathy before slipping away gracefully, eager to cast off their clammy suits and dresses. As Rose hugged and reassured the sympathizers, her eyes were drawn to two figures who hovered well beyond the shade of the funeral tent.

A Negro woman in a black dress stood under a large post oak tree. None of the people leaving the Stuart service seemed to notice her, or if they did, they probably assumed she had paused on her way to the Colored cemetery—a rocky hillside that lay just across the access road. Rose had no way of knowing how long she had been there. When the two made eye contact, Madam La'Moor nodded slowly, turned and walked away.

The second figure was more troublesome. Rose had heard a car approach and park during the service. The sight of Ray Parrish roaming restlessly around his patrol car pulled down an avalanche of fear that Rose had managed to displace for three days. The Chief apparently had something on his mind, but he did not join the line of consolers to reveal it.

When the line dwindled to four, Rose allowed the small group to escort her to her car. While Rose settled into the passenger seat, Molly Brady asked. "Did you hear your girl Janet had her little baby this morning?" Rose shook her head. "Well, she did," Molly confirmed. "A little girl. Over eight pounds, they said. Both of 'em appear to be just fine." She patted Rose's arm. "Maybe that will bring you a little comfort today."

The gravediggers watched the last of the funeral party drive away. The grizzled pair eased out of the city truck, discarded cigarettes, grabbed their tools. Before sinking a shovel into the clumpy red clay, they read the inscription Jack Stuart had vowed would be his epitaph when he'd been tagged with it some thirty-odd years before.

Jackson Bedford Stuart
April 15, 1889-June 4, 1957
"A Mule Trader You Could Trust."

"I never swapped mules with him," the shorter grave-digger said, "but he was a sonuvabitch to work for."

When Jeff and Rose arrived home, the specter of Chief Parrish drove them directly to the kitchen table. As Jeff hung his suit coat over the back of his chair, Rose poured them both a glass of sweet tea.

"You need to leave tomorrow morning," Rose said, as she sat down.

"I'm not sure I should go," Jeff said.

"You have to. I've lost enough in the last three days. I'm not going to let Ray Parrish take you away."

"I saw him lurking around at the cemetery." Jeff said. "If they'd caught Cody, he'da come right down front and hauled me off. He'da loved that."

"I think he's trying to scare us," Rose said. She took her glass to the sink. She peered out the window, half expecting to see a police car racing up the driveway. "It's like Granjack said, 'Cody Hunter's not the kind to stay out of trouble.' They'll get him sooner or later."

"I don't want to leave you alone," Jeff said.

"I appreciate that, son, but I've got plenty to do. Just straightening out the paperwork will take months." She pulled herself away from the window and sat at the table. "I could have Janet help me. Lord knows she'll need the work. She could bring the baby." She reached across and laid her hand on Jeff's. "Then I have to decide what I'm going to do with *my* life."

"Now you can open that gift shop. Or be a travel agent. Work in a library," Jeff said, reeling off alternatives that Rose commonly repeated after a hard day's work. "You used to talk about taking some college courses."

"It's time to fish or cut bait," Rose said. Another Granjackism. His old sayings had been rattling around in her head the last few days.

A long silence hung over the table while they contemplated how drastically their lives had changed in less than a week. Rose walked into the dining room. The large table was covered with a blizzard of paper—insurance forms, bills, tax returns, bank records—all that was left of a business that had been the centerpiece of their lives. She opened a gray metal box and extracted an unmarked business envelope.

She slid the envelope across the kitchen table. "I found this in Granjack's chiffarobe."

Jeff pulled the sheet of lined notebook paper from the envelope. Tears filled his eyes when he saw the cramped, scribbled handwriting.

This is My Will.
I leave everthing to Rose Stuart. If
my sister Jennie wants anything that
came from Mama's house give it to her.
Jackson B. Stuart
March 19, 1957

Give my grandson Jeff my truck and $500.

"He wrote this after his heart attack," Jeff said.

Rose read the will again. "I think he added the last part after we talked Sunday. It's in a different pen."

"I'll bet the old man was cussin' a blue streak when he figured out he wasn't going to make it back to his house," Jeff said.

Rose nodded. "He got the job done before he laid down."

"What are we going to do?"

"As it stands, I don't think anyone can prove anything," Rose said. "We didn't take out much insurance. Wouldn't have *any* if Jack'd had his way. If we get back as much as paid in over the years, that's fine with me."

"No shortage of lumberyard fires," Jeff said.

"I'll have to push the insurance company, or they'll know something's wrong." Rose ran her fingers through her hair. "I don't feel good about it, but I don't see what else I can do." She knew she'd be looking over her shoulder until the whole thing was settled. Maybe for the rest of her life.

Jeff rose abruptly and walked to his room. He retrieved a folder and spread the contents on the kitchen table. As he unfolded the maps, Rose inspected the lists of camping provisions necessary for a car trip across the U.S.

"When did you do all this?" she asked.

"Last winter. I was gonna go with Cody Hunter."

Rose shook her head in horror. Things *could* be worse.

Jeff spread a large road map across the kitchen table. He'd marked two routes—one in red pen, the other in black. "I can either go west and hit Route Sixty-six at Oklahoma City, then cut up north through California," he said, tracing the black line, "or I can take the old Wilderness Road up through Kentucky, then to St. Louis and hit some of the Lewis and Clark Trail along the Missouri and Snake rivers. Whichever way I go out, I'll come back the other."

"Who said you're going out there?" Rose asked. But her voice lacked conviction. She knew when she first saw the will exactly what it meant.

Jeff didn't even look up from the map. "I've got a truck and five hundred dollars, Mama. I've gotta go somewhere, and it ain't gonna be Wilmington. I know where I can get work in Oregon."

"When are you coming back?"

"I'll stay at least a year. I need to see all four seasons."

Rose heart sank. "That's too long. Can't you just make it a summer thing?" If he was back by September, he could still get into some kind of school.

Jeff raised his eyes from the map. "This isn't a vacation, Mama. This is a chance to see what my choices are. It might be my only chance."

"You're so young," Rose said, and knew she shouldn't have.

"Half my class is going into the Army," Jeff said, quickly. "They could go to war."

"But at least they'll be with other boys. With someone responsible for them."

Jeff looked at his mother as though he were ready to call the men in the white coats and butterfly nets on her. "Anything worth doing has to be done alone," he said. Granjack again.

Damn that old man anyway, Rose thought, then instantly repented. Defeated, she said, "Just so long as you know you can come home *anytime* if you have trouble . . . run out of money . . . or you just want to."

"Sure," Jeff said casually, returning to his map.

Rose removed all the paperwork from the dinner table, and the two began assembling the items on the lists. When Jeff dialed up a rock'n'roll station on the radio, the music seemed to invigorate them both. Occasionally the DJ would play a slow song by the Platters or Elvis's "Love Me Tender," and Rose would glimpse the magic that captivated the kids. Each time her spirit faltered, she reminded herself of the fat man with the badge who could ruin Jeff's life. There was no alternative to flight, and Granjack had dictated the path. Controlling from the grave.

Jeff chatted cheerfully to raise his mother spirits and his own. They worked feverishly until the dining room table groaned under the load and hunger demanded they stop. It was only when they sat down for a quiet supper that the hazards of a journey across a strange and perilous continent without ally penetrated Jeff consciousness. The solution came in a flash. When Rose fell asleep on the couch watching "The Eddie Fisher Show," the boy pursued a plan that seemed damn-near divinely inspired.

CHAPTER FORTY-FIVE

"Are you crazy?" Marty gasped, spilling Schlitz Beer on a comic book depicting Popeye and Olive Oyl in distorted carnal embrace. "What the hell did you lose in Oregon?"

"I got contacts there," Jeff said. "And I figured that was about as far from Rockton as I could get without a boat."

When no one answered the doorbell at the Baptist parsonage, Jeff had walked around back. Marty nearly had a stroke when Jeff knocked on the fallout shelter door. The Curator was drinking warm beer and sorting through his collection of "Eight-Page-Bibles," the miniature comic books that showed various cartoon characters—Popeye and Olive Oyl, Dick Tracy and Tess Trueheart, Little Abner and Daisy Mae—engaged in illicit contortions while pursuing lascivious plot lines. It was time to abandon the bunker. The Rev had vowed anew to unleash the bulldozers, level the building, and sow the iniquitous soil with salt. Marty was burying the remnants of his once-grand archive in a large tin box in the woods. An Auto-Copulatory Time Capsule.

Marty's reaction to Jeff's proposal to strike out on a trans-continental trek in an antique Ford truck in little more than thirteen hours was predictable. "It's fuckin' insane!" the Curator wheezed. "You've never been out there. Leaving *tomorrow*? I can't get ready that quick. You can't just show up some place you've never been and expect to find work. It's impossible..." Marty's voice trailed off as his mind caromed from one insoluble problem to another.

Jeff countered. "I know people who'll hire us soon as we get to Oregon. We can camp on the way. I got money and supplies—you don't need to bring nothing but your sleeping bag. Jesus, Marty, how many times have you pissed and moaned about how bad you want to get out of this town? Here's your chance. We can be like those guys in the book. Dean and...Sol—"

"Sal. Sal Paradise and Dean Moriarty," Marty corrected, distractedly. "The hell of it is, those two guys always started out with all these hopes and dreams. But every time they came back in failure. It never worked out like they planned."

"That's just a book, man," Jeff protested. "It's time to make a move. Your future in Rockton has gone to hell and ain't coming back. From now till you die, you'll always be the preacher's kid who got nailed in the post office with an armload of jerk-off books."

"I'm getting outa this town come fall," Marty snorted defensively.

"Yeah, marchin' off forty miles to a two-bit prep school with soldier suits and Sunday school," Jeff spat back. "Toy guns *and* Bibles!"

Marty's spirit plummeted through the cement floor. For two months he had managed to banish serious thought of his September conscription. He'd talked about it, even laughed about it. But he'd never admitted to himself that he would actually walk through the iron gates into a life of shaved heads and servile discipline. *Somehow,* his heart had pleaded, *something* will come up.

"This is your chance, Marty. It's now or never."

Marty stood and distractedly paced off the small room. "Damn, it would be a blast, wouldn't it," he said. "We could drive when we wanted to, find a place we liked, stay awhile. Answer to no-damn-body. I've got some money put back. We could pick up some work along the way if we run short."

"We won't," Jeff said quickly. "I've got enough to get us there and back if we never get work."

"The Rev and the old lady would positively *shit,*" Marty said, sounding as though that alone would justify the trip.

"You're free, eighteen, and a high school graduate," Jeff declared. "You can go where you damn-well please."

"Yeah. There's a lot of chicks between here and the Pacific Ocean, and I hear they're a lot different out there. Wilder. Healthier," Marty said, cupping his hands at chest level. Large breasts were apparently part of the West Coast package. "The folks are at a meeting at city hall," he said, carelessly tossing pornography into a burlap sack. "Some kind of book-burning thing. Won't be back till after ten. I'll lay it on them then. I can't wait to see their faces."

"I'm leaving at eight o'clock tomorrow morning," Jeff said firmly. "Show up with your sleeping bag and whatever money you can get hold of."

Jeff stopped at the door and paraphrased a minor red-clay prophet whose words might push a doubting pilgrim across the line. "Marty," Jeff said solemnly, "you don't want to end up on a bar stool at fifty years-old talking to some stranger about the land you shoulda bought, the girl you shoulda married, and the trip you shoulda taken."

Marty nodded grimly. When they shook hands on parting, the boys were sailing on clouds of sublime expectation, blown by the winds of destiny from east to west.

It's a good thing we're leaving in the morning, Jeff thought as he walked across the parsonage lawn. Even Marty should be able to keep his loins girded and his ass in gear for twelve hours.

Jeff's eyes burst open at 2:35 a.m., shaken awake by the Weasels of Dread feasting on his entrails, sucking his courage, paralyzing his will.

How could he have committed to a two thousand mile trip in a clap-trap truck to a territory where he'd never been, knew no one, and could only expect to be treated as a rank stranger? Depend on friends of Cody Hunter for work? Insane! Cody had likely run off with their women and owed them money.

Marty wasn't going to show up in the morning. Marty's rebelliousness stopped well short of venturing into a world where nobody knew or cared who his father was. The weasels dredged up memories of Marty's broken promises and undependable behavior dating back to first grade.

What if he got in a wreck, or got sick on the way? There would be no one to help. Alone.

How could he leave his mother after what she'd just been through? How could he be so selfish?

Why not stay in Wilmington? It was less than a day's drive away. There'd be a place to sleep and food to eat. Close to the beach and other kids. When this Cody thing blew over, he could slip back into town and start his life up right where he'd left off.

The boy moaned aloud when he thought of his grandfather, in his grave for less than a day. How could he leave this house, this land, so soon after Granjack's death? Did the old man really mean for him to take the truck and strike off west? Probably just a drunken whim.

The weasel's banquet continued until exhaustion dragged the victim under. The boy didn't know what he would do come daylight, but the idea of jumping into an ancient truck and driving alone two thousand miles into a hostile land terrified him beyond words.

And he prayed no one would ever discover what a coward he was.

CHAPTER FORTY-SIX

Jeff quit his treacherous bed before sunup. His mind spun in erratic circles as he showered and dressed, unable to fix on any course long enough to judge it. He feared going to Oregon, hated the thought of holing up in Wilmington, and he couldn't stay in Rockton. All that pushed him forward was the humiliation of backing down from a plan he had pronounced defiantly only a few hours before.

As he gazed around the bedroom that had never seem so warm and comforting before, he prayed for an unequivocal *Sign* to guide him. The most obvious Sign would be Marty's appearance, packed and eager to roll West. Of course, he hadn't told Rose of inviting Marty along.

"Ready for your big trip?" Rose asked cheerlessly, as Jeff walked into the kitchen. She apparently had no more sleep than he. He grunted and nodded vaguely.

Breakfast was a grim chore with neither party showing any enthusiasm for the eggs, sausage, hash browns and biscuits. They discussed how they would convey the title of the truck, and what to do if he encountered trouble on the road. He would take two hundred dollars with him; she would wire the rest by Western Union when he was settled. Newspaper says you might run into rain. Take the extra tarp.

Throughout the meal the boy considered calling Marty's house, but he didn't. He had a gut feeling that this must all play out in its own way.

"You'd still be welcome at Aunt Lolly's," Rose said softly, as she cleared the table. Jeff shook his head.

Jeff backed the truck as close as he could to the front door. Although eight o'clock approached like a runaway train, he did not hurry to get the truck loaded. Keeping an ear tuned to the highway, he moved his provisions from the dining room table. Each time he heard a car approach his dirt road, he held his breath until the sound faded down the paved highway. While Rose cooked chicken and gazed sadly from the kitchen window, the boy arranged and rearranged his camping gear and supplies. Several times he retrieved tools or supplies of questionable use from the house or shed. Eventually, he found that no matter how slow he worked, there was nothing left to do but throw the canvas tarpaulin over the truck bed, tie it down, and declare the job done. It was 8:15 a.m. No Marty.

Jeff checked the water in the radiator and jumped when the screen door slammed. Rose, pale and gaunt as a wraith, walked from the house with a hamper of food. She opened the passenger door and blocked the avalanche of baggage that tumbled toward her. She shoved it all—fly rod, portable radio, guitar, sleeping bag, maps, AWOL bag—back in the cab and attempted to reorder it. The large, unwieldy guitar defied placement. She grabbed the instrument by the fretboard and backed out of the cab. Grasping the guitar by the neck with both hands, she cocked the guitar body behind her right ear, took a short stride with her left foot, then swung with all the strength, malice, and righteousness her slender body could generate. The guitar body impacted the right front fender with a loud discordant CLUNK.

Jeff, checking the oil under the hood, jerked away from the explosion. The back of his head clipped the upraised hood, confusing him further. It was only after Rose's second and third blows against the fender that he realized what had happened. He rubbed the angry knot on his head as he faced his mother.

Rose stood with the fretboard still clutched in both hands, the strings dangling over the shattered wooden body on the ground. A bewildered half-smile flickered across her face as she shrugged off any understanding of what had just happened or who was responsible.

Before a word could be uttered, the sound of tires sliding off the pavement and onto their dirt road interrupted the bizarre scene. Although hidden by the trees, mother and son charted the car's progress by its straining motor. The providential nudge that Jeff had searched for since rising approached full-bore.

It was a *Sign* all right: a Mojo, a Hoodoo, and a Bad Moon Rising all balled into one. Jeff's soul fell to the ground and rolled under the left front tire of Police Chief Ray Parrish's squad car as it slid broadside in front of Granjack's truck.

"Mornin', folks," the Chief drawled through his open window. His florid face took a weak stab at a smile. Parrish took his time getting out of the car. No hurry, nobody was going anywhere, anyway.

Jeff felt dizzy and steadied himself against the truck fender. Rose calmly dropped the guitar neck and stepped to the front of the truck. She set up solidly beside her son. "Mornin', Ray," she said. "What brings you out here?" Her voice was as flat as Parrish's haircut.

"Well, I been wantin' to talk to you folks for the past several days," Parrish began. He lit a Lucky Strike and paced beside his car as he spoke. "But it's been a tough time for y'all, and I didn't want to tread on your feelings." The Chief glanced in the back of the truck. "Somebody gettin' ready to take a trip here?"

"Jeff's going camping up around Boone for a few days," Rose said. "He wants to get off by himself. You understand."

"Oh, I understand," the Chief said. "Lotta gear there." He raised his right haunch and set it down heavily on the squad car's front fender. "You see, I've had this feelin' Jeff might be plannin' a trip that would take him considerably further than Boone. When I got word on Wednesday a sheriff up in East Tennessee had captured our mutual friend, Mr. Cody Hunter, I knew I needed to talk to you folks. I just couldn't bring myself to do it until now." He nodded toward the truck bed. "I'm glad I didn't put it off till after lunch."

"I can't see how any of that concerns us," Rose said, as though discussing nothing more serious than a change in the weather.

"I'm makin' arrangements to have ol' Cody sent down here so we can all discuss that little dust-up we had last Saturday night. I'd like to have Jeff around for that."

"Do you have a warrant?" Rose's voice reflected more curiosity than contention.

"No," Parrish admitted, "but I can get one anytime I want. We got cause aplenty for that."

Jeff held his breath, and for a long moment there was no sound but the birds jeering from the trees.

"I'm willin' to cut Jeff some slack," Parrish said finally, staring at his cigarette, "if he'll own up to his part in this thing."

"I don't know anything about any of that," Jeff said solemnly.

Parrish slid off the fender, flipped his cigarette to the ground and stepped on it. "Suit yourself," he said sourly, jerking open his car door. "You've been informed you're a suspect in a felony. You try to leave town, I'll declare you a fugitive and have you arrested."

"Just a minute, Ray," Rose said, her voice rising slightly. "I think we have something in common here that overlays any business about Cody Hunter."

Parrish leaned over the open car door. "I can't imagine what that would be, Miss Rose."

"A kind of..." Rose searched for the words, "mutual desire to avoid becoming in-laws."

The Chief rested his right foot on the door panel and thought for a moment. He shook his head. "Can't see no chance of that happenin'. My girl's done swore off Jeff for good. She can't even say his name without spittin'."

Rose took a step forward and cocked her head to the side. "Just how long do you think that'll last? They've been breaking up regularly for the last three years. But they always fall back into one another's laps, don't they?"

The Chief was clearly uncomfortable with the metaphor; his right hand made a pass at his crotch then brushed across his gun butt. He shook his head to clear it of visions of teen-age carnality that had aggravated him all spring. "I reckon if I send the boy to prison for a couple years," Parrish said, reclaiming the offensive, "that'll slow down their courtin' a mite."

Rose's eyes narrowed to dime-thin slits. "Jeff's not going to prison. And you know that anything to do with court and lawyers will take a long, long time. A lot longer than it'll take Jeff and Vicky to get back together."

Rose and Ray stared at each other while Jeff made an effort to look virile and avoid fidgeting.

"Remember, Ray," Rose said, "you and I have been throwing cold water on them for years, and we've never been able to separate them."

The Chief winced visibly as the apparition of amorous dogs leaped to mind. White furrows of anger formed on a forehead fast turning purple. Does she know she's talking like that?

Jeff was stunned by this turn in the conversation. He had enough sense to keep his mouth shut, but he grew distinctly uneasy each time Parrish's hand fluttered around the butt of his gun.

"I got a proposition for you," Rose said. "There's no court papers on Jeff, so there's no reason why he can't take a camping trip. If he stays gone for," Rose studied the cumulus clouds piling up off to the west, "say, a year. That'll give Vicky time to snatch up a new boy friend. Plenty of time to forget all about Jeff."

Parrish pulled his foot out of the car and hitched up his belt. As he gazed off into the woods, his right foot absently traced a circle in the red dust. There was no tellin' how this whole can of worms with Hunter and Stuart would finally shake out—hell, Sam Langston was backsliding on testifying against Hunter, and Tennessee hadn't agreed to extradite the son-of-a-bitch yet. But no matter how he turned all that over in his mind, Ray couldn't get past the sanctity of blood. The law is the law, he concluded, but Vicky is *my little girl.*

"Two years in the Army oughta be long enough to straighten everthing out," the Chief said. "He can volunteer for the draft—"

"No!"

Two heads swiveled toward Jeff. "I *won't* go in the Army!" he said. If he'd learned nothing else from Cody Hunter, he'd learned that. "I'll stay out of town for *two* years. I'll swear *never* to see Vicky again—but I'm not going in the Army."

"Boy, I don't care where the hell you go, so long as you're gone for two years." The Chief clambered quickly behind the steering wheel. "I better never see you sniffin' around my house again." Christamighty, Parrish thought, as he cranked up and swerved angrily down the dirt road, couldn't I have thought of a better way to say that?

The Stuarts waited until the squad car had pulled out of sight before they burst into an eleventh-hour-reprieve celebration. When the comprehension of what she had done, what had been avoided, dawned on her, Rose sat down on the running board to compose herself. Jeff felt strong enough to push the truck cross-country.

The urgency persisted; they shared the fear that the Chief might change his mind, reappear. As he climbed into the cab, Jeff swore to his mother he would eat vegetables, ignore hitchhikers, to his own self be true, and do the thousand things that would keep him healthy, safe, and Christian until he returned. Both Stuarts repeated that two years was not a long time, but only the driver believed it. Then, there was nothing to do but leave.

Rose watched the truck roll down the driveway and disappear behind the trees. She strained to hear as Jeff pulled onto the paved road, shifted from low to second to high. Then silence. The profound relief she felt only minutes before had dissipated as quickly, as completely, as the truck's dust cloud. She knew that by nightfall all that would remain would be the aching emptiness that would attend every waking moment until she saw her son again.

It doesn't have to be two years, she reasoned. Vicky could leave town, get married. Jeff could come back earlier. Or she could drive out to wherever he was working. She had never seen anything beyond glimpses of Virginia and South Carolina. If she didn't go soon, she never would. She would start planning a trip.

Rose had one foot on the porch when she realized she could not face the empty house. A mountain of obligation awaited—bounden duties, endless tasks.

They could wait. As she climbed behind the wheel of her station wagon, she vowed to attend to a promise that had never made it on to any of the thousand "To Do" lists she had drawn up in the last twenty years, but had never strayed far from her consciousness.

Rose rolled her windows down, and set sail for Spainhour Piano Showroom in Oak City. She wouldn't buy anything until the insurance and books were straightened out, but she would at least price a good upright piano. Maybe "used," she hedged. Around ten o'clock, she would visit Janet in the hospital and see that little baby girl. After that, she could stop by the Twin Circle Grill and pick up some barbecue sandwiches and onion rings and take them to Delphina's for lunch. Although the seer had become stingy with advice, she was still a good listener. And Delphina had seen her cry before.

Jeff drove out of town attended only by the sound of the truck in high gear and the hum of tires on pavement. His mind was full and needed no competition from the radio. He had no trouble suppressing a momentary urge to drive by the Ryder house. He realized that they wouldn't have traveled many miles before Marty would require more care and reassurance than he was willing to offer. Better to go it alone.

Twelve miles out of Rockton, Jeff pulled to a stop at the crossroads. He didn't hesitate. Nothing short of God's right hand descending from a cloud and directing him to Route Sixty-six would have altered Jeff's path. He turned north toward the Cumberland Gap, upper Midwest, Badlands, then the Lewis and Clark Trail. The route the Old Man would have traveled.

Jeff fished a chicken leg from the hamper as the first fat raindrops slapped his windshield. Homesick already, he started writing a song. By the time he reached Corbin, Kentucky, the rain had eased, and "Drivin' Through Teardrops" had changed from a Hank Williams country-weeper to a Chuck Berry rave-up. He'd be rolling through a lot of towns with pawn shops in the next two thousand miles. Inside one of them was a guitar some bluesman had lost track of. A guitar that could teach him a thing or two.